CHASING THE HORIZON

SCOTTY CADE

Dreamspinner Press

Published by
Dreamspinner Press
5032 Capital Circle SW
Suite 2, PMB# 279
Tallahassee, FL 32305-7886
USA
http://www.dreamspinnerpress.com/

Cover Art
© 2014
Reese Dante.
http://www.reesedante.com
Cover content is for illustrative purposes only and any person depicted on the cover is a model.

ISBN: 978-1-63216-001-0
Digital ISBN: 978-1-63216-002-7

Printed in the United States of America
First Edition
June 2014

Readers Love SCOTTY CADE

Sunrise Over Savannah

"…this is a beautiful story. Well written, deep characters, lots of drama, especially toward the end."

—Love Bytes Same Sex Romance Reviews

"This was a very emotionally charged book, and I simply loved all of the men Mr. Cade put in this story."

—The Novel Approach

The Mystery of Ruby Lode

"My attention was grabbed from the first page to the last. I give this a book 5 sweet peas, 5 stars, and a 2 thumbs up rating."

—Mrs. Condit & Friends Read Books

"The storyline and plot are brilliant."

—MM Good Book Reviews

Unconventional Courtship and *Unconventional Union*

"Taken as a whole, both *Unconventional Courtship* and *Unconventional Union* make for a highly enjoyable read."

—Hearts on Fire

"Beautifully written with characters that live and breathe off of the written page, *An Unconventional Union* is one of my favorite books I've read this year. Mr. Cade … gave this reader several hours of pure reading enjoyment, and I can't wait to see what he has in store for us!"

—Top 2 Bottom Reviews

By SCOTTY CADE

Final Encore
The Mystery of Ruby Lode

Sunrise Over Savannah
Chasing the Horizon

An Unconventional Courtship
An Unconventional Union

LOVE SERIES
Bounty of Love
Foundation of Love
Treasure of Love
Wings of Love

Published by DREAMSPINNER PRESS
http://www.dreamspinnerpress.com

As always to my husband, Kell. He is the most understanding, supportive, and unselfish person I know and sacrifices many things to allow me to follow my dream. At the risk of sounding gay as a goose, in the famous words of Barbra Streisand, "Oh my man, I love him so."

I would also like to thank my dear friends Hawken Morrison and Justin Lavigne, upon whom two of the characters in this book are based. Hawken is a handsome, sweet, and gentle man who can scare the hell out of you if you don't know him. Justin is our good-looking pocket gay and made sure that I referenced his "pools of honey" colored eyes. I love you both.

CHAPTER
ONE

GARNER HOLT stood behind the helm of his Beneteau Oceanis 55, a moderate wind blowing through his shoulder-length, sun-streaked brown hair. *AquaTherapy*, as he'd so aptly named her, was heading south toward Key West, cutting through the clear azure waters of the Hawk Channel, just off the south Florida coastline. *AquaTherapy*'s sails were tuned perfectly to the southwest winds, and she was cruising along at a brisk six and a half knots, heeling a comfortable eighteen degrees.

The closer Garner got to his destination, the lighter his heart felt and the better his mood became. He turned his head upward as the warm mid-December afternoon sun blanketed him with her glorious rays. He inhaled deeply, and his lungs filled with crisp, salty sea air.

God, I love the feeling of freedom when I'm on the water.

With seeming inevitability, though, that thought caused Garner's mind to drift back to a time when things weren't so simple, and freedom was the last thing he felt. The lightheartedness waned, and he couldn't help but wonder why he'd spent so many years chasing his tail instead of chasing the horizon. He knew it was partly hereditary. Both of his parents had been overachievers. His mother—now retired and living on Long Island—had been a world-renowned pediatrician. His father, who'd died at age sixty-seven, had been a very successful commercial mortgage broker, who had worked night and day. The one pleasure he'd indulged was his love for sailing, which he'd passed along to his only son. Garner's own insecurities probably accounted for the rest of it. That and a need to make his ambitious parents proud.

As *AquaTherapy* made her way down the coast, the old familiar feelings of anxiety and inadequacy snuck back in. When he'd gone off to college, he'd been almost obsessed with his education. He'd put everything on the back burner, including his love for sailing and his family and friends. His only goal was to succeed. And as luck would have it, his sacrifice and commitment hadn't gone unrecognized. He'd graduated at the top of his class and was immediately hired by Mount Sinai Medical Center in New York City. After only four years, his Ivy League education, strong work ethic, and unmatched dedication earned him the title Head of Psychiatry, the youngest doctor ever to hold that coveted position. But as with all positions of power, it wasn't without its drawbacks and its costs.

Garner cringed when he thought back to the grueling schedule that had left him absolutely no time for a personal life. That, combined with his extremely independent personality meant any sort of relationship was a disaster waiting to happen. He'd tried a few times, but after his last boyfriend told him where to shove his job, he'd given up and decided it wasn't worth the headache—or the heartache.

By the end of his eighth year at Mount Sinai, his career had definitely been on track, but the pressure and stress were finally starting to take their toll. He'd barely survived that year and went into his ninth battling severe burnout and exhaustion.

Garner felt the stab of a residual sadness when he recalled that February morning when he didn't get out of bed. That morning had stretched. For two weeks. He'd been so overcome with neglected depression and exhaustion he'd simply shut down. The minute he was on his feet again, he'd started the process of early retirement.

A smile quickly replaced the sadness as he remembered how free he'd felt when he'd sold everything, bought *AquaTherapy*, and set out to find new winds to fill his sails.

Joy, freedom, and a sense of finally being in control of his own destiny had overtaken him when he'd pulled out of New York harbor and rounded the point at Sandy Hook, New Jersey. He'd felt as free as he did right this very moment. After spending an incredible couple of months on the water, taking his time meandering along the eastern seaboard, exploring the Delaware and Chesapeake Bays, and picking up the

Intracoastal Waterway in Norfolk, VA, Garner had finally started to discover who he really was and not who he'd forced himself to be.

"You and I are a good team," he said out loud, patting *AquaTherapy*'s hull. "Except for that little delay in Savannah, which turned out to be a blessing in disguise, it's been smooth sailing for the both of us."

Picturing Hank and Thompson's handsome faces, Garner smiled. He'd been temporarily derailed when his engine failed in Savannah, Georgia, and he'd had to be rescued by a very handsome BoatUS Captain named Hank Charming. He was towed to the Thundercloud Marina, where the marina mechanic uncovered a manufacturer's error that couldn't be repaired. His boat required a new engine, and that came with a six-week lag time.

After the initial shock of being stranded for six weeks wore off, Garner tried to figure out what he was going to do to keep himself entertained. Luckily, he didn't have to wonder too long. The day before he'd been towed in, the owner of the marina, Thompson Gray, had lost his dockhand and was in dire need of a replacement. Following a brief meeting, Thompson offered him the job, and he gladly accepted.

After working with Thompson during the day and dating Hank Charming at night, Garner realized the guys had a very strong emotional connection to one another. He soon learned they shared a very complicated past, an even shakier present, and little or no chance for a future. They interacted on a daily basis when needed, but their past was clouded with misconceptions and untruths that were slowly eating away at both of them. In the end, with Garner's help, Hank and Thompson were able to find their way back to one another and were now happier and stronger than ever.

Garner suddenly realized he missed his new friends. While acting as their unofficial therapist, he had become very close to them both, and that had surprised him. Much to his astonishment, he'd left Savannah with mixed emotions and a heavy heart. He'd never planned to stay—he had a horizon to chase—but that didn't make leaving them any easier. On the morning he'd pulled out of the marina, they'd all promised to stay in touch, but Garner knew only too well that life sometimes gets in the way of the best intentions.

Garner sighed and looked up at the powder blue sky. "And here I am. Sailing along with no complications. Just the way I like it."

WITH *AQUATHERAPY* now cruising along on autopilot, Garner put all these old feelings out of his mind and focused on what was ahead of him. He stretched out in the cockpit and basked in the Florida sunshine anticipating the future. He listened to the latest NOAA weather report on his VHF radio; the weather was going to be clear and picture perfect for the last couple of days of his journey. Suddenly very eager to get to Key West, he decided to sail straight through the night and make it to his destination by tomorrow morning.

"Just one more day," he said to the ever-present dolphins dancing alongside his boat. "We're almost home free, boys and girls."

WHERE HAS the day gone? Garner sipped a glass of Sancerre, watching the spectacular sun hover above the western horizon. The yellows, oranges, and magentas were all blending into one magnificent blur that danced on the water, and then slowly sank into the abyss.

After dusk, with his GPS and radar set to alert him to any imminent danger, Garner sailed through the night, the bright moonlight shimmering like diamonds as it reflected off the deep, sapphire-colored water. He dozed every now and then, tweaked his sails as needed, but mostly gazed at the billowy blue velvet sky against the distant lights of the Florida coastline.

When the morning sun peeked above the horizon, Garner smiled and thought of Hank and Thompson back in Georgia, probably watching the same sun rising over Savannah. He kissed his index finger, held it up in the air, and wished them a heartfelt good morning.

By seven thirty, Garner was almost giddy. He was only five miles away from Key West, so he radioed ahead and received his docking instructions from the harbormaster. With sails furled and *AquaTherapy* motoring along at five knots, he pulled into the Conch Harbor Marina, sporting a smile as broad as the dawn.

Following instructions, he pulled along a T-head pier and, with the help of a dockhand, secured his boat and connected the water and electricity.

By eight thirty, Garner had traded the fleece, blue jeans, and boat shoes he'd worn overnight for shorts, a T-shirt, and no shoes. He was on the dock barefoot, rinsing the dried salt off his boat, when he saw someone walking down the dock in his direction. As the stranger got closer, Garner could see that the man's head was shaved and he was wearing low-hanging black jeans, but no shirt or shoes. His skull, as well as every other part of his exposed body, including his feet, was covered in brightly colored tattoos.

As the man continued toward him, Garner could see that he appeared to be pierced in every visible orifice, sporting a stainless-steel nose ring, a loop in his left eyebrow, studs up and down both of his ears, and a bar with balls on either end in his bottom lip. Garner did his best not to stare, but he couldn't help it; the man reminded him of a pierced and tattooed Mr. Clean.

Looking farther down, Garner saw that the stranger's nipples were pierced, as was his bellybutton. A chill ran the length of Garner's spine, and he shuddered when he thought about what else might be pierced that he *couldn't* see. And just to push the entire look over the edge, the man wore silver-dollar-sized solid black discs in his stretched earlobes.

Garner started to feel uneasy, and his heart rate began to increase. He quickly looked for any other boaters milling around the dock who might offer a little support if he needed it, but there was no one to be seen.

His next thought was of some sort of weapon. Garner doubted he could hose the guy to death—should the need present itself—but anything else he could possibly use for a weapon was aboard *AquaTherapy*.

When the guy was about ten feet from him, Garner's felt the adrenaline pumping through his veins at breakneck speed. He didn't make eye contact but tightened his grip on the hose and held his breath. *Shit! He's coming right at me. Calm down, you sissy. You lived in New York City for how long?*

Garner spread his feet apart and moved the hose to his left hand, fisting his right. *I might go down, but not without a fight. Just four feet away. Three Feet. Two feet. One foot.*

When Garner could finally see the figure in his peripheral vision, the scary dude lowered his head and walked right past him.

Garner exhaled with relief and willed himself to calm down. He nonchalantly turned his head and followed the stranger with his eyes, but the guy kept on walking until he reached a fishing boat named *ReelCrazy* three slips down and hopped aboard. *Appropriate name!*

CHAPTER
TWO

H AWKEN "H AWK" Bristol slowly opened his eyes and blinked a few times, trying to bring something, anything, into focus. *Where in the fuck am I?* He turned his head to scan the room and felt a stabbing pain that started at the base of his neck and quickly consumed his entire skull. *Shit, that hurts!*

He instinctively licked his dry lips and decided he would kill someone for a glass of cool water to quench his cotton mouth. *And man do I have to pee.* But before he could think about any of that, he had to figure out where he was.

While trying to scan the room without moving his aching head, Hawk gingerly reached up and turned on the lamp beside the strange bed. He instantly froze when someone—or something—stirred next to him. He turned his head carefully and blinked a few more times, attempting to bring the object into focus. As his vision slowly cleared, he saw a man lying on his back, naked except for a leather harness, and covered in someone's dried come.

Fuck, Hawk! What did you do this time?

He studied the burly figure intently, struggling to jog his memory, but no matter how hard he tried, nothing concrete came to mind. After a while he thought he vaguely remembered the man's face but certainly didn't know his name or how in the fuck they'd ended up here. Wherever the hell *here* was.

He gently laid his head back down on the pillow and closed his eyes, trying to recall the events of the night before. *Stopped for a quick drink on the way home.* He remembered that much. *So far so good, Hawk—nothing wrong with that.* Then he remembered some nice older bear of a man buying him a tequila shooter. *That's when all the trouble started. Holy shit!* Slowly, the events of the night started to unfold.

Hawk squeezed his eyes tighter against the vivid memories, but they forced their way in anyway. The Jägermeister. Stripping on the bar. *And... oh hell no!* The back-of-the-bar blowjob came rushing back to him. *Oh crap, Hawk. You did it again!*

No longer able to ignore his overflowing bladder, Hawk sluggishly sat up in the bed to begin a search for a bathroom, doing his best not to wake the man lying next to him. He slowly swung his legs over the side of the bed and winced at an unexpected stab of pain. *Fuck! My ass hurts.*

Once upright and relatively steady, he checked around for his clothes. Clothing was strewn everywhere, including a leather jockstrap and leather chaps hanging from a curtain rod. *Those aren't mine.*

Hawk finally spotted his red T-shirt on the floor next to a chair with an empty bottle of lube and a box of condoms sitting on the arm. *That's why my ass hurts.* He quietly crossed the room, picked up the red T-shirt, and silently cursed when half of it remained on the floor. He reluctantly dropped the piece of cotton, shaking his head in disgust as he flashed back to the shirt being ripped off him.

Appalled at himself, Hawk looked around for anything else he might recognize. He spotted a familiar black, silver-studded belt on a pair of black jeans hanging on a doorknob across the room. *Mine!* He tiptoed over to get his pants and was relieved when he glimpsed a bathroom through the half-open door. Hawk lifted his jeans off the knob, silently slipped in, and closed the door behind him. He checked his pockets for his keys, wallet, and cell phone and was relieved when they were all there. He leaned against the door and closed his eyes.

Almost there, Hawk. All you have to do is get out of here without waking the guy.

Carrying his jeans, Hawk crossed the bathroom and stood in front of the toilet. He looked down and was horrified to see he was still wearing a condom, complete with last night's sperm deposit filling the tip. *Round two? I sure hope I gave as good as I got.* Then he panicked when he realized he hadn't seen a condom on the mystery dude.

Fuck, Hawk! Did you let him fuck you bareback?

He slipped the latex off and was relieved when he saw a used condom in the trash can next to the toilet. Hoping it was from last night, he added his and quietly relieved himself. He debated on whether to flush or not and decided against it, still hoping to make an escape without the morning-after rituals. He drank from the faucet and splashed his face, taking a few extra seconds to wipe his now unsheathed penis and dry off. He dropped the towel on the floor and slowly opened the bathroom door. He peeked into the bedroom—*Still out cold, thank you, Bear God*—and scanned the room for his underwear, boots, and socks. The rest of his clothes were nowhere to be found, and Hawk cursed under his breath. *Those were my favorite fucking boots.*

He stooped down to look under the bed, and suddenly the harnessed lump in the bed started to stir. *Fuck the boots!* He made a split-second decision and bolted for the door.

Naked as the day he was born, Hawk ran down a set of stairs, taking them two at a time as if he were a small child. His pants were flapping behind him, and his belt buckle was rattling loud enough to wake the dead. He stopped at the bottom of the stairs just long enough to put his jeans on and look for an exit. Spotting the way out, he looked around and breathed a sigh of relief that there was no one between him and freedom.

With renewed energy, Hawk burst out of the door and squinted against the morning sunshine. He immediately started scanning the area to try and get his bearings and saw the prominent sign over his head: La Te Da. He whistled. *Way to go, Hawk. At least you weren't slumming.* He'd spent the night at one of Duval Street's most upscale inns.

Then he quietly cursed under his breath when he remembered La Te Da was on the opposite end of Duval Street from where he lived.

People stared openly as Hawk took the walk of shame, hobbling down Duval Street barefoot, hung over, and in desperate need of coffee. Of course, he knew they had no way of knowing he'd woken up with a total stranger, still wearing a used condom. Or that he couldn't find his underwear or his favorite boots. He figured they were staring for the same reason most people starred at him: because he was a big, scary guy with a shaved head, piercings in every visible orifice, and covered in tattoos.

Hawk mostly tuned out the gawking morning tourists, though. He was too hung over to care as he walked toward the marina at the end of Duval where his boat, which also happened to be his home, was docked.

His head was still throbbing when, six blocks later, he stepped into the Urban Spoon Coffee Shop and saw his best friend, Justin Morrison, behind the counter.

"Whoa!" the barista said when Hawk walked up to the counter. "Look what the cat dragged in." He lowered his voice. "You look like shit."

Justin stepped out from behind the counter with his hands on his hips. Then he raised one finger to his chin and gave Hawk the once-over. "You know the policy, dipshit. No shirt. No shoes. No service."

"Fuck you, Justin, just give me my usual."

Hawk's best friend smiled coyly and sauntered back behind the counter. "Coffee's on the house if you give me a little blow-by-blow, so to speak, of your conquest last night. You know, just a little something to get me through my lifelong dry spell."

Hawk didn't answer. He stood tall, simply glaring at Justin.

"Oh come on, Hawk, please?" Justin yelled over the whirling coffee grinder. "At least give me a hint."

Hawk felt his blood pressure rising, but he kept his cool. He wasn't so sure he wouldn't be doing the same thing if the shoe, or lack thereof, was on the other foot.

Justin put a cup of coffee on the counter and rested his chin in his hands. "Did your date involve strip poker?"

"What kind of stupid question is that?" Hawk snapped, taking a sip of the hot liquid and scowling from the burn.

Justin scrunched his face and gave him a disappointed look. "Because you lost your shoes and your shirt, idiot."

Oh, I get it! Hawk had to smile a little at that one.

"So are you gonna tell me?" Justin asked again.

Starting to get annoyed, Hawk leaned over the counter and whispered, "I can't tell you."

"Why the fuck not?"

"Because I don't fucking remember."

"Oh, Hawk, again?" Justin questioned. "You were so out of it you don't remember anything? Or did you black out completely?"

"Don't know. Don't remember much," Hawk said. "But I know something happened because I still had a full condom on when I woke up, and my ass hurts like hell."

"OMG," Justin said, throwing his head back in laughter.

"Keep it down." Hawk looked around furtively. "Do you have to make sure everyone knows my business?"

"Honey," Justin said, holding up his index finger. "My mamma used to always say if you don't want folks to know you did something, don't do it."

"Fine!" Hawk slapped a five-dollar bill on the counter, took his coffee, and headed for the door.

Before he slammed it behind him, Hawk heard Justin yell, "Coffee's on the house, but I'll keep this as a tip. Call me later."

Another six blocks and Hawk's feet were getting sore from walking on the pavement barefoot, so he hailed a pedicab to take him the rest of the way.

By the time they reached the marina, Hawk's skin was damp, his palms clammy, and he was starting to tremble all over. It took every bit of concentration he could muster to pay the young man who'd just pedaled him almost all the way down Duval Street, without hurling.

He climbed out of the pedicab on shaky legs and gingerly made his way into the marina and down toward the piers. When he was halfway down his dock, he spotted a new sailboat a few slips up from his. He squinted against the morning sun, trying to read the name.

AquaRemedy? *No, that's not right.* Aqua... *something.* Therapy? *Yeah,* Therapy. AquaTherapy.

Busy trying to read the name of the boat, he almost missed the guy with the hose in his hand, rinsing it off. Even from a distance, Hawk could see the guy was good-looking and well built, but his body language and the way he moved said nothing but "uptight." He was so stiff, it almost looked as if someone had forced a huge dildo up his ass and ordered him to hold it in without touching it. The closer Hawk got, the stiffer the guy got.

At that point, all Hawk wanted to do was get to his boat and lie down before he either passed out or blew chunks all over the dock, but as he approached, the stranger was watching him with a look on his face that struck Hawk as odd. He brushed it off, not in the mood to deal with anyone, dropped his head as he walked by without acknowledging the guy, and went straight to his boat. He somehow made it as far as his bed before he collapsed.

HAWK OPENED his eyes and sat bolt upright. *What the hell?* Something was vibrating against his thigh and making a muffled sound. *Cell phone, you idiot.* He sighed and rubbed his temples to try to alleviate the dull ache behind his eyes. The phone stopped ringing, and Hawk lay back down. He glanced at the clock—6:42—and then the porthole. It was dark outside. *Is it evening or morning? Did I sleep through the night?* Before he could decide, the phone went off again. He straightened his leg and fished the damn thing out of his pocket.

"What?" he said, lifting the phone to his ear.

"I thought I asked you to call me later," Justin quipped.

Hawk sighed. "What's up, Justin?"

"I just wanted to make sure you were okay. You looked pretty rough when you stopped by here this morning."

So it was evening and not morning. "I'm fine, thanks."

There was silence on the other end of the line.

Hawk groaned. "Really. I promise, I'm fine."

"Hawken, you know I worry about you. You can't keep up this pace."

"Come on, not now, Justin."

"When, then?" Justin snapped.

"*Never* would be a good time for me."

"That's pretty doable since the only time I ever see you is when you're running away from a trick or you need a caffeine fix... or a combination of both."

Hawk opened his mouth to protest, but before he could speak, Justin added, "You're my best friend, Hawk, and I can see you're on a collision course for something really bad. I can just feel it."

Hawk sighed in surrender. He knew he'd been on a merry-go-round of sex and alcohol for the last few years, but what the fuck? A collision course for something bad? He dismissed the statement without a second thought. He was just having some no strings attached fun.

"Look, Justin. You're right, I have been neglecting you, and I'm sorry for that," Hawk offered. "I promise I'll do better, but you've got to give me a break, okay? You're not going to change me, so please stop trying."

More silence.

"'Kay," Justin eventually replied, sounding defeated and worried.

Hawk knew Justin worried about him, and it touched him, but his life was his to live as he saw fit, and no one was going to tell him otherwise.

"Listen," Hawk said. "First thing tomorrow morning, I have to take the boat over to the fuel dock for a fill-up and get it ready for a fishing charter, but as soon as I'm done, I'll come by the coffee shop and we can grab a bite to eat together. How about that?"

Before Justin could answer, Hawk added, "And I promise I won't stand you up this time."

Justin huffed into the phone. "The jury is still out on that one."

Hawk hated hearing the disappointment in his friend's voice, because somewhere deep down, he knew he deserved it.

Justin's voice chimed in again, perkier this time. "But I have a better idea."

Here it comes. Hawk took a deep breath, dreading what might come next. "And what is that?"

"You can go with me to see the Divine Miss Richfield at the Crystal Room Cabaret tonight. She's only here for one night, and I really want to see her."

Relieved that it wasn't anything to do with the way he'd been living his life on the edge or a way to *save* him from himself, Hawk exhaled but didn't give in too easily. "You know I hate drag shows."

Justin huffed again. "Oh come on, it's one night—a few hours, really. And it would be fun to just hang out like we used to do. You know, before you took to self-medicating your emotional issues, gallivanting with every Tom, Dick, and Harry, and ignoring me."

Hawk exhaled but didn't say anything. *The guilt train is pulling into the station. All aboard!* "Okay, fine," he conceded. "But I'll meet you there."

"Yay! You won't regret this," Justin screeched into the phone. "You'll love her. I saw her in P-Town last year, and she's really hilarious."

Hawk sniffed. "I'll go, but don't expect me to like it. In fact, I think I'm regretting it already."

"The show starts at ten thirty sharp, so please be there no later than ten fifteen," Justin said, and then the line went dead.

Hawk dropped the phone on the bed beside him and rolled over to stare at the wall. He thought back to Justin's warning. "Am I on a collision course for something bad?" he mumbled. After mulling that over in his head for a few minutes, he came to his own conclusion. "No more than usual! But I am on a collision course for a shower and some food." He rose to his feet and made a beeline for the head.

CHAPTER
THREE

"You're almost a blond now, Holt," Garner mumbled as he glanced at his wavy, shoulder-length locks in the mirror. His hair was now way more blond than brown from all the sunny days he'd spent on the docks at the marina in Savannah, not to mention his days at sea. But he also realized he was only going to get blonder the longer he stayed in Key West and chuckled when he thought about the blond jokes that Hank and Thompson would certainly bestow upon him.

He leaned into the mirror as he applied moisturizer to his evenly tanned and mostly unwrinkled skin, mentally patting himself on the back for remembering to apply sunscreen on a regular basis.

He took a step back from the mirror, studied his slender face and strong jawline, and frowned. *God. I may not have many wrinkles, but the older I get, the more I look like Dad.* He felt the familiar wave of sadness and guilt that normally washed over him when he thought about his father, but over the years he'd learned to keep them at bay. Mostly.

He forced the feelings back down as he scanned his naked body in the mirror and felt a little bit of pride. "Not bad for thirty-six," he said. "At least the old physique hasn't turned on me yet." He followed his broad shoulders and muscular chest down to his small waist, flat stomach, and naturally strong legs. "I guess all those years at the gym really paid off."

He'd spent almost nine years behind a desk, and during that time, he'd been obsessed with the gym, so afraid he was going to get fat and flabby.

He stepped out of the head and stood in front of his open closet door. He folded his arms across his chest and patted his bare foot. *It's your first night in Key West, Holt, and you only get one chance to make a first impression, so what's it going to be?*

Deciding he wanted to fit in, he settled on a pair of comfortable, well-broken-in jeans that rode low on his hips and a neon green Nautica T-shirt. He stood in front of his full-length mirror. *I guess this will have to do.*

It was still a little early, so Garner decided to have a drink before he ventured out for his first night on the town. He opened a bottle of chardonnay, poured himself a glass, and climbed the companionway stairs to the cockpit. He settled in front of the steering wheel, kicked his shoes off, and propped his feet up.

It was a beautiful evening. Mild in temperature and with only a hint of the spectacular sunset coloring the western sky. Garner took a sip of his wine, leaned his head back, and closed his eyes, soaking in the last warm rays. At the sound of footsteps on the dock, Garner's curiosity got the best of him, and he opened one eye to see who was approaching. He raised his head and sat up straight when he saw Mr. Clean casually making his way down the dock. As the stranger approached, Garner began to feel very silly. The guy didn't look nearly as scary as he had this morning and not the least bit intimidating. Yes, he was still bizarre looking, but as he got closer, Garner could see that he was dressed in form-fitting blue jeans, a tight gray turtleneck, and black high-top tennis shoes.

Normal, everyday attire, he thought. *No spiked leather vest and pants with chains leading to his wallet. No shit kicker boots either. Just ordinary clothing.*

When he reached the stern of *AquaTherapy*, it appeared as if he was going to stop. Garner's heart skipped a beat in anticipation. But their eyes locked, and Garner held the stranger's gaze. After a few seconds, the stranger simply nodded, flashed a smile, and kept going.

Garner nodded back and followed the stranger's movements down the dock.

What struck Garner as odd was the stranger's familiar, hollow stare. His crystal blue-gray eyes produced the same effect Garner had experienced when he'd gazed into Thompson Gray's emerald eyes for the first time. The flecks of gold and the depth of green in Thompson's eyes had had a major impact on Garner back in Savannah, but despite the rich color, they too had been hollow, almost devoid of any emotion.

After the man disappeared through the marina gate, Garner continued to stare as if he could still see him. He was startled out of his thoughts by his cell phone ringing. He unclipped the phone from his belt and, without looking, slid his finger across the bottom of the phone and put it to his ear.

"Hello."

"Glad to hear you're still alive," the voice on the other end of the line said.

"Thompson?" Garner said, breaking out of his trance and smiling into the phone. "I was just thinking about you."

Thompson chuckled. "Do I dare ask why?"

"Probably not," Garner replied.

"Oh geez," Thompson said. "You're right. I probably don't want to know."

"How the hell are you guys? Hank okay?"

"We're great. Missing you, though."

"I miss you guys too," Garner said with sincerity.

"Where are you?" Thompson asked.

"Just got to Key West this morning."

"That's great," Thompson said. "Now that you've arrived, if you're going to stay put for a while, Hank and I would like to try and figure out a time when we can both get away so we can come see you. If you still want us to, that is?"

"Hell yeah," Garner replied. "I can't wait to see you guys."

"Hold on, let me put you on speaker," Thompson said. "Hank wants to say hi."

A few seconds later, Garner heard Hank's voice. He sounded so happy it brought a smile to Garner's face. "Hey, Gar, how's sunny Key West?"

"So far so good," Garner replied.

"Oh come on, is that all you have?" Hank teased.

"Give me a break. I just got here, and I'm a slow starter."

"Who are you trying to fool?" Hank asked. "I remember the day we first met. Slow starter, my ass."

Garner chuckled. "Okay. Guilty as charged."

Thompson cleared his throat. "Hey, guys? I'm listening. For Pete's sake, the last thing I want to hear about is how you two flirted with one another the first day you met."

Garner heard Thompson huff like he'd been elbowed in the ribcage, followed by a muffled "Ouch."

"Okay, fine," Hank said over the speaker. "But at least tell us about the trip?"

Garner filled them both in on the details of his voyage, and before he knew it, they were saying their good-byes with promises of seeing each other very soon.

Garner stood and shoved his phone into his pocket just as the last remnants of the sun dipped below the horizon, leaving behind only hues of orange and yellow filling the western sky. He stared at the colorful display for a few minutes, downed the last of his wine, and took the empty glass down below. He checked himself in the mirror one last time. "As good as it's gonna get," he whispered to himself before grabbing his keys and heading topside again to begin his first night in Key West.

As he walked along the dock, Garner recognized a new bounce in his step and realized he was looking forward to being with people again. Being on the water alone had been one of the best mind-clearing practices he'd ever experienced, and this particular leg of his trip had given him plenty of time to reflect on Hank and Thompson and the part he'd played in helping them. But as a psychiatrist, he also knew how important human contact was to the spirit. Mr. Clean's bizarre mug popped back into his mind again, and he chuckled. *Well, some human contact, that is.*

Shaking his head to scatter the image of shaved heads, tattoos, and piercings, he tried to focus on what he wanted for dinner. "A real dinner?" he said to himself, feeling excited about his evening.

After a few blocks, Garner turned onto Duval Street. The heart of Key West was buzzing with activity, and he didn't know where to look. Standing in the middle of the street, he almost felt like he was in a mini Times Square. Bright lights filled the early evening, and the sounds of the city mixed with music; cheerful voices and laughter were alive and bursting with anticipation.

Glancing up and down the crowded thoroughfare, trying to determine where to go, Garner was mesmerized by the sights. There were tanned, muscular, half-naked men in every direction, some paired off and holding hands while others were obviously cruising the crowds, looking for, well, whatever they were looking for.

Garner chuckled. It had been a very long time since he'd been to Castro Street in San Francisco, where this sort of thing was expected, but this was Florida for God's sake, the home of retired grandparents.

As he stood on the street taking it all in, his voyeurism was abruptly interrupted by a loud noise much like the honking sound one would identify with a kid's birthday party clown. When he turned, he realized his initial summation wasn't very fair off. He instinctively jumped back just in time as a very large drag queen in full regalia flew by on a bicycle, honking a horn and shoving a flyer in his face. He accepted the flyer rather than get run over and read an advertisement for a drag show later that evening at The Crystal Room Cabaret in a place called La Te Da. He smiled, folded the flyer, and stuck it in his pocket.

Deciding it was definitely time to move on, Garner surveyed Duval Street in each direction, and after careful consideration, chose the direction with the most activity. He weaved into the oncoming foot traffic and matched the pace of the other lollygaggers. Suddenly, he felt like a kid in a candy store. Being... well... Garner, the reaction took him totally by surprise, but instead of analyzing it as he normally would, he just went with it. Before very long he felt energized, and the previously identified bounce in his step was even more pronounced. His boat shoes almost floated above the concrete. There was something interesting to see in every direction, and he reveled in the sights. After ten or so blocks, he absentmindedly reached up and rubbed the back of his sore neck. The perpetual smile on his face broadened as he realized he'd been moving his head from side to side for so long, afraid to miss anything, he'd totally given himself a crick.

Once again folding into the ever-moving crowd and feeling comfortable with the rhythm of the night, Garner casually strolled along the crowded sidewalk. He soaked up the informality of his temporary new home, slowing every now and then to take in the beauty or bizarreness of a piece of art in a gallery window, and then he'd once more pick up his pace until something else caught his eye.

About an hour into his leisurely stroll, Garner's stomach not so subtly made itself heard and began to protest the lack of attention. He quickly shifted his focus and began to search for cafés and restaurants that caught his eye, stopping to check out the menus posted proudly on the busy sidewalk. He eventually settled on a little restaurant called Square One, suddenly hungry for herb-roasted chicken and good ole home-style mashed potatoes.

Garner stepped inside and looked around. He noted the place was very crowded but still had an intimate feel, and so far, he was very happy with his selection. He slipped the handsome host a twenty and asked for a small table tucked away in the corner with a view of the dining room and smiled appreciatively when he got exactly that.

After ordering a glass of wine, a salad, and the roasted chicken that had prompted his patronage as well as set his mouth watering, he sat back and simply watched. The romantic restaurant was filled with couples holding hands and cooing, some straight, some gay or lesbian, but everyone obviously feeling very comfortable with their public displays of affection. Garner thought about how far society had come in just his lifetime and realized that in some small way, his generation had helped to carve out a better life for today's gay youth. He took a small bit of satisfaction in that.

With more than half of his journey on the water behind him, Garner was more relaxed than he'd been in a very long time. But again, instead of analyzing it, he went with the totally foreign feeling and smiled when he suddenly thought about his friends back in New York. "Uptight" was the word they most frequently used when asked to describe his personality. But right here, right now, uptight couldn't have been further from the truth. He suddenly thought about the rainbow sticker his best friend Greg had adhered to his boat the day he left New York. When he'd found it, he'd known exactly who'd put it there, and he'd called Greg and given him a shitload of grief. The only response he'd received was "If you're going to cruise your uptight ass around God knows where, at least people need to know you're gay. How else are you gonna get laid?"

The sticker hadn't exactly gotten him laid yet, but it had had its benefits. It had been the way Hank identified him as gay when he'd come to tow Garner's boat to a marina for repairs, which in turn had put him right in the middle of an emotional love triangle with Hank and Thompson that had tested his libido, not to mention his skills as a psychiatrist. But in the end, it had all worked out the way it was supposed to, as do most things, and while it hadn't gotten him laid per se, it had brought Hank and Thompson together. So in the end, he guessed Greg was right.

In the next few minutes, his dinner came and was well worth the wait. Best roasted chicken he'd ever had, and he savored it to the last bite. After one more glass of wine and a few bites of Key Lime Pie, he paid the check and ventured out once again onto Duval Street.

He looked at his watch and saw it was nearing nine thirty. He pulled out the piece of paper he'd shoved in his pocket and read the details about the show in The Crystal Room Cabaret at La Te Da. The flyer read, "Join us at the Crystal Room Cabaret at La Te Da, featuring John Webster and the many faces of the Crystal Room. And tonight only, direct from Provincetown, our Special Guest, none other than the Divine Miss Richfield."

"What else do I have to do?" he said under his breath, checking the address and starting out for the club. "What the hell, it sounds like fun."

When he reached his destination, he almost wished he'd had dinner there. Not because the food at Square One wasn't absolutely fabulous, but the ambiance of La Te Da just seemed more—for lack of a better term—him.

Staring at the building in front of him, he now realized that La Te Da was more of an entertainment complex rather than simply a drag bar. There was a restaurant, a quiet little bar, a drag bar, and a dance bar as well. The complex also offered high-end accommodations. From the sidewalk, the restaurant looked absolutely charming. Candlelit tables with white linen tablecloths and black toppers were glowing in the outdoor dining area, each table appearing to be in its own private dining room, sectioned off by long billowing shears of white fabric dancing on the light evening breeze. *Charming. So romantic and absolutely charming.*

From the street, he read the menu and knew he would make a point to dine here soon. He glanced at his watch again, and since the show didn't start for another forty-five minutes, he decided to have an after-dinner drink in the little bar. Ordering a glass of port, he took a seat at the end of the bar and watched the patrons come and go. It seemed strange to not know a single person anywhere he went, but at the same time, it was exciting. In his mind, each time someone walked into the bar, it was an opportunity to possibly make a new friend.

His thoughts were interrupted by a soft voice. "New in town?" the bartender asked, raising an eyebrow and replacing the napkin under his half-finished glass of port.

"Yes, as a matter of fact I am," Garner replied with a slight smile. "Do I look that obvious?"

"Not really," the bartender said. "Just haven't seen you around and, well, Key West is a very small town." He stuck his hand across the bar. "Austin Newkirk."

Accepting the outstretched hand, Garner gave it a tight shake. "Garner Holt. Nice to meet you."

Garner had always thought you could tell a lot by a man's handshake, and in this case Austin's was firm and strong, just the way he liked it. And the man wasn't at all hard on the eyes. His olive complexion was set off by jet-black hair that shone like silk in the low light of the bar, and he had the deepest hazel eyes Garner had ever seen. Garner was definitely an eye man, and Austin's changed from green to brown to gold, depending on how they caught the light.

"So," Austin said, "vacationing, or are you Key West's newest resident?"

Garner chuckled and took a sip of his port. "A little of both, really."

Austin cocked his head to one side.

"I just pulled in on my boat early this morning," Garner explained.

"Ah… so just passing through?"

"Maybe. Maybe not," Garner replied. "My original plans were to cross the gulfstream and head to the Bahamas and then eventually to the Caribbean, but I have no timeline, so I'm taking it as it comes."

Austin wadded up a bar towel and tossed it into the sink. "Sounds like a pretty damn nice life."

"It is," Garner agreed. "But I paid my dues."

Someone took a seat at the other end of the bar, and Austin held up one finger. "Hold that thought. I'll be right back."

Garner nodded and watched the handsome bartender closely as he casually strolled down to the other end of the bar. His first thought was about how Austin's ass muscles flexed under his fairly tight black slacks. But then, as usual, his years of being a psychiatrist kicked in, and he did a little analyzing. What hit him next was the air of confidence Austin carried when he walked. He was definitely a man who was comfortable in his own skin. *Nice.*

When Austin returned, customers all taken care of, he brought the bottle of port over and held it up in front of Garner with a raised eyebrow.

"Sure."

"This one's on me," Austin said as he poured.

With Garner's drink refreshed, Austin rested his elbows on the bar and looked directly into Garner's eyes. "So where were we?"

Garner chuckled. "Oh hell, I don't know."

Austin smiled. "I know exactly where we were. You were about to tell me if you are staying on in Key West for a while or just passing through."

Garner held his port glass up in a mock toast. "Very good. Handsome and smart."

Holy shit, did those words just leave my mouth?

"So you think I'm handsome, huh?"

Garner felt the blush slowly consume his face and wanted to slide off his barstool and hide under the bar. "Sorry," he said. "I don't usually say stuff like that, but this town is having a strange effect on me."

"Don't fret," Austin said. "It happens to the best of us."

"You too?" Garner asked.

"Fuck yeah." The bartender offered a clearly reminiscent smile. "I came here on vacation for a week, went home, quit my job as a junior accountant, packed up everything I own, and moved here... what?" He seemed to be doing a mental count. "Twelve years ago."

"Any regrets?" Garner asked.

"Not a one," Austin shared. "I found a job at a CPA's office as soon as I arrived but got really bored, so I quit and... well, here I am. Been managing this place for over ten years now."

"We seem to have something in common," Garner said. "I left my profession as well, but I just decided to retire instead of doing something else."

"Must be nice."

"Yeah, well, like I said, I paid my dues. Long hours and absolutely no social life."

"What did you do?"

Garner hesitated.

Austin seemed to pick up on his reluctance. "Never mind," he said, slapping the bar lightly. "Folks come to Key West to forget or even escape, so scratch that question."

Garner relaxed again. "Head of Psychiatry at Mount Sinai Medical Center in New York City."

Austin whistled. "I'm impressed."

"Oh don't be," Garner said, sliding his hand in circles on the bar, remembering his past life. "It was an all-or-nothing job, and I got tired of the 'nothing' part. Very long hours, budget cuts, limited staff, and did I already mention no social life? It sucked big time."

"So I take it you're single?" Austin asked.

"Yeah, I'm single," Garner replied. "You?"

"Met my partner here about a year after I arrived, and we've been happily together ever since."

Garner experienced a wave of disappointment and then immediately felt stupid. *Why am I feeling let down? Maybe because he's an interesting guy, you moron?*

"Good for you," Garner said, pushing those foolish thoughts out of his head. *What is up with me?*

He straightened on his barstool and looked Austin in the eye. "So what does he do?" he asked, not sure of what else to say.

"He's the headliner in The Crystal Room Cabaret," Austin said proudly.

Garner tried to mask the surprised look on his face but obviously didn't do a very good job of it.

"I know what you're thinking," Austin said. "The guy is married to a drag queen?"

"Well, ah... no," Garner stuttered. "I wasn't thinking that at all."

Austin raised an eyebrow.

"Okay," Garner confessed. "Maybe I was thinking that a little, but I wasn't judging. I'm just a little surprised is all."

Austin smiled, obviously having some fun at Garner's expense. "Hey, man, don't sweat it. I get that all the time."

"I'm really not judging, I swear," Garner said, trying to sound convincing.

"It's okay. Really."

"Will you tell me about him?"

Austin looked up toward the ceiling. "Let me see. He's gorgeous for starters. But more than that, he's kind, compassionate, and an all-around great guy. He just happens to put on a wig, gown, and high heels and play dress-up five nights a week to entertain tourists. And he makes a damn good living at it."

Garner couldn't help but recognize the pride in Austin's voice when he talked about his partner, or the look of contentment on his face. "I'm happy for you guys," Garner said. "I really am. He sounds wonderful."

Austin started to reply, then held up a finger and moved a little way down the bar. Garner turned in the same direction, and his mouth dropped open when he saw Cher walk up. Austin leaned across the bar and gave her a great big kiss.

Garner did a double take. *Did I just see Cher?*

He took a closer look, squinting his eyes tightly, and then shook his head in disbelief. *Yep, that's Cher all right.*

Austin whispered something into Cher's ear. She glanced in Garner's direction and smiled. Garner immediately looked away, half expecting her to break into a live rendition of "Gypsies, Tramps and Thieves."

When Garner looked back, he saw Austin hold his hand out, and Cher reached her sequined-glove-encased hand across the bar and slipped it into his. *Holy shit! Austin's bringing her down here.*

Garner gulped, not really knowing what to do. Then Cher was standing right next to him, still holding Austin's hand.

"Garner, I'd like you to meet my partner, John Webster," Austin said. "Jack, this is Garner. Garner uh… Holt? Right?"

Garner nodded, unable to form the words to respond. *How does one greet a man in a dress?*

Giving up on etiquette, he simply stood and stuck out his hand. "Nice to meet you, John."

"Likewise, and call me Jack, please," Cher—no, Jack—said in a deep voice. "I hope you're planning to see my show tonight?"

"As a matter of fact, I am," Garner said in a shaky voice.

"Well, don't wait too long, honey." Jack tossed his long black hair over his shoulder, curling his tongue, and sucking in his cheeks. "The show starts in five minutes, and I'm a 'Dark Lady' if you show up late."

Garner chuckled. "Got it. All I have to do is settle my check, and I'll head right over."

Cher nodded. She leaned over the bar and stole another kiss.

"Break a leg," Austin said with a smile.

Cher turned and looked over her shoulder. She tossed her hair again and waved her hand in the air. "In these heels, I'll be lucky if I don't break them both."

After Garner settled his check and said his good-byes to Austin with a promise to return soon, he ventured into The Crystal Room Cabaret. To his surprise, upon entering he realized the cabaret was fairly large but intimate at the same time. In line waiting to be seated, Garner took his time and took it all in. He saw that the theater was designed in three levels. The main level, where everyone entered, and two lower levels, all levels leading down to what he assumed was the stage, currently hidden behind royal blue velvet draperies trimmed in gold and silver. Looking from left to right, he saw banquette seating in the same royal blue velvet lining the walls on each level and royal-blue-skirted, high-top tables with barstools on the lower level directly in front of the stage. It reminded him of a smaller version of Caesar's Palace in Las Vegas.

When it was his turn to be seated, Garner was tapped on the shoulder and did a double take to find himself being escorted to his table by a tall but very beautiful Britney Spears. Much to Garner's surprise, he was led toward one of the high-top tables directly in front of the stage, but he stopped short when he almost ran into Bette Midler having a disagreement with Bette Davis over who was the biggest diva. He quickly apologized and took his seat, not wanting to get in the middle of their shtick. Britney took his drink order, and he sat back to take in the sights. The place was a who's who of celebrities, all decked out in their finest. Doing a quick scan of the room, he spotted Lady Gaga and Mae West taking drink orders and Carol Channing, Phyllis Diller, Liza Minnelli, and Barbra Streisand milling about the crowd greeting guests. And last but not least, a seven-foot Amy Winehouse was going from table to table with a very large can of hairspray, offering to spray everyone's hair. Of course these were *not-so-cheap* imitations, but man were they entertaining.

Shortly after Garner's drink came, the lights dimmed, and the live band started an overture of show tunes. Minutes later, the MC introduced the incomparable John Webster. The crowd hushed until you could have heard a pin drop. Suddenly, the music started and Garner immediately recognized the intro to "If I Could Turn Back Time." When the curtain opened, Jack was standing center stage in an exact replica of the black leather body suit Cher wore on the aircraft carrier during the video. Garner's mouth dropped open in amazement, and from where he was sitting, he would have sworn he was watching the real thing. Garner studied Jack's performance very closely, and every mannerism and movement was spot-on. Each lip-synced word had obviously been practiced for endless hours and was definitely hitting the mark. Garner found himself continually checking out Jack's crotch area, or lack thereof, curious as to where he was hiding his junk because it was nowhere in sight.

The song ended with the crowd up on their feet and thunderous rounds of applause. Garner found himself on his feet right along with the rest, whistling and clapping like he'd just seen the real Cher. The room eventually quieted, and everyone sat back down as Jack sauntered to center stage and picked up the microphone. "Thank you. Thank you so much," he said, bowing his head and curtsying. "Welcome to The Crystal Room Cabaret. My name is John Webster, and along with our regular cast of lovelies, we hope to thoroughly entertain you this evening."

The crowd went wild again, and Jack motioned for their attention with his index finger. "But… but…." The crowd slowly quieted again. "In addition to our usual star-studded lineup, we have a legend on our boards this evening. Who, you ask?" Cher brought her hand up to cup her ear, and the crowd all yelled "Who?"

"Okay, I'll tell you," Cher teased. "None other than the very funny and demented Divine Miss Richfield, directly from P-Town."

The crowd erupted again, and Jack bowed his head once more. When the room quieted, Jack spoke again. "David, let's turn up the lights and see who we have with us tonight."

The house lights came up slowly, and Garner felt a rush of panic when Jack's eyes locked on his. "What a handsome crowd we have this evening," Jack continued, making his way into the audience and offering his hand to Garner.

The audience roared and applauded when Garner nervously stood and, as if on autopilot, allowed Cher to lead him to center stage. His heart was pounding, and he was sure his face was as red as a beet. Once on stage, he stood very still, and for the first time in a very long time, he was scared shitless. He squinted against the spotlights, and his body began to tighten up limb by limb. Suddenly, he felt like one big awkward pile of flesh and bones and had no idea what to do with himself. He absentmindedly shoved his hands in his pockets and planted his feet firmly on the stage as if to keep from bolting.

"Relax, honey," Cher told him, looking him up and down. "Isn't he the cutest thing you've ever seen? Tell the audience where you're from."

Garner bounced from one foot to the other. "Manhattan," he squeaked out in a barely audible voice.

Cher tossed her hair over her shoulder and smiled. "What brings you all the way from the big city to li'l ole Key West?" she asked.

Unable to think of another answer, Garner said, "M-my sailboat."

The crowd roared again, and Cher chuckled. "Well put," she said, sucking in her cheeks. "A man of few words, I can see."

By now Garner knew he was blushing horribly, stuttering incomprehensibly, and making a complete and utter fool of himself. *Oh come on, Gar, get it together. You can handle this.*

"What do you say, gang?" Cher said to the crowd. "Is it time for Crystal virgin karaoke?"

The crowd exploded into a roar once more and started chanting "Virgin… virgin… virgin."

Appalled at what he'd just heard, Garner considered running, but as in his worst nightmares, his feet wouldn't move. Besides, Cher had fished one hand out of his pocket, obviously sensing that he might just bolt, and had a firm grip on him.

Someone plucked his other hand out of his pocket, and he turned to see Marilyn Monroe shoving a microphone into it. His blood pumped through his veins at record-breaking speed, and he broke into a sweat.

"Do you see that teleprompter over there?" Cher asked, pointing to a large screen near the sound booth. "Just follow my lead and sing the 'Sonny' part, okay?"

Before Garner could protest, he heard the band start the intro for Sonny and Cher's "I Got You Babe."

He felt Jack squeeze his hand as he started singing in his real voice.

"They say we're young and we don't know, we won't find out until we grow."

Garner saw the words moving up on the teleprompter and followed along as best he could. When Jack finished his part Garner knew he was up, but his damn mouth wouldn't work.

"Okay, okay, boys," Jack said as the band stopped. "Let's give Garner a few seconds to catch his breath, so to speak. We did just spring this on him."

Garner released a breath at his short reprieve and took the time to try and calm his reckless nerves. His mind was on overload, and he was getting light-headed, but just when he thought he might pass out, his professional training kicked in, and he quickly started to analyze the situation.

I'm stuck up here with nowhere to go, so I might as well relax and make the best of it. I know this song, so that's not a problem, and no one in this damn audience knows me, so what have I got to lose?

After talking himself down, he started to relax a little. *What do I have to lose? I did come to Key West to loosen up and have a little fun. Why not go with it? Fuck it!*

Cher said something he didn't pay any attention to and the intro started again. Garner opened his eyes, straightened his backbone, and looked directly into the spotlight.

After Jack was done singing his part again, the teleprompter read "Sonny," and Garner opened his mouth.

"Well... I don't know if all that's true, 'cause you... got me and baby... I got you."

The crowd was now up on their feet swaying and clapping, and Garner felt their energy urging him on. He knew he was a little behind the music, and suddenly, he wanted to do better.

Jack and Garner sang the chorus together, and it was Jack's turn to sing his verse.

While Jack sang, Garner took a deep breath and felt surer of himself this go round. With his next verse quickly rolling up on the teleprompter, he prepared to sing. This time he was right on top of the notes and even adlibbed a little bit.

Jack smiled in surprise and squeezed his hand as they sang the entire song. The more Garner relaxed, the better he sounded.

By this time the audience had the tabletop candles in their hands and they were swaying from side to side singing along. When the song ended, the place exploded. Garner knew he was smiling from ear to ear and couldn't help it. Garner and Jack took several bows, still hand in hand, and then Jack spoke. "Let's give it up for Garner Holt, everyone," he yelled into the microphone. "What a good sport. Welcome to Key West."

Garner felt his smile broaden as he waved and allowed Jack to lead him back to his table.

"Good job," Jack leaned in and whispered in his ear as he took his seat.

The rest of the evening was a star-studded lineup of all the best gay icons ever and the hilarious monologues of the Divine Miss Richfield, all very entertaining. When the show was over, Garner went back to the bar to say goodbye to Austin and was instantly met with a round of applause from everyone who'd just seen him in the show. As he walked through the bar looking for a seat, people slapped him on the back and told him how good he was, smiled seductively at him, and slipped pieces of paper in his pockets.

He finally found a seat at the far end of the bar and plopped down on the stool, suddenly exhausted.

Austin walked over, placed a white bar napkin in front of him, and added a glass of port. "On me," he said, slapping both hands on the bar and smiled broadly. "You earned it. I hear you put on quite a show in there."

Garner felt the blush again consume his face, and he smiled weakly, uncharacteristically downing the glass of port. He winced from the burn, and when he could finally speak, he said, "I'm not sure whether I should deck you or thank you. I embarrassed the hell out of myself, but I think I got a pocketful of phone numbers. But seriously, Austin. You could have warned me, man."

Austin chuckled. "If I'd have warned you, you would've made a beeline for your boat and sailed right out of here."

Garner chuckled. "I guess you're right. But maybe a little hint might have helped. For the first five minutes, I looked like a deer in headlights up there."

"Fear not, my new friend," Austin teased. "It happens to everyone." He nodded at the empty glass. "Another?"

Garner thought about another drink, then decided against it. "Nah. I just really came in to say good night. I think I'm in the mood for some dancing. Any suggestions?"

"Hell yeah," Austin said with confidence. "Just down the street on Duval is a club called Aqua. Best dance bar in Key West."

"Perfect," Garner said. "Sounds like a plan."

Austin stuck his hand across the bar. "It was really nice to meet you," he said. "Don't be a stranger."

Garner accepted the outreached hand and the two men shook. "The pleasure was all mine," he said sarcastically, throwing a twenty on the bar. "But don't worry, I'll be back. And please say good night to Jack for me."

"Will do. See you soon!"

CHAPTER
FOUR

HAWK'S DINNER had taken longer than he'd anticipated, and he'd run the last few blocks, determined to get to the club on time. Completely out of breath, he stepped up to the ticket counter, held up his index finger, and mouthed the words "One, please."

Ticket in hand, still breathing heavily, he looked at his watch. *Two minutes to spare. That should blow him away.*

Seconds later, a topless Miley Cyrus wearing a huge Styrofoam wrecking ball came over. He described Justin to her, and she quickly escorted him over to one of the banquettes in the far corner of the club. Justin was perched on his throne, sipping his vodka tonic and waving frantically. "Wow, I'm impressed," he said. "You made it before the curtain went up."

Hawk smiled with a sense of pride he didn't usually allow himself and slid around to the back of the banquette next to Justin. He ordered a beer from Bette Midler and kissed Justin on the cheek.

That move apparently made Justin happy because he smiled and started to chatter about everything from his day to how excited he was to see Miss Richfield. Taking a long pull off his beer, Hawk listened intently as he scanned the club to see if he recognized anyone or saw anything that might interest him. He nearly spit out his beer when he locked on to the uptight guy from the marina, sitting at a table front and center. "Well, well, well," he mumbled under his breath. "Look who knows Dorothy."

"I know, right?" Justin said. Then he obviously realized Hawk wasn't commenting on his rambling. "Wait, what? Who's Dorothy? What are you talking about?" Justin followed Hawk's gaze and suddenly stopped talking.

Without turning away from what held his attention, Hawk said, "It's a term closeted gay men used a long time ago to find out if another man was gay or not."

"I don't get it," Justin said.

"You know Dorothy from the *Wizard of Oz*, right?"

"Of course, everyone knows Dorothy."

"Dorothy and Judy Garland were gay idols. Hence the expression 'Does he know Dorothy?' Get it?"

When Justin didn't answer, Hawk glanced at his best friend and got a sarcastic smile in return. "What an absolutely lovely story."

Turning back to the uptight guy, Hawk said, "I'm glad I could help educate you."

Justin huffed. "I think this is a new record, Hawk."

"What do you mean?"

"It took all of ten minutes for you to find something or someone else to occupy your attention."

"That's ridiculous," Hawk responded, knowing perfectly well what Justin meant.

"Oh please," Justin said. "Don't even try to deny it. I've seen that look in your eye before."

"Well this time you're way off," Hawk responded, turning once again to face his best friend. "I don't even know the guy."

Justin slapped the tabletop, rattling their drinks. "Isn't that the way it always is with you? You don't know him now, but you will sure as hell know him later."

Hawk hated that Justin knew him so well. "No—I mean yes, you're right. Usually that's how it works, but not this time!" Hawk said curtly, then turned to get another look at the uptight guy. "The truth is I know of the guy, but I don't really know him. He's got a boat at my marina, and I saw him when I was walking home this morning."

Justin chuckled. "You mean when you were doing the walk of shame with no shirt or shoes?"

Before Hawk had time to respond, the lights went down and the music started. He closed his eyes and exhaled. *Man, I couldn't have planned that better.*

Justin leaned over and whispered, "Just so you know, we're not done with this conversation."

"Yippee," Hawk said through clenched teeth.

The curtains opened and Cher stood in a single spotlight.

THE FIRST act ended with a big production number starring Barbra Streisand singing "His Love Makes Me Beautiful" from the movie *Funny Girl*, complete with a pregnant bride.

When the curtain went down and the lights came up, Justin was glaring at Hawk. "So," he said. "Are you going to tell me what's with you and that guy, or am I going to have to go over and ask him?"

Hawk sighed. "There's really nothing to tell."

Justin gave him that familiar look of disbelief he often wore when Hawk tried to hide things from him.

"Fine," Hawk said with a defeated tone. "You remember how I told you his boat was at the marina a few slips down from mine when I got home this morning? From the look on his face when I was walking toward him, I think he thought I was going to rob him or something."

"What do you expect, Hawk?" Justin proclaimed. "Strolling in at sunrise with no shirt or shoes. I saw you this morning, remember? You looked like you'd been rode hard and put away wet. And... based on what's been going on with you for quite some time now, you probably had been."

That stung just a little bit, but Hawk quickly recovered. "I guess you have a point," he said. "But something about the guy really bothered me. He was stiff as a board and gave me this weird look. He kept his eyes on me until I got on my boat."

"Let's face it, Hawk, you're a scary guy. Even in your Sunday best. Imagine how the guy felt being new to the marina and seeing you in that condition at that time of the morning."

"But he just looked so uptight."

"You're my best friend, Hawk, and I would have looked uptight given the circumstances. Give the guy a break. He didn't look too uptight just now."

"He did at first," Hawk replied. "But then he seemed to loosen up and really get into it."

Justin leaned back and rested his arm on the back of the banquette. "I agree, and I think you need to stop by his boat and introduce yourself and maybe apologize for scaring the guy. Let him know you're not an ax murderer."

Hawken thought for a second and realized that Justin was probably right. "If he stays on at the marina for a while, I'll stop by. But for all I know he might just be passing through and gone by tomorrow."

"Good boy," Justin said.

The lights dimmed, and the music again filled the club.

By the end of the night, Hawken had been thoroughly entertained. Miss Richfield was funny as hell and had totally lived up to Justin's promise. He couldn't remember the last time he and his best friend had had such a good time or the last time he'd laughed so hard.

He and Justin hung back at their table for thirty minutes or so after the show, just talking and enjoying each other's company. He remembered why he loved the guy so much and why they'd become best friends. They were polar opposites at every turn, but for some reason, it worked for them. They would sit for hours debating topic after topic until they were both so exhausted they'd agree to disagree.

Hawk wasn't ready for the night to end, so he suggested they head to the little bar and have a nightcap. He wanted to spend more time with Justin, but he was also secretly hoping he might run into Garner Holt.

He and Justin took a seat at the bar, and Hawk casually looked around.

"I don't see him either," Justin said, eyeing him.

Surprised that he'd been busted again, Hawk smiled weakly. "Oh give it a break, Butt-rah." Butt-rah was a nickname Justin's brother had given him when he was a child, and he despised it. In the beginning, Hawk knew just when to use it for effect, but it had since become a term of endearment, although Justin still hated it.

Justin glared. "Really? Are we going there so early in the evening?"

Hawk smiled. "I was just checking out the crowd. So give me a break."

"Uh huh," Justin said, obviously annoyed over the nickname. "Why can't you just admit you're intrigued by the guy?"

"Because I'm not."

Justin gave him that look again. "Come on, Hawk. Maybe just a little. Admit it."

Hawk knew he could never fool Justin, so he offered a coy smile. "Fine." He held his forefinger to his thumb with a tiny space in between. "Maybe just a wee bit."

Justin gave him a satisfied smile that for some reason warmed him to his toes.

While Justin continued his endless chatter, Hawk put his elbow on the bar and rested his head in his hand, giving his best friend the once-over for the first time in a very long time. As Justin rambled on, Hawk absentmindedly listened to his pocket gay, as he often called him because of his slight stature. Justin was a small guy, but Hawk never confused small with weak or frail. His pocket gay was compact, but ripped and naturally muscular. Seeing Justin perched on a barstool facing him reminded Hawk of just how ripped Justin was. As he moved his arms gesturing here and there, ranting about one thing or another, his biceps and chest muscles visibly flexed under his tight-fitting T-shirt.

Hawk knew Justin didn't date or even go out very often, but he'd never been able to figure out why. From a few comments here and there, Hawk suspected something had happened to Justin when he was younger that had left a lasting impression, but he'd never gotten the nerve to ask, nor had Justin ever volunteered.

At some point Justin stopped talking, flashed a big smile, and focused on Hawk with an amused expression. And when Justin smiled, really smiled, he almost glowed from the inside out. Tonight that familiar glow, coupled with Justin's twinkling eyes and shiny dark hair, reminded Hawk just how handsome his best friend really was. His rich brown eyes were the color of pools of honey, and at the moment they were filled with curiosity and mischief.

"You haven't heard a word I've said, have you?" Justin asked. "What are you looking at?"

"You." Hawk grinned. "I'd just forgotten how charming and handsome you really are and how much fun we always have when we're together." Hawk straightened suddenly. "Let's go dancing," he said, surprising even himself. *Where in the hell did that come from?* Hawk was not much of a dancer, but he knew Justin loved to dance, and tonight, for some reason, he wanted to make his pocket gay happy.

"Really?" Justin said. "I haven't been out dancing in so long."

"Then finish your drink and let's go." Hawk slapped his hand on the bar. "Where should we go? You pick."

The guy on the barstool next to Hawk leaned over. "I didn't mean to eavesdrop, I swear, but I just heard the bartender a little while ago telling some guy that Aqua was *the* place to go for dancing these days."

"Thanks," Hawk said. "I've heard that too. It's right down the street on Duval, isn't it?"

"That's what the bartender said."

"Thanks, I appreciate it."

Hawk turned to Justin. "Okay with you?"

Justin downed the last of his drink. "Sure. Let's blow this joint!"

GARNER STOOD in line waiting to get into the club. Even from the outside of the building, the *thump thump thump* of the music vibrated through his body. His foot tapped, and his hips naturally swayed from side to side with the beat of the music. He was lighthearted and happy.

When he got to the head of the line, he paid the cover, stopped at the bar and ordered a Scotch, neat, and took a seat in a corner against the wall with a view of the dance floor. He was in a people-watching mood, and from what he'd seen in line, this place wasn't going to disappoint.

For the first thirty minutes, Garner scanned the bar and saw a barrage of people. There were bears in leather harnesses, drag queens dressed to the hilt, preppy older men in shorts and golf shirts, and twinks. In addition to all the men, he saw lesbians and heterosexual couples, everyone converging under one roof. *You gotta love America.*

While Garner was enjoying all the sights, a nice-looking guy at the bar made eye contact with him, smiled, and dipped his head in Garner's direction. Not in the mood to cruise or get laid, Garner smiled and then quickly looked away. He took another sip of his Scotch and was making yet another scan of the club when he stopped short and almost spit his Scotch down the front of his shirt. Mr. Clean had just walked in with his arm over the shoulder of a very little, handsome brunet. *Well look at that. Mr. Clean has a date.*

From the shadows of his perch, Garner felt like a voyeur as his gaze followed Mr. Clean and the brunet around the club. They ordered drinks from the bar, and then his date took him by the hand and led him to the dance floor, drinks still in hand.

From the look of things, Mr. Clean was not at all into dancing. His date, however, was a different story. The buff little brunet was moving with the music, spinning around and backing up to Mr. Clean, twerking, and then spinning around again, hips gyrating with the best of them. Garner switched his attention to Mr. Clean. He looked unhappy and very uncomfortable. He moved a little from side to side but couldn't seem to find the beat.

As he attempted to keep up with the music, his piercings reflected the strobes and spinning lights over the dance floor, and his shaved head began to glisten from the sweat forming there.

Suddenly, Garner realized that he no longer found Mr. Clean scary or intimidating. In fact, not only was he not the least bit scary or intimidating, he appeared to be downright awkward and exposed.

Garner continued to study the guy intently. As the music thumped and the lights whirled overhead, the contradiction between Mr. Clean's physical appearance—with all the tattoos and piercings—and his obvious emotional discomfort in his current situation made the guy seem vulnerable in a weird sort of way. Garner unexpectedly saw something really attractive about him, and it shocked the hell out of him. He liked the contradictions—and everything else he saw.

The song came to an abrupt end, and Mr. Clean quickly stopped dancing. When he turned to exit the dance floor, his expression had softened and relief was plastered all over his face. He took a step forward, then abruptly stopped. As if seeking Garner out, Mr. Clean scanned the room. He stopped when their eyes met.

The intensity of the stare almost knocked Garner off his seat. He gripped the barstool with his free hand and dropped both legs to the floor, spreading them in an attempt to steady himself. *What the fuck?*

Garner's heart raced as if he'd just been caught with his hand in the cookie jar, and a wave of panic rushed through his body. He knew he hadn't *technically* done anything wrong, but he had sort of been stalking the guy since he'd noticed him. But none of that mattered now. The only thing that mattered was the intensity of the guy's stare. Garner knew he should look away, but for some odd reason, he was held in place by a force stronger than his will. He matched Mr. Clean's gaze, and for Garner, the connection was like no other he'd ever experienced. In his mind, the entire club faded away, and it was just the two of them gazing into one another's eyes.

The music blared again, but Mr. Clean didn't start to sway or even attempt to dance. He remained firmly in place and seemed as unable to break the strong connection as Garner was. He didn't move until his date took him by the hand, kissed his cheek, and started to lead him off the dance floor. But Mr. Clean craned his neck toward Garner, obviously not wanting to break the connection either. Garner watched as the man twisted and contorted until he disappeared into the crowd.

The spell now broken, Garner mentally winced at the immediate loss. He frantically searched the crowd for just one more glimpse and saw only the top of a shaved head maneuvering through the quickly thickening crowd.

Led by some strange force, Garner stood up on his toes and followed the movement of the bare head until it was out of sight. He sat back down and tried to hold on to the overwhelming feelings that consumed him.

What the fuck, Garner? You don't do this kind of shit. You don't even know this guy.

His rational brain was struggling to maintain control while his emotions were running rampant. Despite the reprimand he'd just given himself, he kept an eye out until he spotted the shaved head again and locked on to it. Heart racing, he tracked the man through the crowd of partyers while he tried to rationalize what had just happened as some sort of fluke—anything other than a real connection.

Garner was unsuccessful on all counts and driving himself crazy with irrational resolve. Nothing he had ever been taught or learned through his many years of studying and practicing psychiatry could validate or explain the matched intensity of what had just happened between him and a total stranger. He was almost at the point of panic when he lost sight of that shaved head again. He decided right then and there that no matter how crazy it seemed, he had to go after this man, if only to eliminate the mystery that surrounded him.

He willed himself to stand and forced his feet to carry him forward. He stopped short when someone put a hand on his shoulder. His heart skipped a few beats, and he held his breath with anticipation as he imagined Mr. Clean, after seeking him out, now standing behind him. He released his breath and turned around slowly.

The butterflies dancing in his stomach stopped and his heart sank when instead of Mr. Clean, he saw the guy who had made eye contact with him earlier in the evening.

The guy was studying him quizzically, but Garner was too worried about losing track of Mr. Clean to care. He quickly looked back over the crowd, hoping to pick up on the shaved head, but the stranger stepped into Garner's line of vision and stuck out his hand in greeting. "Hey, I'm Joey."

Garner didn't want to be rude, so he exhaled, sat back down in defeat, and nervously accepted the outstretched hand. "Garner. Garner Holt," he said, wishing the guy were invisible.

"I hope you don't think I'm a stalker," Joey explained. "But I saw you walk in earlier and wanted to meet you."

The *stalker* comment instantly made the hairs on the back of Garner's neck stand up. But he relaxed when he realized how silly that was in light of what he'd been doing. *If you only knew whom* I've *been stalking.*

"No worries," he said instead. "Nice to meet you, Joey."

"Can I buy you a drink?" Joey asked.

Desperate to search for his Mr. Clean but not wanting to be impolite, Garner lifted his glass and checked the contents. "Sure," he said. "Dewar's, neat."

As soon as Joey headed for the bar, Garner went back to desperately scanning the crowd. With his target nowhere in sight, he briefly thought about ditching Joey and going after the object of his desire, but deep down he knew that was something he could never do. So he sat there, defeated and frustrated, and waited for Joey to come back with the drinks. With any luck, Joey would come back, hate him, and disappear as quickly as he'd showed up.

HAWK ALLOWED Justin to lead him off the dance floor, through the jam-packed bar, and out to the patio, where he stopped and abruptly turned Hawk around. "What was that all about?"

"Damn if I know," Hawk said, still not sure what had just happened.

Justin grabbed Hawk by the biceps. "I knew there was something between you and that guy."

Hawk, still a little rattled, shook his head. "It was the weirdest thing, Jus. One second you and I were dancing, and the next I felt someone's stare, turned around, and locked on to the guy's eyes. It was like I went into this trance, and I kept picturing him looking down at me with those intense eyes as he fucked the hell out of me. I couldn't move, not because he was holding me down, but because I didn't want to move. Each thrust felt like a lightning bolt rushing through me, filling me with some super strength. I… I just didn't ever want him to stop. It was like nothing I've ever experienced before."

"Good God, Hawk," Justin said. "I saw the whole thing unfold right in front of me, and, man, you've got it bad. I kept trying to lead you off the dance floor, but you wouldn't budge."

"I'm sorry, Jus. I need to go back in there and see if I can find him. You know me. Shit like this doesn't happen to me. Something weird as hell is going on here, and I need to find out what it is."

Justin's expression suddenly changed. "Okay, are you dumping me yet again for a one-night stand?"

Hawk thought for a few seconds. "If I'm lucky I am," he said honestly. "But please come with me. I need my wingman tonight."

Justin smiled and took Hawk by the hand. "Fine. Let's go see if we can scope him out."

Hawk stopped short. "Then what?" he asked.

"You introduce yourself and take him home and let him have his way with you."

"Hey, you're right." Hawk said. "Why should this be any different? I'll just do my usual shtick and wink at him, grab his crotch, and take him home and let him fuck my brains out."

"You forgot 'and then disappear.'" Justin slipped his arm around Hawk's waist. "That's the Hawk I know and love," he said. "Go get 'em, tiger."

Hawk laughed. "God, I hate that you know me so well."

Hawk and Justin walked back into the club, fighting the mounting crowds and heading for the last place Hawk had seen Garner. After ten minutes of stepping on people's feet and slipping behind this one and that one, the crowd thinned a little, and Hawk stopped dead in his tracks. Garner was still sitting where he'd last seen him. His perplexed expression made Hawk feel a little better and mirrored the way Hawk felt.

"There he is. Go knock his socks off," Justin said, squeezing his hand and pointing to an empty spot at the bar. "I'll be right over there if you need me."

Hawk nodded and took a deep breath. He took two steps in Garner's direction and then froze when a guy walked up and handed Garner a drink. He immediately turned around and started walking quickly in the other direction. When he reached the bar, he slapped Justin on the back. "Okay, time for plan B. Get me a drink."

Justin turned around with a surprised expression on his face. "Damn, that was quick. Did he shoot you down already?"

"I didn't get the chance," Hawk said, looking over his shoulder.

Justin followed his gaze and saw Garner sitting in the corner sipping on a cocktail with another guy.

"Who? How?" Justin rambled.

"I have no idea," Hawk answered. "I was on my way to talk to him when this guy walked up, handed him a drink, and sat down next to him."

Hawk slammed his hand down on the bar, drawing an annoyed look from the bartender, but successfully getting his attention. When their drinks finally came, Hawk downed half his beer in one swig. "Can we go back outside?" he pleaded. "I can't breathe in here."

Not five minutes after Hawk and Justin found a place to sit, Hawk saw Garner and his friend walk through the double doors. "Fuck, are they following us or what?"

He kept an eye on Garner and watched him sit at a barstool along the back wall with the guy standing next to him. His eyes suddenly met Garner's again, and the same explosion went off in his brain. Garner held his gaze once more, everything around Hawk fading into the background. For one split second, it was just the two of them. Then suddenly the hairs stood up on the back of Hawk's neck when the guy with Garner draped his arm over Garner's back and leaned in and kissed him on the lips.

Without thinking he turned to Justin and threw his arms around him and covered Justin's lips with his own. Justin tried to push him away, but Hawk held fast. "Just go with me on this," he mumbled against Justin's tightly closed lips, gripping the back of Justin's head and trying to shove his tongue down Justin's throat. When the kiss ended, he looked back over at Garner and smiled coyly. When he saw the expression of disappointment on Garner's face, he immediately regretted his actions.

"What the fuck was that about?" Justin hissed, smacking Hawk on the arm.

"I'm sorry," Hawk said, feeling embarrassed and shocked. "I saw that guy kiss him, and I don't know what came over me. Let's get the fuck out of here. I've had enough of playing cat and mouse for one night."

"Hell no!" Justin said. "You can go if you want, but I'm finishing my fucking drink."

Not wanting to leave Justin alone, Hawk sat down and took another pull off his beer, his mind reeling. As he glanced back over his shoulder, he saw Garner walking out with the guy who had just kissed him.

GARNER SAT in the same position, nervously scanning the club and trying to pretend he was interested in the small talk Joey was attempting to make.

"I'm gonna take a walk outside," he told Joey. "I really need some air."

"Sure. Mind if I join you?" Joey asked. "I could use some air as well."

Fuck. "Sure," Garner said, standing and making a beeline for the patio, Joey right on his heels.

By the time Garner reached the patio doors, his heart felt like it was going to jump out of his chest. The outdoor space was much bigger than he was expecting and just as crowded as the interior.

Eventually, Garner found a spot along the back wall with an expansive view of the patio. He again scanned the area until he spotted Mr. Clean also perusing the crowd. When their eyes met, Garner felt the butterflies dancing in his stomach. He absentmindedly wiped at a line of sweat that had formed on his forehead and tried to decide how to proceed.

Lost in Mr. Clean's gaze, Garner vaguely felt an arm slip over his shoulder as Joey's face came into view and interrupted his eye contact with Mr. Clean. Before he had time to process what was happening, Joey's lips were covering his.

No! Garner stiffened and pushed him away. When Joey attempted to slide his tongue into his Garner's mouth, Garner lost it. "What the fuck?" he said, looking around Joey and trying to reconnect with Mr. Clean. His heart sank when the object of his obsession turned his attention to the brunet and proceed to make out with him like a teenager.

Garner said the first thing that came to his mind. "What the fuck do you think you're doing?" he hissed.

Joey looked shocked. "I'm sorry, I thought…."

"You thought wrong," Garner said, standing so abruptly the barstool went flying behind him. He stormed toward the exit and felt more than saw Joey following him.

"Wait," Joey said. "I'm sorry, I thought…."

Garner didn't stop until he got to the entrance of the club. He spun around, and Joey was right behind him with an embarrassed expression on his face. Garner waved his finger in front of Joey. "Look, I'm sure you're a very nice guy, but I don't appreciate unwanted advances from someone I just met. Thanks for the drink."

With that he turned and made a grand exit onto Duval Street, heading for the marina. His brain was whirling a little from the Scotch and the events of the evening.

How could he go from being deathly afraid of a guy one minute to being so attracted to him the next? A mental picture of Mr. Clean again popped into his brain. The shaved head, the tattoos and piercings, and the big black disks in his ears.

My God, he's not even my type. I've never had so much as a henna tattoo.

He reached the marina mentally exhausted, wanting nothing but his bed. He stopped at his boat and glanced over at *ReelCrazy*. He shook his head still not knowing what to make of the evening's events, but he'd surely get to the bottom of it tomorrow. Mr. Clean lived two boats down, and he was damn sure going to knock on his hull in the morning and straighten this whole thing out. But right now all he wanted was sleep. He boarded his boat, turned off all the lights, and climbed into his bed, pulling the covers up over his head. His last conscious thought was "Welcome to Key West."

HAWK WALKED Justin home, apologized a hundred times for his rash behavior, and then set out for the marina. He took his time, making a point of staying out of the hustle and bustle of Duval Street and enjoying the quiet he found in the picturesque neighborhoods of old Key West.

Once he found a comfortable rhythm, his mind drifted off, and Hawk started to replay the entire evening in his weary head, starting with the Crystal Room Cabaret and the uptight Garner Holt singing "I Got You Babe" with a six-foot drag queen dressed like Cher.

When Hawk had realized the MC was heading towards Garner's table, he knew this was going to be good. But he could never have prepared himself for what he saw next. The poor guy stood in the middle of the stage with Cher, his eyes squinting against the spotlights, his body riddled with tension. Hawk even remembered feeling a little sorry for him when he started bouncing from one foot to the other, obviously uncomfortable with the attention being bestowed on him.

When Hawk had heard Cher say, "It's time for Crystal virgin karaoke," he'd choked on his beer.

When the band started the intro for Sonny and Cher's "I Got You Babe," Hawk thought the guy was going to pee himself, but when his turn to sing came and he just stood there, Hawk's pity had turned to something else altogether. He'd been completely focused on him.

He might be uptight as hell, but he's pretty damn good-looking just the same.

Then he'd watched Garner in disbelief as he straightened up, opened his eyes, and looked directly into the spotlight with a newfound confidence. And… it had looked damned good on him.

When Mr. Uptight started to relax and sing… well, Hawk started to really see him in a different light, and the attraction reached all the way down to his groin.

Shit! He's not even my type. What's up with this?

When he'd seen Garner later at Aqua, there was that immediate connection. *How do you analyze that?*

In his entire life, he'd never felt anything as energizing as when he'd first locked eyes with the guy. But the most puzzling thing was how he'd reacted when he saw that guy kiss Garner.

Replaying that scene in his head over and over, he wondered why he was so enamored. He didn't know Garner. As a matter of fact, their initial meeting—of sorts—wasn't under the best of circumstances, so what was the attraction?

He searched his mind as he strolled along, and it kept bringing him back to the first time he saw the stranger at the marina. But no matter how hard he tried, all he could actually remember about the brief encounter was the uptight vibe the guy was throwing off, like a window shade pulled down so far, it was about to pop and spin endlessly out of control.

In his mind's eye, Hawk tried to recall anything else that might have had an impact on his subconscious mind, but he kept coming up with nothing.

Then it hit him like a ton of bricks. His mind quickly flashed back to a particular expression on Garner's handsome, suntanned face. *Oh great, Hawk, now you think he's handsome too.* He tossed that thought out of his already saturated brain and kept analyzing every other detail he could remember about the guy's face from the very first time he'd seen him. *The guy was afraid of me! When he first saw me barefoot and shirtless, heading in his direction, he was actually afraid of me. Why didn't I remember that?*

He focused on the mental image and his jeans were suddenly getting tighter. He grabbed his crotch to reposition himself and damn if he didn't have a hard-on.

Damn, Hawken, you're one fucked-up dude. The fact that the guy was afraid of you is turning you on. That's a first and weird as hell.

When Hawk finally made it to the marina, he walked down the dock and slowed in front of *AquaTherapy*. For a split second, he thought about knocking on the hull and settling this once and for all, but as he scanned the boat for any sign of life, he saw nothing. There were no lights shining through any of the portholes, no music playing, nothing to indicate whether Garner was there. And even if he was in there, he was probably fucking that guy from the club, and that's the last thing Hawk wanted to confirm or even think about right now.

"Time to call it a night, Hawk. Remember, you have a charter tomorrow morning," he mumbled as he lowered his head and walked to his boat.

CHAPTER FIVE

GARNER WOKE to the sound of the wind whistling through his rigging and the waves lapping against the hull of his boat. He glanced at the clock. *Ten thirty!* He sat up and looked out of the porthole. The sky was gloomy and gray with very ominous clouds hanging low, and based on the way flags were ripping back and forth, the wind must have been blowing at least twenty knots. He plopped down on his back and rested an arm over his forehead. *Ten thirty? I haven't slept this long in ages.* He remembered tossing and turning all night, waking frequently, recalling the strangest dreams. But for the life of him, he couldn't remember one of them now.

Garner lay quietly, trying to jar his memory. In the stillness of his bed, he could feel *AquaTherapy* heaving in the wind; the lines stretching in one direction caused *AquaTherapy* to creak under the stress, and then she would heave in the other direction. *I better get up and check the rigging.*

Once topside, the first thing he did was glance in the direction of *ReelCrazy*. His heart fell to the bottom of his stomach when she wasn't in her slip. *He's gone!* Was Mr. Clean only passing through?

A loud rumble of thunder in the not-so-distant skies reminded Garner of the task at hand. He pushed the overwhelming feelings of disappointment aside and focused on securing his boat against the howling wind.

With his boat secure, he noticed a cruiser on the other side of *AquaTherapy* was lying heavily against the dock from the force of the wind. He knocked on the hull a few times and yelled over the howling wind and waited. No one came out, so he adjusted the lines himself, trusting he wasn't overstepping. He hoped someone would do the same for him if the situation were reversed.

Just as Garner was slipping the last line around the cleat, the skies opened and the rain came pelting down in bucket-loads. By the time he got from the dock into the covered safety of his cockpit, he was soaked to the bone and a little chilled to boot. He stripped down to his underwear and went down below for a towel and a dry change of clothes. With his boat and the boat next to him now secure to ride out the storm, he sipped his coffee and tried to sort through the disappointment he was feeling about Mr. Clean and his boat being gone.

Before he had too much time to talk himself out of the disappointment, he heard a loud thump and felt a jar as if something had hit the floating docks. He put his coffee down and stuck his head through the companionway door, looking in all directions. The rain was falling so hard it was almost impossible to see through the clear vinyl surrounding the cockpit. He heard another thump and felt the dock shake again. It sounded and felt like a boat was trying to dock, not having much luck and slamming into the pier. No wonder in this wind. *Only a fool would try and dock a boat in these conditions.* He squinted against the pelting rain, and his heart nearly jumped out of his chest when he saw the stern of *ReelCrazy* trying to get into her slip. *He's not gone.*

As elated as he was, he panicked at the thought of Mr. Clean trying to get the boat into the slip in these weather conditions. He quickly dug through his gear until he found his two-piece rain slicker, suited up, pulled the hood up, and headed outside to try to help.

Garner didn't think it was possible, but it felt like the rain was coming down harder than it had been earlier. When he reached *ReelCrazy*'s slip, Garner saw a shaved head sitting atop a yellow rain suit. Mr. Clean was on the flybridge, and two guys on the lower stern seemingly petrified from fear and not offering any assistance at all. Mr. Clean waved, obviously relieved to see someone there to help him, but didn't acknowledge Garner in any recognizable way. Garner felt a little stab of sadness, but then remembered his head was totally covered by his rain hood.

It appeared Mr. Clean was trying to line up for another approach, but Garner could clearly see the problem. The boat was taking the wind on her starboard beam, which meant that each time Mr. Clean would line up the stern and attempt to back into the slip, the wind would take the bow and pivot it to port, creating an odd angle that prevented the boat from maneuvering successfully into the confined space.

Watching the next attempt, Garner was very impressed. Mr. Clean compensated appropriately for the force of the wind by positioning the stern upwind of the slip with the bow hard to starboard. By doing this, he was aiming to allow the wind to push the stern into position and give him time to gun the engines and back into the slip before another gust blew the bow too far to port. Unfortunately, the wind was blowing way too hard for even the most competent sailor to outwit.

Garner got an idea. He ran down the starboard finger of the slip and yelled to one of the guys to go up onto the bow and throw him one of the bowlines already secured to the cleat in preparation for docking.

But much to his surprise, neither man budged or even seemed willing to venture out onto the bow. Knowing Mr. Clean wasn't able to leave the bridge, Garner yelled to the guys again, this time with a more authoritative tone. "The only way you're gonna get into this slip is if you throw me a bowline so I can secure it to the piling to keep the bow from pivoting! Now do it!"

One of the guys looked at him, and Garner nodded for reassurance and then yelled again. "Just follow the gunwale until you get to the bow and get me that line! And hold on!"

The minute the guy stepped onto the gunwale, his friend made a mad dash and hurled over the other side of the boat. When Mr. Clean lined up for his third attempt, Garner signaled and the guy tossed the line. Catching it on the first try, Garner immediately secured it to one of the pilings, and Mr. Clean gunned the engines. *ReelCrazy* pitched backward into the slip, and Garner tightened the line as the boat rushed in, preventing the bow from pivoting. That did the trick.

He yelled again, instructing the passengers to throw him the other lines, but again neither of them moved. With the boat now successfully in the slip, Mr. Clean scurried down the flybridge stairs and threw Garner the lines one by one until the boat was secure.

Without saying a word, Mr. Clean climbed back up to the flybridge and shut down the engines and electronics, then returned to the cockpit to take care of the passengers, both of whom were now hurling over the side. Not knowing what else he could do, Garner rechecked all the lines. He knelt to readjust the last line, and when he stood and turned, he was looking straight into mesmerizing slate-blue eyes.

"I really appreciate your help," Mr. Clean said, offering his hand.

Garner accepted the outstretched hand and, after shaking it, removed his rain hood.

Those slate-blue eyes immediately widened as he recognized who had helped him dock. "Garner Holt," he said, barely loud enough for Garner to hear over the howling wind.

He knows my name. "Wait! You know my name?" Garner asked.

Mr. Clean flushed. "Saw you at the Crystal Room Cabaret last night before...."

"Before I went to Aqua?" Garner asked hesitantly.

Mr. Clean opened his mouth to speak, but both men turned simultaneously when the boat's passengers roared as they vomited over the side. Mr. Clean looked at Garner and rubbed his shaved head. "Fuck! They started this about an hour ago and haven't stopped."

"That sucks for all of you" was all Garner could think of to say.

In the wind and pelting rain, the two men stood, looking at one another like it was sunny and calm and there weren't two guys right next to them in agony, spewing their guts out.

"About—about last...," Mr. Clean stammered.

But before he could finish his sentence, his shaky voice was interrupted again as both guys roared in unison, even louder this time, one slapping the side of the boat.

Mr. Clean turned toward the intrusion and then looked back at Garner with an expression that could only be described as frustration.

Garner laid a hand on his shoulder. "Why don't you get these guys taken care of and then come over to my boat?" he suggested. "We can talk more then."

Mr. Clean nodded. "Sounds good," he said, turning to leave.

Garner wrapped his fingers around Mr. Clean's bicep, stopping him midturn. "Before you go, please tell me your name?"

Mr. Clean stopped and ran a hand over his shaved head again. Garner made a mental note that it was something Mr. Clean did when he was nervous.

"I'm sorry, man. I'm Hawken, Hawken Bristol. My... my friends call me Hawk."

Garner smiled, relieved to no longer have to refer to the man as Mr. Clean. "Good to meet you, Hawk," he said, squeezing Hawk's bicep before releasing it. "I'll see you in a bit."

"Hawken Bristol. Hawk," he said to himself. "What a great name."

Garner hopped onboard *AquaTherapy*, stripping down to his underwear in the cockpit before he went below. He took a hot shower and dressed in blue jeans and a long-sleeved red T-shirt, made another pot of coffee, and waited for his visitor with anticipation.

HAWK WAS totally distracted as he helped the fishermen to the dock and then walked them one by one to solid ground. As soon as they stopped throwing up, he loaded them with more Dramamine and, an hour later, sent them on their way.

"I can't believe they talked me into going out in these conditions," he huffed, mentally kicking himself in the ass. "Although in all fairness to them and me, the marine forecast wasn't near as bad as the current conditions."

Hawk walked back to his boat, attempting to block the sheets of rain stinging his face and unprotected head. He climbed aboard and started to remove his raincoat. "Look at the bright side, Hawk. At least you don't have to wash down the boat."

Stepping under the protection of the cockpit roof, Hawk was now safely out of the direct line of fire. He removed his boots and poured at least a couple cups of water out of each, before taking off his rain pants. Not the least bit surprising, when he got down to his underwear, he was soaked through and through, not to mention being a little chilled from the wind. He stepped into the refuge of the dry cabin and headed straight for a hot shower.

He stepped under the hot stream of water and allowed the jets to soothe his stressed-out body, massaging the nerve endings one by one like steamy liquid fingers.

With all the tension of the day running down the drain along with the hot water, Hawk was feeling more relaxed by the minute. The sight of Garner Holt removing his hood in the pelting rain, his palm pressed tightly against Hawk's arm and their eyes locked on to one another's yet again, flooded his mind. "Garner Holt," he said under his breath, liking the way it rolled off his tongue. Hawk had hoped to see Garner today to apologize for startling him and to get a handle on this thing between them, but he'd had no idea it would be under these circumstances.

Hawk squeezed body wash onto his hands, rubbed them together vigorously, and started lathering his entire body. When his hand dropped down to his groin, he lathered his dick and allowed his hand to slide up and down his shaft. The sensation brought a mental picture of Garner pounding his ass like there was no tomorrow, and he forced himself to stop, not wanting a fantasy as much as he wanted the real thing. He was suddenly very anxious to see Garner again. Hawk finished his shower and, deciding to go commando, dressed in a pair of comfortable button-fly Levi's, his favorite black vintage Henley, and a pair of flip-flops.

Hawk opened the cabin door and stepped into the cockpit. He was now warm and dry, but he instinctively wrapped his arms around himself against the howling wind and pouring rain. He looked at his wet slicker suit hanging on the boathook and just couldn't fathom putting it on again. He grabbed the golf umbrella he'd used to shuttle his fishermen to shore and decided to take his chances. He looked over at Garner's boat and a chill ran up his spine that he knew had nothing to do with the wind and rain.

Hawk popped open the umbrella, ducked underneath, and stepped off his boat. He'd barely made it to the *AquaTherapy*'s finger dock when a gust of wind blew his umbrella inside out. He banged on the hull of the boat and struggled to right his umbrella. By the time he'd done so, he was again soaked to the bone.

Garner appeared through the companionway door and hurried to unzip the canvas and clear vinyl panel enclosing his cockpit. "Oh, man, you're soaked."

Hawk tossed the umbrella through the opening and climbed onboard. "Fuck! Man, is it blowing out there or what?" he said, fighting the wind to zip up the opening.

Garner gave him a pitying look. "Come on, let's get you down below and dried off."

"A towel should do the trick," Hawk said with water dripping off his nose ring.

"Look at you," Garner chuckled, giving him the once-over. "I think you need a little more than a towel."

Hawk looked down at his soaking wet shirt and jeans. "I guess you're right."

Garner waved a hand thought the air. "Follow me. I've got some sweat pants and a T-shirt that should do the trick."

Hawk kicked off his flip-flops, followed Garner down the companionway stairs, and waited on the rubber mat, not wanting to drip on Garner's teak and holly floor. He looked around the boat's main cabin and smiled at the leather appointments, highly polished brass lanterns, and oriental rugs filling the space. *Man, this makes my boat look like a floating trailer.*

Minutes later his host returned with a bath towel, a stack of clothing, and the most gorgeous smile Hawk had ever seen. Without hesitation Hawk pulled the wet Henley over his head and tossed it up to the cockpit. Garner's expression turned into something resembling amazement as he studied Hawk's tattoos and piercings. Garner's grin was still etched in Hawk's memory. His heart was going *thump thump thump* as he unbuttoned his jeans, peeled the wet denim down to his ankles, stepped out of them, and stepped through the companionway door. For a split second he cursed himself for deciding to go commando, but when he looked up at Garner's face, the amazement had turned into something totally different. Hawk would know that look anywhere. It could be described as pure, unadulterated lust.

When their eyes met, Garner held out the towel with a visibly trembling hand while clutching the rest of the clothing to his chest with the other. Hawk dried his head and face and then moved the towel down his body slowly and deliberately as he dried his chest and torso, avoiding his quickly hardening cock. He ran the towel down his legs and feet, never breaking eye contact. He straightened and held out the towel. "Get my back for me?" he asked in a sound just above a whisper.

Hawk turned and displayed his colorfully tattooed back as Garner took the towel.

Hawk felt a trembling cloth-clad hand gently caressing his back and shoulders, making slow vertical passes. Hawk smiled when he felt the soft cloth slide down to the cheeks of his ass and continue in the sweeping motion. He suddenly felt cold when the hand and towel withdrew, leaving him craving that simple touch. He quickly turned, needing that connection again, but instead of Garner's touch, he got Garner's eyes, and Hawk lost it.

In one swift move, Hawk took the clothing out of Garner's hands and threw it to the side. He cupped Garner's head with his broad hand, forcing him to lunge forward. And when Garner was close enough that their noses were almost touching, Hawk brought their lips together in a crushing onslaught of passion that came from somewhere deep within his core.

Garner ran his hand over Hawk's shaved head, obviously welcoming the advance. Hawk sighed deeply and slid his tongue between Garner's lips, seeking entry. Garner opened and accepted his frantically searching tongue, and Hawk made an unrecognizable sound that he refused to call a whimper. Hawk combed every inch of Garner's warm mouth, and he thought Garner tasted like no other he'd ever kissed. His unique flavor was a combination of coffee, hot chocolate, and mint leaf, all wrapped into one flavor package specifically designed to send any caffeine-addicted chocolate lover and mint freak jumping off the proverbial wagon with desire. Hawk forced his tongue in deeper, needing to taste more, needing to feel more, as if he were searching for Garner's soul.

Hawk's tongue was still deep inside Garner's mouth when he lifted the man off his feet and carried him to the couch. They both jumped when thunder cracked loudly, adding to the eerie howls of the wind through the sailboat's riggings. The force of nature surrounding their little cocoon only seemed to heighten the desire flowing between them.

Yearning for more bodily contact, Hawk pushed Garner down onto the couch and pinned his hands over his head. He broke their heated kiss only long enough to get Garner's shirt off, tossing it aside and diving back in for more, desperate to taste Garner again. Hawk held Garner's wrists in place with one hand while his other hand roamed over Garner's chest and abs. Garner arched his back when Hawk stopped and lingered at one of his nipples. He lightly brushed over the erect nub with his callused thumb, teasing and tantalizing as he circled the sensitive area.

"If I beg will you do that again?" Garner hissed into Hawk's mouth when Hawk pinched the nipple between his thumb and forefinger hard and then released it and rubbed again.

"Hell yeah," Hawk groaned as he did it several more times before moving to the other.

Garner was rocking his hips up and down, and Hawk could feel Garner's erection pulsing through the confines of his blue jeans.

Again breaking the kiss, Hawk moved down to the spot between Garner's neck and shoulder and began nibbling, then kissing and licking.

Garner once more arched his back, leaning his head into the assault and thrusting his erection against Hawk's body.

"Pants off," Hawk mumbled into Garner's neck. "Want your pants off."

Hawk stood and pulled Garner to his feet. He unbuttoned the denim and slid the zipper down, opening the front and exposing the outline of Garner's rock-hard erection, still hidden by his boxer briefs. He then slid his hand inside the thin layer of cotton and wrapped his fingers around Garner's throbbing cock. He moved his hand down frantically, reaching for Garner's balls, and then back up again, repeating the move over and over. He stopped and rubbed his thumb over the tip, smearing the evidence of Garner's arousal around the head. Garner pulsed in his hand with each stroke as he moaned into Hawk's ear.

Garner suddenly pushed Hawk away with enough force to send him back a few steps and anxiously started to peel his own blue jeans and briefs off.

"Bed!" Hawk hissed, stepping back up to Garner and kicking the discarded clothes to the side.

"Soon," Garner hissed. "But not yet."

Garner slammed Hawk's six-foot-two-inch frame back onto the steep companionway stairs like he was nothing more than a ragdoll and then immediately fell on top of him, crushing their lips together once again. Hawk was stretched out on the stairs, his ass resting on the second step and his long legs extending far past the bottom step. Garner was still on his feet positioned on top of him, but they were lined up perfectly, their three-inch difference in height disappearing completely. Hawk ran his fingernails down Garner's back until he hit Garner's ass and then forcibly squeezed and massaged his cheeks.

Garner rubbed Hawk's shaved head, then dropped to his nipple rings, which he tugged and pulled, sending Hawk into a tailspin.

Unable to control himself, Hawk pushed himself off the stairs, holding on securely to Garner. They landed on the floor, Hawk on top.

"I could fucking eat you alive," Hawk groaned, eliciting a desperate moan from Garner.

Hawk knew exactly what he wanted and was going to get it in the end, but right now he was enjoying this play for dominance way too much to concede so early in the game. He felt sure Garner was used to being in control, and Hawk was determined to give him a run for his money, at least for now.

They rolled over and over on the Oriental rug, exploring one another's bodies. Hawk's back soon hit the base of the sofa, forcing them to roll in the other direction, and they both stopped when they found themselves pinned between the banquette and the cocktail table with Hawk again on the bottom.

"Bed! Now!" Garner snarled, rolling back in the other direction.

When they were in the clear, out from under of the confines of the cocktail table, Garner stood, holding his hands out and pulling Hawk up with him. Hawk forced Garner up against the wall and held him there. He licked his way down Garner's smooth, tanned chest, nibbled on his stomach, and stopped and inhaled the scent of Garner's trimmed pubic hairs.

Garner's unique scent filled Hawk's nostrils, and he reveled in the musky, clean, manly aroma, taking long, deep breaths. Hawk wrapped his lips around Garner's fully erect cock and swallowed him up to the hilt. Garner's hands landed on Hawk's shoulders for support as his legs began to tremble.

Hawk circled his tongue around the head of Garner's cock and focused on the sensitive area underneath. When Hawk swallowed him again, Garner tensed and whimpered. Garner's strong arms slid under Hawk's shoulders, pulling him back up until their lips met once more.

Hands moving feverishly, eager for more skin contact, they staggered along the hallway, sending the mounted brass lanterns swinging and swaying from the sheer force as they bumped and ground their way to their final destination. When they reached the aft cabin, Hawk backed Garner's legs against the bed and shoved him down with such force, his body almost bounced back up again. Hawk knelt on the bed, grabbed Garner's legs behind the knees, pushed them up and apart, and again took

Garner into his mouth. Garner was still rock hard as Hawk took him all the way in, drawing another moan from him.

Garner sighed deeply. "Jesus, Hawk," he gasped as Hawk moved up and down his length. The noises coming out of Garner drove Hawk crazy with desire. Normally, Hawk was a selfish lover, taking what he needed from start to finish, but something about Garner's reaction to his touch and the sounds escaping his lips made Hawk want to do everything he could to make sure those wonderful sounds didn't stop. Garner was like no aphrodisiac Hawk had ever experienced.

Desperate to have his tongue down Garner's throat again, Hawk lowered Garner's legs and licked his way all the way to his mouth. But in a move that impressed even Hawk, Garner effortlessly flipped him onto his back and looked down at him with a sinister grin. Garner whistled as he ran his eyes seductively up and down Hawk's body with such desire it almost made Hawk come at the sight.

Garner planted his hands on either side of Hawk's shoulders and slowly brought his lips down to one of Hawk's nipples, rolling the nipple ring around in his mouth, tugging gently, then releasing it and moving on to the other. Hawk's trembling hands were pressed against the bed, and Garner laid his on top of them to steady and reassure Hawk.

Garner slid down and took Hawk into his mouth, repeating the moves Hawk had used on him. *Damn! He's every bit as good at sucking dick as I am.* "Fuck! That feels good!" Hawk arched and hissed as he felt the sensation all the way down to his toes.

Wrapping his hand around Hawk's cock, Garner moved it in unison with his mouth, up over the head and down again, echoing the motion. Hawk fisted the sheets and closed his eyes so tightly he saw stars. He threw his head back, rolling it uncontrollably from side to side as he held on for the ride. Just when he thought he couldn't stand it any longer and was going to blow, Garner pulled off, slid his hands under Hawk's calves, and lifted his legs over his head, holding him firmly in place. He ran his tongue under Hawk's balls and licked at the tender spot between his balls and his opening, teasing and tantalizing with each stroke. When Garner's tongue darted to his opening and licked and probed, Hawk hissed, "Fuck yes!"

Hawk's still-trembling hands grabbed his ass cheeks and spread them apart, giving Garner as much access as possible. After a few minutes of Garner's tongue probing in and out, Hawk was already on his way to heaven, but when Garner ran the stubble of his chin against Hawk's opening, he sent him up and beyond. Every nerve ending was on fire, and as if Garner sensed Hawk's heightened sense arousal, he quickly soothed the area with his tongue. He repeated this process, driving Hawk to the brink of ecstasy.

Lost in the moment, no longer caring about fucking with Garner's head and fighting for the dominant role, Hawk wrapped his hands around his ankles and pulled his legs farther above his head. "Condom!" Hawk snarled, wiggling his ass against Garner's face.

Garner leaned over to the bedside table and opened the drawer. He withdrew a condom from the box and ripped it open with his teeth, taking his deliberate time rolling it on, staring right in to Hawk's eyes. When the condom was in place, Garner again leaned over to the bedside table. "Fuck," he exhaled in a curse.

"What?" Hawk responded in a harsh tone, his impatience getting the best of him.

"The lube's in the head."

"Forget about it, man, I don't need it."

"What?" Garner asked in surprise. "I'm not going to fuck you without lube."

"Don't want it, just fuck me now!"

Garner shook his head, then spit into his hand and rubbed it around Hawk's opening, spit again, and grabbed his sheathed cock and stroked.

Garner knelt over Hawk and positioned both of Hawk's feet against his chest. He pressed inside slowly, and Hawk hissed from the initial burn. Garner hesitated, Hawk presumed to give him time to adjust, but Hawk didn't want to adjust—he wanted it hard, and he wanted it now. He released his ankles, grabbed Garner's hips with both hands, and pulled Garner into him. Hard.

"Fuck yeah!" Hawk screamed, thrashing his head from side to side. The force of Garner entering him was an overwhelming mixture of pain and pleasure, and he loved it, craved it, and needed it. The stretching and the burn brought joyful tears to Hawk's eyes, and Hawk blinked in an attempt to hold them back.

"Fuck me hard! Please!" he begged, pushing Garner away and forcefully pulling him back in again.

It apparently didn't take Garner long to figure out exactly what Hawk wanted because in seconds his legs were completely over his head, and Garner's hands were planted securely on either side of him and he was up on his toes in a push-up position, driving hard into Hawk over and over.

Each pounding coaxed a loud moan out of Hawk as he absorbed and reveled in the pleasure of the pain. Hawk's legs were suddenly pushed farther back and pinned on both sides of his head. That move forced another moan out of Hawk, but when the sound escaped his lips, it was muffled by Garner's lips covering his.

Hawk groaned into Garner's mouth when he felt the sudden emptiness of the man withdrawing completely, but before he had time to protest, Garner rammed back in with such vigor Hawk was forced against the head of the bed, neck bent and shoulders pinned firmly against the headboard.

Garner released Hawk's legs, eased back, and planted his knees on the bed at Hawk's thighs. He pushed Hawk's left leg over to the side, held his right leg by the ankle in a vertical position, and pounded harder and deeper.

The change in position hit Hawk's sweet spot and had him on the verge of coming. "Jesus fucking Christ," Hawk ground out. "That feels incredible."

The constant rhythm of Garner driving his cock deep inside him was pushing him closer and closer to his release. Just as he was about to give in to the pleasure, Garner withdrew and rolled him over and pulled him up to his knees. Garner's fingernails dug into Hawk's hips as he entered him from behind with the same vengeance and force he'd used earlier. Hawk let out a loud moan as his head was forced against the headboard again.

"Is this how you like it?" Garner asked, pounding harder and harder, his fingernails digging into Hawk's thighs.

"Yesss!" Hawk hissed, bracing himself for the next thrusts. "Harder. Faster. Please!"

Garner obliged and picked up his pace. Hawk's head was pounding into the headboard and his ass was taking a beating and he loved every minute.

The desired abuse was getting the best of Hawk, about to send him over the edge. He attempted to take himself in hand, but Garner forced his hand away. "Mine," he said, reaching around and taking Hawk into his hand to stroke in rhythm with each thrust.

"Holy fuck!" Hawk ground out, desperately fighting to hold back his imminent release. When he gave in to the pleasure, he came in spurts, over and over until Garner milked him dry.

Seconds later Hawk felt Garner stiffen, still pumping feverishly.

"Hawk!" Garner yelled and then bit down on Hawk's shoulder as he came in waves deep inside of him.

With both of them now panting for breath, Garner collapsed on top of Hawk. In return Hawk dropped onto his stomach, wincing as his skin came in contact with the cold, sticky remains of his release. Garner eased out of Hawk and slowly fell to his side. The feeling of fullness now gone, Hawk immediately missed having Garner inside him, but he was too exhausted to complain. He turned onto his side and snuggled his ass into Garner's stomach. Garner threw an arm over his waist and pulled him in tightly. Hawk was confused by the nirvana he was experiencing while lying in the stranger's arms, but he was determined not to overanalyze. He forced himself to enjoy the feeling and simply sighed and closed his eyes.

GARNER LAY still, listening to the lapping of waves against the hull and the steady, rhythmic breaths flowing out the man in his bed, the man he'd thought was going to rob him just the day before and the same man with which he'd just had the roughest sex of his life. He was still in shock, and his mind was reeling from his own behavior during what had just transpired between them. He could never remember being so turned on in his entire life, and the harder Hawk wanted it, the more turned on he became. *What the fuck?* he thought. *Who knew?* But he quickly decided to save the self-analysis for another time.

Right now there was something that interested him much more than self-discovery, and he might never again get the chance to secretly observe the man lying next to him, apparently sleeping like a baby.

He stared at Hawk's perfectly shaped and close-shaved head, admiring the colorful tattoos, but struggling to try to make out what they were in the dimly lit cabin. His gaze slowly drifted down to the shiny studs running down Hawk's left ear, ending at the black discs in Hawk's stretched earlobe. *Why on earth?*

Before Garner could roll that question over in his mind, lightning flashed through the porthole, followed by a loud roar of thunder. Hawk stirred a bit and backed up against him a little closer, but didn't open his eyes or appear to wake up.

Garner continued to study Hawk with the same curiosity with which one would study a newborn baby to make sure all the fingers and toes were where they needed to be. But Hawk was no baby, and although he had all his fingers and toes, he had a shitload of other appendages and interesting things to study.

This time, Garner started at the piercing in Hawk's left eyebrow. He closely examined the inch-long stainless steel bar, paying special attention to the tiny skull and crossbones on each end before dropping his attention to the silver hoop in Hawk's thin and almost regally shaped nose.

That's pretty understated compared to the skull and crossbones.

Next was the bar just below his bottom lip and the one he couldn't see, but knew was there, piercing his tongue. His gaze dropped lower and stopped and focused on the round silver hoops with the small shiny black balls adorning each nipple. *God! That must have hurt.* Moving on, he next focused his attention on the small hoop in Hawk's belly button. He knew the head of Hawk's penis was also pierced, but from this position he couldn't see the hoop there either.

How in the hell does he ever get through airport security?

Looking back up, Garner noticed a tattoo on Hawk's left shoulder. It was some sort of skull with a peacock tail. Below that, leading down his arm, was a huge diamond and what appeared to be a Viking head. And lower still, on his bicep, were horseshoes surrounding an image of a horse and a woman's head. On his forearm was a big dagger in flames and leading down to his hand were a rat and a firecracker.

There seemed to be some sort of tattoo covering every visible part of his arms and legs, though all Garner could see now was his left side. From where he was lying, he couldn't identify any of the tats on Hawk's left leg, but one tattoo on the top of Hawk's left big toe caught his attention.

Garner squinted to try and make out what the hell it was and after quite some time, realized it was a camel. He thought about the significance of a camel on Hawk's toe and then it hit him. "It's a camel toe," he whispered, covering his mouth when he realized he'd said that out loud. Garner did his best to muffle the laughter that was trying to escape his mouth, but apparently he was unsuccessful.

"I'm very impressed," a rough, sleepy voice said. "I normally have to explain that tattoo to people."

"Sorry," Garner whispered, releasing his hold on Hawk's waist as Hawk turned onto his stomach and rested his head on his folded arms. "I didn't—" Garner stopped when he saw the large, colorful peacock covering Hawk's back. "Wow," Garner said. "That's an incredible tattoo."

"Thanks," Hawk replied. "It's one of my favorites. Took two years to complete."

"I don't think I've ever seen a more gorgeous peacock," Garner said, staring at the bird's face. "It looks almost proud, and the colors are so vivid." Leaning back to get a better look, Garner added. "My God, it spans your entire back and shoulders. I'm almost afraid to touch it."

"Don't be," Hawk said. "It doesn't bite."

Garner slowly raised his hand up and touched the peacock's head, tracing the outline of the tattoo consuming Hawk's entire back and shoulders.

"You were going to say something earlier?" Hawk asked inquisitively.

"Oh, I was going to apologize for waking you."

"You didn't."

Roars of thunder joined the lapping sounds, filling the cabin with an air of intrigue and suspense, and neither of them seemed to want to disturb the ambiance by talking.

When the thunder settled, Hawk spoke. "Did you see everything you needed to see?"

Shit! He wasn't sleeping. "Busted again," Garner said. "And to be truthful, the answer is no. I'm really fascinated by... well, everything. But how did you know I was watching you?"

Garner heard the slightest chuckle escape Hawk's lips. "Man, I'd have to be dead not to feel those eyes studying me."

"I'm sorry, I thought you were asleep. I certainly didn't mean to make you uncomfortable."

Hawk laughed out loud, rolled over onto his back, and looked up at Garner. "You don't think you're the first person to look at me like I'm some sort of freak, do you?"

Garner felt the blush heat his cheeks. "I guess you have a point. But for the record, I don't think you're a freak at all."

Hawk closed his eyes. "Go ahead, dude. I know you have questions."

"Well, if you don't mind me asking. Why all this?" Garner asked, waving his hand down Hawk's body.

"Why what?" Hawk asked, his eyes still closed.

"All the piercings and tattoos?"

"Why not?"

"Point well taken," Garner said. "Did any of this hurt?"

"Sometimes," Hawk said. "Some areas are more sensitive than others."

"I guess that makes sense. Is all this addictive once you start?"

Hawk took a long time to answer, as if it were the first time he'd ever been asked the question. "The tattoos are more addictive to me than the piercings. I think I may be at my limit with the piercings. But certainly not the tattoos."

"But the tattoos are all permanent," Garner said. "Do you worry that one day you'll regret getting them or wonder what they are going to look like when you get older?"

"To be honest, I don't feel like I actually have a choice with the tattoos. When I get a new tattoo, I don't feel like I've added something, I actually feel more like I uncovered something that was already there, a new part of me. You know? And as far as what I'll look like when I get old, all I can say is I believe in living for today. To me, my piercings are no different than someone who gets a nose job or some other type of cosmetic surgery—eventually it all goes south."

Garner thought about his answer and decided it was honest and somewhat thought-provoking. But he was still captivated by how it all started, and he wanted to know more. "So what came first, the piercings or the tats?"

"The ear piercings came first, believe it or not," Hawk answered. "When I was about nineteen, I think."

Nineteen? Garner's education told him that since Hawk had waited so long, it probably hadn't started with adolescent rebellion. Most kids who rebel against one thing or another do it early and mostly for the shock value. "It doesn't sound like rebellion to me, so what started it all?"

Again Hawk seemed to be thinking about the question. He shrugged. "Maybe there was a little bit of rebellion, but that wasn't the driving force."

"If not rebellion, then what?" Garner asked.

"I'd wanted a tattoo since I was very little, and surprisingly my parents didn't shut me down right away. I guess they thought it was a whim, and I would forget about it as soon the next thing came along. But after I pestered the hell out of them day after day, they finally sat me down and explained that tattoos were something permanent and getting one was a decision I would need to make as an adult. They said as parents they didn't feel like they should allow me to do something that was so permanent until I was old enough to understand the consequences."

Impressed, Garner nodded. "They handled that pretty well. My parents would have shit a brick if I'd said I wanted a tattoo when I was that young."

"They were pretty cool considering they were both ministers."

Garner didn't see that one coming. "Ministers?" he questioned.

"Yep. My mother was a pastor and my father was a deacon. Don't get me wrong, they were strict, but not so strict that I couldn't express myself."

The wind was still howling, and Hawk was now rubbing Garner's forearm ever so lightly, which was making Garner very sleepy. "Okay, so one more question then I'm done."

Hawk looked up at him with skepticism.

"Promise," Garner said. "It's a two-part question, but the last one for now."

"*For now*, huh?" Hawk mumbled, closing his eyes again. "I figured as much, but shoot."

"Does it piss you off when people stare at you?" Garner asked. "And... do you think people are scared of you because of the way you look?"

Hawk smiled. "Weren't you the first time you saw me?"

Damn! "Busted a third time," Garner admitted. "I thought I concealed being in fear for my life pretty well."

"Seriously, dude? Now that I think back, the look of terror on your face was pretty damned obvious. I was just too hung over to notice at the time," Hawk said, smiling. "But to answer your question, no, it doesn't bother me when people stare. To be honest, for the most part I don't even notice the stares anymore. I've been unique in my hairstyles and the way I dress since I was very young. I guess I'm sort of blind to it after all this time."

Satisfied for now, Garner laid his head back and closed his eyes. "Thanks for indulging me," he said sleepily.

The combination of Hawk rubbing his arm, the sound of the wind, rain, and occasional thunder, and the rocking of the boat lulled Garner into a sound sleep.

When he woke some time later, he reached over without opening his eyes and found an empty spot next to him. He listened for a second and realized he was once again alone in the quiet of his cabin; the storm had obviously gone along with his sexual partner. He rolled onto his side, wrapped his arms around the pillow Hawk had laid his head upon, and inhaled deeply. Hawk's scent was still lingering, and Garner closed his eyes, savoring the smell. He felt a wave of sadness wash over him and wondered why he felt alone for the first time in a very long time.

Garner eventually dozed off again, and when he woke for the second time, he found the feeling still lingering, like the essence of a recent lover.

CHAPTER SIX

HAWK HAD slipped out of Garner's bed naked as the day he was born and crept to the salon. He'd climbed the companionway stairs and slid the door open as quietly as possible. The whole scene had felt like a flashback from the morning before, just like so many of his other duplicitous departures under the cloak of darkness. He'd felt a pang of guilt but quickly brushed it away.

This is your MO, Hawk. Why change it now? Maybe because you felt some kind of connection to this one, not to mention you just had some of the best sex in your life?

He'd gathered up his clothing and stepped into his wet blue jeans, cursing under his breath when the damp, clammy denim came into contact with his warm, dry skin. For a split second, he'd even thought about going below again and crawling back into the warm arms that had held him there just a few minutes ago, but he'd quickly pushed that thought out of his head. He'd pulled the wet cotton Henley over his head and gasped out loud, biting his bottom lip but sucking it up and pushing through the initial shock. He'd stepped into his flip-flops, slipped through the zippered door, and fought the wind and pelting rain back to his boat.

Once again under the protection of his cockpit roof, Hawk quickly stripped out of those godforsaken wet clothes. He dried as best he could with his wet shirt and then stepped into his cabin and headed straight for the head. He showered and slipped into a pair of worn sweat pants. Shirtless, he went to the refrigerator. When he opened the door, the light cast an eerie glow over his galley and salon. Surprised at how gloomy he felt, Hawk glanced at the clock on the microwave oven and then looked through the galley porthole. Although it was only three in the afternoon, the dark, ominous clouds hanging low over the island made it look like dusk.

He retrieved two beers and popped the first top on the way to the couch, dropped, and downed the entire can in one gulp. Leaning back in the darkened salon, Hawk crossed his legs and popped the second top. He took a sip and then held the cool can against his stomach. He closed his eyes and rested his head on the back of the couch. An image of Garner instantly burst into his mind. The man was doing pushups on top of him, forcing his cock in and out, tantalizing him with every stroke, his rich brown eyes burning with desire. Hawk felt a surge of electricity travel through him and land right in his cock, causing an instant erection.

He downed the second beer, tossed the can to the floor, and pulled his sweats down then kicked them completely off. He spit into his hand, grabbed his cock, and pumped. He stuck the fingers from his other hand into his mouth and slid them down to his asshole, wincing when he came in contact with his very tender opening. He pushed through the initial discomfort and slowly slid two fingers inside, massaging and moving in unison with the hand pumping his cock. In his mind's eye, he pictured Garner on top of him, pounding into him, and he remembered the way it felt to be taken by his uptight stranger.

It took only minutes for his heart rate to double and the hypersensitive nerve endings in his dick and asshole to go into overdrive, sending him into a full-blown sexual frenzy. He instinctively started to gyrate on the fingers massaging his insides and pumped feverishly on his cock.

"Fuck yeah!" he hissed, throwing his head back and releasing his load, coating his chin, chest, and stomach in spurts of warm liquid. "Fuck!" he repeated, running his tongue over his chin, tasting himself as he squeezed and worked every last drop of his release onto his stomach.

"Damn! I've got to start using lube," Hawk said out loud as he closed his eyes, winced, and gingerly slid his fingers out of his ass. He sighed and stilled as his heart rate began to slow and the waves of his orgasm dissipated.

A vision of Garner's handsome face again popped into his mind. "Fuck no!" he said, turning his head from side to side in an attempt to rid himself of the vision. "I've got to get out of here before I sex myself to death." He hopped up and headed for another shower.

Twenty minutes later Hawk was standing in his salon, dressed in his standard black T-shirt, torn jeans, and badly worn Doc Martens, the smell of Old Spice filling the small cabin. He looked out and saw the wind and rain had stopped and the skies were starting to clear. He dug his cell phone out of his pocket and speed-dialed Justin. His best friend answered on the first ring. "Hawk?" he whispered.

"Hey, what's up, Butt-rah?"

Dead silence on the other end of the phone.

"Jus… you still there?" Hawk asked.

"Yes, I'm here and you know I hate that name," Justin answered in a very curt but very low tone. "And you also know I'm not supposed to answer my cell phone at work. What's wrong?"

"Nothing's wrong, why do you assume something's wrong every time I call?"

"Because of late, unless something's wrong, you never call. And never at this hour."

That comment stung, but Hawk brushed it off and continued. "Everything's fine, okay? And… I know you hate that nickname, but I love it, and I only use it as a term of endearment."

"Fine," Justin said in a hushed tone.

Hawk pictured his pocket gay behind the coffee counter with his back to the customers, hunched over his phone, his hand over his mouth, whispering but looking over his shoulder constantly to make sure his boss didn't catch him.

"So, you want to meet me somewhere for a drink?"

"What? It's only—" Justin paused, obviously looking at his watch. "—four o'clock."

"Yeah, almost happy hour," Hawk teased. "If it makes you feel better, you can meet me somewhere and not have a drink until five o'clock."

Justin chuckled. "You're in an awfully good mood. You must have gotten laid again."

"Oh, come on. Can't a guy be in a good mood that has nothing to do with sex?"

"Most people can, but *not* you, Hawken Bristol," Justin said.

"Ohhhhh—a knife directly to my heart," Hawk teased. "So you want to meet me or not?"

"Sure. I get off work in about thirty minutes. Where?"

"How about the Bourbon Street Pub?" Hawk asked. "I haven't been there in ages, and they have two for one from five to seven."

"Okay," Justin whispered. "I'll meet you there. Now let me hang up this phone before I get fired."

"See you in a bit," Hawk whispered back, not sure why he was keeping *his* voice down.

HAWK WAS sitting at the bar when he saw Justin bounce in with his usual flare. He waved and patted the empty barstool next to him as Justin made his way through the crowded bar, stopping to say hello to everyone he knew. He suddenly remembered how well liked Justin was and how many casual friends he had compared to Hawk. Justin's friendship was it for him. Hawk wasn't very trusting, and not that many people cared for his over-the-top appearance anyway, so it worked out just fine.

Hawk thought back to when he'd first moved to Key West. Most guys—well, to be honest, most people—had stayed clear of him, he assumed because of the way he looked. Justin had been different. He was the first person Hawk had met who didn't look at him like he had two heads and had walked right up to him and introduced himself and never once mentioned a single tattoo or piercing. Justin had treated him like a regular person, and they had become fast friends. His pocket gay was an all-around nice guy, and Hawk had never heard anything to the contrary.

Hawk looked at Justin working the crowd, his tight little muscular body bouncing from person to person, his smile beaming as he laughed and flirted, teasing his way through the bar. Hawk wondered again why Justin never dated. He seemed to have a ton of acquaintances, but as far as Hawk knew, he was Justin's only good friend. He decided tonight was the night he was going to find out.

When Justin finally made it to his barstool and gave Hawk a hug and a kiss on the cheek, he realized what an odd pair they must make to everyone who saw them together. Justin was as handsome, conservative, and put together as any New York model, as opposed to Hawk's freakish appearance and demeanor. He shook his head in wonderment at the fact that they'd been friends for going on six years.

Of course, they'd had their issues of late. Especially since Hawk had supposedly gone down a road of casual hookups and wild sex Justin didn't think was good for him. But Hawk knew Justin's bitching was out of concern, and although it drove him mad, he understood and tolerated it because he genuinely loved the little guy.

"How many have I missed?" Justin asked, running a hand through his short dark hair.

"You're only one behind," Hawk assured him. "This is just my second."

"I'll have two vodka tonics," Justin said to the bartender.

"That's my boy," Hawk said, reaching over and rubbing Justin's shoulder. "Should I be concerned?"

"Whatever for?" Justin said sarcastically. "Maybe for the fact that I got reamed out royally by my big ole lesbian bull dyke of a boss because I answered my cell phone again?"

"Oops," Hawk said, pulling a swig off his beer.

The bartender dropped two drinks in front of Justin, smiled, and waited.

"Oops my ass." Justin cocked his head toward Hawk and told the bartender, "Put these on his tab."

Hawk nodded and the bartender disappeared to the other end of the bar. "I'm sorry, Jus, I don't really know your schedule anymore, so I have no idea when it's okay to call or not."

Justin looked at him like he was an alien and shook his head. "I have the same schedule I've always had, asshole."

Hawk looked down at his empty beer bottle. "I'm sorry. I guess I haven't been a very good friend lately."

"Give me your cell phone," Justin ordered.

"What?"

Justin repeated his request.

Hawk dug his phone out of his pocket and did as he was asked.

Justin slid his fingers across the bottom of the screen and tapped a few times. When he finished, he handed the phone back to Hawk.

Hawk looked at the screen and saw that the calendar was open. He tapped the days and realized Justin had just added his schedule from seven thirty in the morning to four thirty in the afternoon on Wednesday through Sunday.

"Thanks, man. I promise I'll use this."

"Make sure you do, because I don't want to have to go to jail for planting my foot up some bull dyke's ass."

Hawk threw his head back and howled. "Got it. Besides, you're too pretty to go to jail."

"Tell me about it," Justin said, looking Hawk up and down. "Enough about me, let's talk about you."

"What?"

"You have that just-laid look again. Who and when?"

Hawk's lips curved into a smile, and he shook his head. "Damn, Jus, are you spying on me? If not, you must be kin to *The Mentalist* or something. How can you always know what's going on with me?"

Justin looked him up and down again. "Because I know you very well, for starters, but every time you get laid, you get this really relaxed expression, and all the stress drains out of your face."

Hawk shook his head in disbelief. "I'll remember that and try to always look stressed out just to throw you off."

"Seriously," Justin said. "I'll bet it was with that guy from last night, right?"

Hawk slammed his hand down on the bar, causing their drinks to rattle. "Now I know you're spying on me."

"Oh man, this is going to be good," Justin teased. "Out with it."

Hawk gave him the Reader's Digest version about how and what had transpired earlier in the day, but of course left out all the sexual details.

"Wow, dude," Justin said, shaking his head. "It's not like you to shit in your own back yard. Unless…?"

Hawk turned to Justin and immediately recognized the "I know you're keeping something from me" expression on his face. He'd seen it many times before and dreaded what was coming next. "I really don't want to know what you're thinking, so stop it and let's move on," he warned.

Justin flashed his famous all-knowing smile. "You like this guy and you want to see him again."

"You're crazy," Hawk replied.

Justin downed the last of his first drink and took a sip of the second. "Well I'll be damned."

"Just stop it, Butt-rah," Hawk said rather curtly. "You're way off base with this one."

"Now I know I'm right 'cause you only get that tone with me when you're feeling defensive about something."

"Fuck," Hawk cursed under his breath, staring at his empty beer bottle. "Am I that fucking transparent and predictable?"

"Yep" was all Justin said.

Before Hawk said another word, he held up a finger and the bartender came running over with another beer. "Okay, so I had a good time and maybe I will fuck him again, but that's all there is to it."

"That's saying a lot coming from Mr. Hit and Run. Are you sure about that?"

"Positive. The guy was a good fuck, and I wouldn't mind tapping that again. That's all. Plain and simple. And besides, you know I'm not the dating kind."

"Whatever you say," Justin mumbled wryly. "Whatever you say."

To get the attention off *his* love life, Hawk tried to change the subject. "How come we talk about my love life all the time? Enough about me! How come you never tell me anything about your love life? In all the years I've known you, I've never seen you go out on a date or ever go home with anyone."

Justin took another sip of his drink and put it down on the bar. "Because I don't date" was all he said.

Hawk rested his arms on the bar and turned his head to look at Justin again. "I know you don't date, Jus, but what I don't know is why."

The blood seemed to drain out of Justin's face. His expression became somber, and he started fidgeting with his cocktail napkin.

"Come on, Justin, I know you pretty well too. For years I've had this feeling that something bad must have happened to you and that's why you don't trust very many people. But what I don't understand is why you don't trust me. I haven't pried because I figured when you got to know me, you would eventually tell me, but every time I bring up your dating, or lack thereof, you change the subject."

Hawk paused and waited for Justin to say something, anything, but he just looked straight ahead, like he was seeing something in the mirror behind the bar that Hawk wasn't.

Hawk tried again. "Look, I realize you know most of Key West; hell, I witnessed it again when you got here. But as far as I know, I'm your only really good friend. Why is that?"

Justin gulped the rest of his drink and put the glass down. His hands were now trembling, and he closed his eyes and held on to the end of the bar. He turned to Hawk and looked him in the eyes. "I do trust you. Does that make you happy? And the answer is... because I was raped. Satisfy your curiosity?"

Justin turned on his barstool, stood, and made a beeline for the door.

GARNER SAT in front of the television with the remote control in his hand, sipping a glass of chardonnay while he flipped from channel to channel, but nothing seemed to hold his interest.

A couple of hours ago, he'd seen Hawk bouncing down the dock, looking as happy as a lark, on his way to God only knows where, dressed like he was looking for some serious man-on-man action.

"Why should that bother me?" Garner asked himself out loud. "Every indication says this guy has some serious baggage, and I should avoid him like the plague."

And what about your shitload of baggage? You're a loner in your thirties who sucks at relationships and gave up your high-powered career to chase the horizon. Now tell me that's not baggage. Garner had to chuckle at his own thoughts, but sadly, he was right. What kept bothering him, though, was he couldn't figure out why he was so drawn to this guy.

In a fit of frustration, he shut the television off and threw the remote across to the other side of the couch. The more he thought about the man, the more Hawk piqued the interest of the psychiatrist in him. He could quite possibly be a classic textbook case. His desire for exceptionally rough sex, combined with his appearance, could indicate a guy who'd had a lot of shit to deal with growing up.

If Hawk hadn't told him that his parents were rational, well-educated ministers, he would have guessed—an educated guess, of course—that they had been unmarried teenagers with drug and/or alcohol addictions who cared little or nothing about him or his upbringing. Another possibility might be that he was a child of a single working mother with no real male influence in his life. And any of the above options could have had a negative effect on Hawk and his self-esteem, causing him to act out in appearance and behavior. But the rough sex—that was a totally different story.

There were all sorts of textbook cases that came to Garner's mind when he thought about the sex. One real possibility was sexual and physical child abuse. Some studies show a direct link between a preference for rough sex and adults who were sexually and physically abused as children. In some cases, the victim doesn't believe he or she deserves to be loved in a gentle and loving way and therefore thrives on more brutal sexual activity.

Another possibility with abused children involved the need for domination and power. The adult feels that he or she had no power to stop the abuse when it was happening, so they must exert that power now. But Hawk was totally submissive, so that might not apply in his case.

Fear of intimacy could be a factor, as well as a mental and physical disconnect between love and sex. But the most common psychological explanation was that the pain of rough sex sometimes reassured an abused person that they could still feel something.

Garner was smart enough to know that all this was just speculation, and there was no way to really know unless he sat down with the guy and picked at his brain. *Hell*, Garner thought. *For all I know, the guy may just like rough sex, tattoos, and piercings.* Which basically blew his textbook diagnosis all to hell.

Garner downed his wine and poured himself another glass. He looked through the galley porthole and saw that the storm clouds had moved on, giving way to the stars and moon now shining brightly in the dark evening sky. The harsh wind had also diminished, leaving behind a light easterly breeze that caused the palms on the tree-lined shore to sway gently to the west. Garner ventured up to the cockpit, opened all the vinyl glass panels, and lay down on the bench seat, enjoying the soft, tepid wind as it passed over him.

It wasn't long before the breeze, combined with the gentle lapping sounds against the hull, lulled him into a deep sleep.

"FUCK!" HAWK mumbled under his breath. He dug into his pocket, threw two twenties on the bar, and took off after his best friend. He moved as quickly as he could without making a scene, but Justin had a head start and maneuvered his compact body through the crowded bar at breakneck speed. With his head hanging down and without stopping to talk to a single person, Justin stormed right past all the acquaintances he'd chatted with earlier and busted through the front doors of the club without stopping.

By the time Hawk was outside, he had to break into a jog just to keep Justin in sight. Hawk yelled to him to slow down and wait, but Justin either didn't hear him or was pissed and ignoring him. Hawk picked up his pace again, and when he finally reached Justin, he reached for Justin's arm. His friend yanked it away and kept going.

Hawk broke into full-out run, passed Justin, turned, and stopped with his arms wide open. Justin was unable to stop and ran right into his arms. Hawk wrapped Justin up and held him tightly. "I'm so sorry, man," Hawk whispered into Justin's ear. "I felt sure something had happened to you, but I never imagined this."

Justin made a lame attempt to break free, but Hawk tightened his hold, and the little guy eventually stilled, settling into his embrace. Justin covered his face with both hands and rested his head on Hawk's broad chest. Hawk actually felt Justin's sobs before he heard them and held on tighter, hoping to reassure Justin that everything would be okay.

Duval Street was abuzz, and the tourists seemed to do their best to sidestep the two men embracing in the middle of the sidewalk. To their credit, most of them tried to be discreet, but Hawk quickly realized that even in Key West the sight of a heavily tattooed man with a shaved head and piercings in every orifice holding on tightly to a small muscular sobbing man was a little hard to resist, so he decided to let them have this one.

Justin eventually started settling down, his sobs slowly changing over to low whimpers, but Hawk continued to hold on fast. He was still trying to catch his breath from running two blocks, and his stomach was churning from the beers he'd downed at happy hour, but Hawk wasn't going to let that stop him from taking care of his friend.

When Justin eventually quieted, he slipped his arms around Hawk's back and squeezed with such strength it forced a beer burp out of Hawk's mouth.

The shock of what he'd just done forced Hawk to release his grip. Justin took the opportunity and pushed out of the hold, slapped Hawk across the chest, and started rubbing the burp off his shoulder.

He looked Hawk right in the eye. "Jesus, Hawk! Not only did you make me cry like a baby in the middle of Duval Street, you burped all over my damn shoulder."

Hawk returned the stare, then took a step back and put his hands on his hips. "Well excuse me, your royal highness! My stomach was full of beer, and I had to chase your squirrely ass for two blocks. You're lucky I didn't fart on you while I was at it."

The look of disgust on Justin's face almost brought a smile to Hawk's, but he held it together. "Yeah, you heard me," he said, nodding repeatedly.

Justin showed no expression for a few seconds and then suddenly burst into laughter. Hawk tried his hardest to look pissed, but he couldn't keep a straight face to save his soul. They laughed until they were both doubled over, wiping the tears out of their eyes.

When they were finally able to get themselves under control, Hawk threw an arm over Justin's shoulder. "How about hotdogs and french fries to go? I'm starved."

Justin smiled and nodded without saying a word, and with Hawk's arm draped over Justin's shoulder, they starting walking back toward the marina. They stopped at Hawk's favorite hotdog cart and loaded up with way too much food and were still laughing when they stepped through the gate and onto the dock.

Hawk paused briefly when he passed *AquaTherapy*, and Justin, who never missed a thing, piped up, "Is that his boat? You know we have plenty of food if you want to invite him."

"Yes, that's his boat. And you better stop it, you little shit, before you find yourself taking an evening swim!" Hawk said, continuing on to his boat.

Justin howled again. "God, this is so much fun."

They sat cross-legged on the floor in their sock feet with a pile of empty hotdog wrappers and french fry boxes between them. Hawk had long since unlaced and kicked off his Doc Martens and Justin his Nikes.

Hawk drew a long sip off his bottled water and twisted the top back on. "So will you tell me about it?" he asked hesitantly.

Justin didn't respond. He simply leaned back on his elbows, crossed his feet at the ankles, and stared up at the ceiling as if he were mentally traveling back in time. When Justin dropped his head and looked at Hawk, his face had taken on a solemn expression and his honey brown eyes were dark and cloudy with indecision.

A long, uncomfortable silence loomed between them until Justin finally spoke, his voice low, shaky, and riddled with emotion. "It happened when I was a junior in high school."

Seeing the pain etched in his best friend's face and hearing the hesitancy in his voice, Hawk quickly raised his hand. "Dude! It's okay. I can tell this is painful for you. Let's talk about something else."

Justin looked up to the ceiling again without even acknowledging that Hawk had spoken. "I met him the night of my junior prom." Justin looked back down at Hawk briefly and offered him a weak smile. "I told you I came out of the womb gay, right?"

"Many times," Hawk said, rolling his eyes and nodding while he scooted back against the couch and stretched out.

"So I'm sure it comes as no shock to you that I was out and proud in high school."

Hawk opened his mouth to answer, but when Justin continued on with his story, Hawk figured it must have been a rhetorical question.

"I was teased and bullied a good bit because of it and even beaten up a few times, but it didn't take me too long to figure out that if I faded into the background and didn't draw unwanted attention to myself, I could survive. So when the prom came around, I decided that putting the spotlight back on myself by taking a guy, or even a girl, to the prom was totally out of the question. Besides, the only other openly gay guy in my school was a total dweeb."

Knowing Justin as well as he did, Hawk knew Justin would rather stay home then take a dweeb to the prom and that made him smile.

Justin didn't seem to notice Hawk's change of expression and continued without missing a beat. "But I still wanted to go to the prom, so I volunteered to be on the prom committee. That way I could still go, but it didn't look too weird if I didn't have a date."

"Sounds like a pretty good solution," Hawk replied.

"I thought so," Justin agreed. "The prom was in the grand ballroom of a downtown hotel, and the room was set up with round tables of eight, six students and a teacher/chaperone and his or her significant other. Besides being in charge of the decorations, my job was to stand at the front door and greet everyone and give them their table assignments."

"That doesn't sound like fading into the background to me," Hawk replied.

"Yeah, well, I figured no one would fuck with me outside of school," Justin said sarcastically. "And please keep the commentary to a minimum, this is hard enough already."

Hawk was just about to say, "Fuck you, asshole," when Justin started speaking again.

"So while I was at the door doing my job, a classmate of mine, Hillary Twesman, walked up to the table with her date. She was a truly pitiful-looking little thing everyone at school called Hillary *Toothman* because she had huge horse teeth and way too many of them to boot. She looked like a fucking Kennedy reject. Anyway her date was, surprisingly, quite handsome, and I later found out he was a sophomore at Florida State."

"Was a high school student allowed to bring a college student to the prom?" Hawk asked.

"Probably not, but the school left that mostly up to the parents unless it was pretty obvious."

"Seriously?" Hawk asked, shaking his head in disbelief.

"Yep, but we digress, *again*," Justin snarled, continuing his story. "Much to my surprise, when she introduced us, her date gave me quite a look and held on just a little longer than protocol when we shook hands. The guy's name was Andrew Powers, and needless to say, after that I was quite smitten with him."

Hawk leaned forward. "Because a guy held your hand a little longer than normal?"

"Give me a break. I was a sixteen-year-old virgin."

Hawk did the math in his head. "Sixteen? Shouldn't you have been at least seventeen?"

"Yeah, but because my birthday is in December and I was just a few months shy of turning six when the school year began in September, I started the first grade when I was five."

Hawk nodded in acceptance. "Okay, got it."

"So, I gave them their table assignment and that was the last I saw of him until much later that night."

Hawk cocked an eyebrow but didn't say anything.

"Yeah, I know," Justin said wryly. "So later that night, I needed to pee. I took a break and headed to the men's room. When I got there, one of the two urinals was available, so I walked up and unzipped my tuxedo pants and was digging for my hooha when the guy standing at the urinal next to me looked over and smiled. He just looked so sweet and alluring."

"Hooha?" Hawk asked. "Who calls a cock a *hooha*?"

"Do you want the story or not?" Justin asked in an annoyed voice.

"You're right, sorry."

"Anyway, I smiled back and then did a quick double take. The guy was Andrew. I quickly turned my head and stared blankly at the newspaper in the glass display over the urinal while I pulled my *dick* out"—the sarcasm was obvious—"and started peeing.

"From the corner of my eye, I saw him look over at me again, and then he lowered his gaze and stared at my dick while I peed. I got so nervous it took all I had not to stop peeing midstream. I felt goose bumps forming on my arms, and my blood started pumping through my veins at breakneck speed. It was a feeling I'll never forget," Justin said, wrapping his arm around himself.

"Luckily, he finished before I did. When he stepped away from the urinal, I exhaled in relief, or disappointment, I'm not quite sure which, and closed my eyes and focused on finishing. I heard the water running and then the paper towel dispenser whirling and then nothing. Silence. I convinced myself the entire thing had been in my head and nothing but a stupid fantasy. When I finished peeing, I zipped up, turned around, and boy was I surprised."

Justin paused briefly, took a deep breath, and smiled weakly. Justin appeared to be reliving the entire scene in his head and his expression was one Hawk couldn't quite read. Hawk felt a pang of guilt for asking him to go through this all over again. But oddly enough when Justin spoke this time, Hawk picked up on a tinge of excitement. Hawk leaned back again and raised his hand. "Wait!" he said. "Let me guess. He was still there."

"Yep!" Justin said but didn't elaborate.

"And?" Hawk asked.

"I froze in my tracks. Andrew was leaning on the counter in his expertly tailored tuxedo, looking every bit like a movie star about to hit the red carpet. My God, he was big. If I had to guess, he was at least six-five and two hundred and twenty pounds. You know the type," Justin added. "Football player size."

Hawk nodded.

"His blue eyes were locked on mine, and he was smiling broadly, his perfect teeth sparkling in the florescent lighting of the hotel bathroom. You know, it's funny. This gorgeous guy was staring at me in the men's room, and my first thought was *my God, his teeth are white*." Justin shook his head in disbelief.

"So?" Hawk asked. "Did you two just stare at one another or did someone speak?"

"He said, 'Hey there,' as he folded his massive arms over his chest and stretched his long legs out in front of him, crossing them at the ankles. At that moment in my life, I remember thinking he was the most beautiful man I'd ever seen, and his teeth were so white," Justin said, smiling like he was picturing the man in his mind.

"What's with you and teeth?" Hawk asked.

"I know, right?" Justin said. "Who knew one could have a tooth fetish?"

Justin continued. "Anyway, I smiled back and told him hello, and then being the shy sixteen-year-old I was, I dipped my head, breaking the eye contact. I willed my feet to carry me over to the sink where I nervously began washing my hands. I heard the dispenser whirling again, and when I finished, he handed me a wad of paper towels, his smile still beaming brightly.

"I dried my hands and tossed the paper into the trashcan, and not knowing else to do, I turned to leave. He grabbed my arm to stop me, and with his mere touch, I felt electricity flowing through my body. 'Please wait,' he said. He began to tell me how Hillary had let it slip that I liked boys. *Here goes*, I thought, *now he's gonna beat me up or something.* But much to my surprise, he confessed that he liked boys as well.

"Before I could ask, he told me the only reason he had agreed to escort Hilary to the prom was because their parents were best friends and his mother had asked him to do it because she didn't have a date. Then he told me I was adorable and leaned over and kissed me right on the lips. And that, my friend… was my very first kiss.

"He asked me out for the very next night, and of course I accepted."

Hawk sat up straight at that statement. "What did you parents think about that?"

"They didn't know," Justin shared. "They would have never allowed me to go, so I told them I was going to the movies with a friend, which I'd convinced myself was pretty much the truth anyway."

Hawk shook his head. Although he knew the outcome, he didn't like where this was going.

"Don't judge," Justin said calmly, holding up a finger. "We decided to meet at a movie theater the next night, and I was walking on clouds I was so happy."

"Wait," Hawk said. "You had a car?"

"Yes," Justin said, sounding exhausted. "Does that really matter?"

"I guess not. Okay. Sorry."

"He bought my ticket like a gentleman, and we sat in the far corner of the back row. A subtle brush of his leg against mine led to a deliberate squeeze to my knee. After a quick stolen kiss on the cheek, we were making out like the teenager I was. I'm sure people were watching us, but at that moment in time, I didn't give a shit. Oh my God. Even now looking back, I think he was the best kisser I ever had."

"Not that you had much to compare him to," Hawk said.

"I said looking back now, Hawk. Are you gonna let me finish or not?"

Hawk waved his hand in the air. "Am I not allowed to ask questions?"

"Not until Q&A," Justin said, going right back into the story. "So anyway, we made out for half the movie until he took me by the hand and led me out of the theater and to his car. We left my car at the movies and drove to a spot I'd heard of but had never been to. You know, one of those remote places kids go to make out?"

Justin held his hand up before Hawk could respond. "Rhetorical question, no need to respond."

Hawk nodded but noted that Justin's face was taking on a darker expression.

"He convinced me to get in the backseat so we would have more room to stretch out, and we started to make out again. I remember thinking I had died and gone to heaven. He was holding my right hand with his left and rubbing circles in my palm ever so gently as we kissed. Then without me even realizing it, he slowly maneuvered my hand to his crotch. When I felt his erection through his pants, I panicked and drew my hand back. He whispered assurances in my ear and coaxed me a little and my hand settled on his crotch. It wasn't until he started moving my hand back and forth over his erection that I started to get nervous and withdrew again. He unbuttoned his jeans and pulled them, along with his underwear, down to his knees and started playing with himself. I was intrigued and frightened at the same time. I mean, man, his cock was huge, and of course, at the time, I only had myself as a comparison. I'm not small, but my God, he was massive. Then he lifted my chin and brought our lips together again, and I lost sight of it, but I could still feel him moving so I knew he was still stroking."

Justin closed his eyes and stopped talking. Hawk figured this is where things took a turn for the worst, and he wondered if Justin would continue. He watched patiently as Justin took deep breaths and slowly opened his eyes. The honey brown color had turned to a deep dark brown.

Justin inhaled deeply. "Before I knew it, he was forcing my face down to his crotch, squeezing the back of my neck so hard I couldn't move, demanding I open my mouth. Overpowered and with no other choice I could see at the time, I did."

Justin stopped talking and looked at the ceiling. "I don't know, maybe that's really what I wanted. I've asked myself time after time if I brought this on myself."

"No!" Hawk said. "No matter how far it got or how much you teased, if you said stop, he should have stopped."

Without acknowledging Hawk's comments, Justin continued. "He forced my head down onto his dick, grabbed my hair, and moved my head up and down. God, I remembering gagging continuously and not being able to breathe as he maneuvered my head up and down his cock. That's when I went from scared to terrified."

Justin paused and wrapped his arms around himself. When he wiped a single teardrop from his cheek, Hawk reached out and laid a hand on Justin's leg. "Dude, you can stop if this is too much."

"No," Justin argued, his bottom lip quivering. "This is the first time in over ten years I've talked about it. I need to get this out."

Hawk squeezed Justin's leg in a show of support. "You can stop anytime you want to. It's okay."

Justin closed his eyes and continued with tears now streaming down his cheeks. "That went on for a while but eventually it wasn't enough for Andrew. He lifted my head, and using the weight and sheer size of his body, maneuvered me onto my stomach. He stretched his body out on top of mine and held me facedown in the backseat. I kicked and thrashed, trying to get away, but I was very puny back then, not near as muscular as I am now, and his weight was crushing on top of me. I remember him reaching under my waist and unhooking my khakis and yanking them and my underwear down to my ankles. The last thing I heard was a spitting sound before I felt the worse pain in my life. The fabric of the car seat muffled my screams as he forced his way inside me over and over again. My begging him to stop only seemed to excite him more, and he pumped furiously until he finally came and eventually collapsed on my back. After he caught his breath he pulled his pants up and got off the backseat. When he slammed the car door shut, I sat up and struggled to pull my pants up. My underwear was caught around my knees and the damn things wouldn't come all the way up. I felt his gaze on me, and I looked up and our eyes met in the rearview mirror. His eyes were no longer sweet and alluring, but cold and not the least bit remorseful. All he said was 'Get dressed.'

"He then drove me back to my car and said that if I ever told anyone what happened, he would say it was consensual and it would be his word against mine. He also told me his parents were very well connected in our town, and he felt certain everyone would believe him over me."

"Fucker!" Hawk mumbled under his breath. "Please tell me you didn't accept that."

"Oh hell no," Justin said. "I may have been small, but I wasn't stupid. I knew something he didn't know."

Hawk smiled. "You were only sixteen. That's statutory rape in most states."

Justin closed his eyes and nodded. "Bingo! Anyway, I drove myself home and immediately told my parents what had happened."

"*Yesss,*" Hawk said, slapping Justin's leg again. "How did they react?"

"Exactly how I expected them to. They were outraged, shocked, and although I knew they were disappointed in me, they never let it show until much later. When everything was said and done, I was grounded for a year for lying to them and putting myself in that situation. Anyway, they took me straight to the hospital and told the doctor what had happened. He completed his examination and called the authorities."

"Did they do a DNA test?" Hawk asked.

"DNA tests weren't as widely used back then as they are now, but my dad, not knowing if Andrew would deny the rape or not, had the smarts to insist they take one. In the end, we really didn't need it. Remember Andrew still didn't know I was sixteen and didn't have the sense to deny anything happened.

"Within four hours he was brought in for questioning and forced to take his own DNA test. At first he did exactly as he said he would and told them I came on to him in the movie theater and it was completely consensual, but luckily the medical examination showed otherwise. Imagine Andrew's surprise when he was ultimately arrested for statutory rape of a minor."

"I hope that bastard got what was coming to him," Hawk said, pounding his fist into his open palm.

Justin reached over, plucked a tissue out of the box on the end table, and wiped his face and blew his nose. "In the state where I grew up, the law says, and isn't this sad that I remember this word for word: 'Anyone who engages in an act of unlawful sexual intercourse with a person under age eighteen who is more than three years younger than the actor is guilty of either a misdemeanor or a felony and punishable by up to one year in county jail or by imprisonment in the state prison.' His family connections kept him out of a state-run prison, but he still got a year in the county jail and five years' probation, not to mention the status of sex offender for the rest of his life."

"Fucking A." Hawk wrapped his arms around Justin. "The bastard deserved so much more," Hawk added when they were both upright again. "But at least he paid for his actions."

The two friends sipped their bottles of water in silence for a little while, Hawk not really knowing what to say and Justin looking absolutely exhausted.

Eventually Hawk spoke. "Dude, it all makes perfect sense to me now. I always knew there was something, and I understand now why you don't date or trust people that easily."

Justin cocked his head to the side and opened his mouth like he was going to correct something Hawk had just said and then thought better of it.

"What?" Hawk asked. "After what we just shared, you think there's something you can't tell me?"

"Just because I don't go out on physical dates, doesn't mean I don't date at all," Justin shared with a slight smile.

"I don't get—" Hawk stopped short. "You mean the Internet?"

Justin flashed a smile and nodded.

"How do you date on the Internet?" Hawk asked. "I know you can meet people on the Internet, but you eventually have to meet in person. Right?"

"Not necessarily," Justin said.

"I know I'm the last one that should be talking to you about sex," Hawk said. "But, dude, are you having cybersex?"

"For the last twenty-three months with the same guy," Justin admitted.

"No shit," Hawk said, smiling broadly. "Dude."

Hawk's smile quickly faded when a thought popped into his mind.

"What?" Justin asked.

"What kind of guy has cybersex with you for almost two years without wanting to eventually meet you in person?"

Justin smiled. "The kind of guy who's in the Coast Guard and has been on a ship for the last twenty-two months."

Hawk thought about Justin's answer. "You said twenty-two months. That means he's back on terra firma? What are you gonna do now?"

Justin closed his eyes. "I haven't figured that out yet."

"Jesus, Justin," Hawk said. "You don't know this guy. If you keep refusing to meet him, and he thinks you led him on for two years, he might come looking for you."

Justin held both hands up, palms out. "Relax, Hawk. It's okay, man. He doesn't know my real name or where I live, all he knows is my online screen name."

"Okay, if a guy is really into you, do you think he would just be happy with a screen name for two years?" Hawk asked. "Hasn't he asked for pictures or anything?"

"Yessss," Justin snapped back.

"And…?"

"If you must know, I sent him a picture of a guy who looks similar to me I downloaded off the Internet."

Hawk stood and started pacing back and forth, rubbing his shaved head. "Fuck, Jus, you're a catfish?"

Justin looked down, fumbled with his water bottle, and didn't respond.

"And what do you know about *him*?" Hawk asked. "What if he's not who he says he is either?"

"I know a hell of a lot more about him than just his screen name," Justin replied. "His name is Jeremy Stanton, he's twenty-nine years old, and he's stationed in Charleston, South Carolina."

"Okayyy," Hawk said. "That's what he's told you. Has he sent *you* a picture?"

"Yes," Justin replied rather proudly. "In his uniform."

"You know, we can scan that picture and do an Internet search to see if he's legitimate. And I might add that he can do the same with yours."

"Really?" Justin responded.

"But let's look at this from another perspective," Hawk said. "I'm the last one to judge based on my sexual habits alone, but at least I'm honest. Let's say he's being totally truthful with you. How does it make you feel that you've been lying to the guy for the last two years?"

Justin just continued to fumble with his water bottle. "I know," he eventually admitted. "You're right. But I've been hoping to get the courage to actually meet him in person. And then I could explain everything to him."

"Has he even asked to meet?"

"Of course."

"And…?"

"I told him I was traveling for work and wouldn't be back for a couple of months."

"Oh jeeze, dude. And he accepted that?"

"Totally, Hawk. In fact, he said I've waited for him for twenty-two months, the least he could do was wait on me for a couple more."

"Then what?" Hawk said, throwing his hands in the air.

"I don't know yet," Justin said in a very low voice, looking Hawk in the eye for the first time since they started this conversation. "Hawk, please don't be mad at me. I really like this guy, and I want to meet him. I really do, I'm just not ready."

Hawk exhaled and this time ran both hands over his shaved head. "Jesus, Justin. What am I going to do with you?"

"Help me?" Justin whispered. "And please don't make me sorry I confided in you."

Hawk dropped to the floor in front of his friend and wrapped his arms around his muscular little body. "Yeah, I'll help you." He leaned back and grabbed Justin by the shoulders. "Tell me something. Are all the muscles and constant workouts because of what happened to you?"

"Pretty much," Justin admitted with a slight smile. "I hoped that feeling stronger physically would make me feel stronger emotionally."

"And has that worked?"

Justin seemed to be thinking. "I think so, yeah."

"Good."

Hawk stood again and Justin started clearing up the food wrappers from earlier. "I'm exhausted. I think I'm gonna get out of your hair."

"Come on," Hawk said, grabbing his shoes. "I'll walk you home."

"I don't need to be walked home," Justin protested.

"I know you don't," Hawk was quick to agree. "But I don't feel like going out, but I'm not the least bit sleepy either. Maybe a walk will do the trick. Besides it's only a few blocks."

CHAPTER SEVEN

GARNER WAS startled out of a sound sleep by male voices. He raised his head just in time to see Hawk and another guy stepping onto the dock. As they got a little closer, he recognized the guy as Hawk's date from the night before.

Garner quickly laid his head back down, not the least bit in the mood for an awkward encounter with Hawk and his boyfriend. He silently waited for them to pass by, and when he no longer heard voices, he released his breath and closed his eyes again.

Boyfriend? Apparently Hawk was dating this guy, and now Garner felt like a total heel for sleeping with someone else's boyfriend. He lay there contemplating his situation until his stomach started demanding something to eat. *It's time for a shower and some dinner.*

After a nice long hot shower and slipping into his favorite jersey running shorts and a T-shirt, Garner poured another glass of wine and rummaged through the refrigerator, eventually deciding on a salad, filet, and a baked sweet potato. He cautiously stuck his head out of the companionway door and listened before climbing the stairs. When he didn't hear any sounds, he ventured into the cockpit to light the grill.

He finished preparing his meal, poured another glass of wine, and settled in at the banquette. "Cheers," Garner whispered to himself, holding up his wine glass, feeling a little bit sorry for himself but not really understanding why.

He finished dinner, carried his dishes to the galley, and dropped them into the sink. He had a good mind to leave them there until morning and go to bed, putting this entire day behind him. Then he decided against it and started washing. He heard sounds and looked out of the porthole, and lo and behold, Hawk and his boyfriend were heading out again. "I guess they're heading out for round two," Garner said under his breath. "Good riddance, boys."

Garner finished his dishes, left them in the dish rack to dry, and cleaned the galley. He looked around with the dishtowel still in his hand. *Now what?*

Still not sleepy, Garner went to his liquor cabinet and poured a single-malt Scotch into a crystal rocks glass. With the threat of seeing Hawk again long gone, he ventured topside to enjoy his drink. He stood in the cockpit and stretched his neck outside the canvas canopy. The stars were still shining brightly, and the three-quarter moon was hovering high in the midnight-blue velvety sky. *This is much too pretty to pass up.*

Garner grabbed a cushion and walked out onto the bow. He dropped the pad and stretched out on top of it, looking up to the heavens. He raised his head every now and then to sip his Scotch and was finally starting to relax when he again heard footsteps on the dock.

This time he didn't even bother to look up until the footsteps stopped and a familiar voice said, "Hey."

Garner raised his head and was shocked to see Hawk standing there with his hands deep inside his pockets, bouncing from foot to foot. "Hey to you," Garner replied. "I saw you pass by earlier and figured you were out for the evening."

"Na," Hawk replied. "Just walking my best friend home."

Best friend! "Would that be the same best friend you were making out with at Aqua last night?" Garner asked.

"One and the same," Hawk admitted. "Long story, but not at all what it appeared."

"Got it," Garner said, not knowing why Hawk's response made him so happy. "Care for a nightcap?"

Hawk looked at his watch. "Sure, why not. It's still early. Permission to come aboard, Captain?"

"Permission granted," Garner said as he rose to his feet.

Garner walked along the gunwale to the cockpit with Hawk walking alongside him on the dock. When they reached their destination, Hawk unlaced his boots, toed them off, and climbed aboard.

"What can I get you?" Garner asked.

Hawk looked at the glass in Garner's hand. "I'll have whatever you're having."

Garner stepped down through the companionway door. "One single-malt Scotch, neat, coming right up." He looked back over his shoulder. "Make yourself comfortable."

When Garner returned with Hawk's drink, Hawk was stretched out on the starboard-side bench seat, leaning back with his feet crossed at the ankles.

Hawk accepted the crystal glass and swirled the Scotch around a few times, brought it to his nose, and inhaled deeply. "Nice," Hawk said. "Smoky and rich."

The man knows good Scotch. "Glad you like it," Garner replied as he took a seat opposite Hawk and stretched out much in the same manner.

The two men sat awkwardly in silence, sipping their drinks until Garner finally spoke.

"Nice boat you've got there," Garner said gesturing over his shoulder. "How long ago did you buy her?"

"Didn't," Hawk replied.

Confused, Garner lifted his head and looked over at Hawk. "Didn't what?"

"Didn't buy her," Hawk repeated. "She was willed to me."

"Ohhhh," Garner said, feeling very curious but not wanting to pry. "So how long have you had her?"

Hawk looked up, apparently counting in his head. "A little under seven years now."

"Have you been running charters the entire time?"

"Not really. Not until I got my six-pack captain's license. And that's been just over five years now, I think."

"Six-pack, huh? I'm impressed," Garner said. "That's a very tough test."

"You?" Hawk asked.

Garner nodded. "Yep, but not near as long as you, though. Only about a year now for me."

Hawk took another sip of his drink. "Doesn't matter how long you've have it as long as you got the damn thing."

"Good point!"

Silence loomed between them once again.

Garner was a little amused by the awkwardness. "Look," he said. "Earlier today my dick was so far up your ass I think I licked it with my own tongue when I was kissing you. And now the best we can do is small talk?"

Hawk shrugged.

Garner chuckled out loud. "A man of many words, I see."

"Okay, how's this for conversation?" Hawk asked. "I loved having your dick up my ass."

Garner's lingering smile turned into a guffaw. "That makes two of us," Garner choked out when he could finally speak.

"You're the one who wanted conversation."

"Touché," Garner said.

Hawk raised his head and looked over, giving Garner a wicked smile. "Want to do it again?"

"Hell yeah," Garner replied, standing and offering Hawk his hand.

Hawk stood without accepting Garner's assistance and the two men were toe-to-toe, staring at each other.

Garner leaned in and gently kissed Hawk on the lips. "The only caveat this time is we do it my way," he said, taking a step back and sweeping his arm toward the companionway door.

Hawk paused. "I'm not quite sure what that means, but I'm sure I can handle it," he said with a slight grin, subtly brushing against Garner as he stepped through the door and disappeared down the stairs.

Garner caught up to Hawk and put a hand on his shoulder, stopping him as he attempted to pull his T-shirt out of his jeans. "No" was all Garner said.

Hawk froze. He cocked his head to the side as if he were listening for his next command. Garner wasn't certain, but his first thought was that it appeared Hawk was preparing for a "Dom/sub" situation, and one he seemed to be perfectly comfortable with. Garner hated to disappoint him, but if that's what Hawk was truly hoping for, he was in for a huge disappointment.

Garner put his hands on Hawk's waist and slowly turned him around. Now facing him in the lamp-lit salon, Garner stood up on his tippy toes and gently pressed his lips against Hawk's while at the same time reaching down to grip Hawk's T-shirt and pull it out of his jeans. Without skipping a beat, Hawk lifted his arms over his head and Garner broke the kiss long enough to pull the shirt off and toss it to the floor. Now Garner was able to get a good look at Hawk's tattooed chest. To his amazement, Hawk's pectorals were covered with birds, all in various stages of flight. *Sparrows?* He wasn't quite sure. He buried his face in Hawk's neck, kissing and licking all the way down to the man's broad, bird-covered chest, inhaling a combination of soap, cigarette smoke, and a classic scent like maybe Old Spice or something similar.

Garner smiled against Hawk's skin when the image of the sailor coming back from the sea in the Old Spice commercial popped into his mind. How stereotypical that Hawk would be wearing Old Spice. But in actuality, so far there had been nothing stereotypical about this man. If anything he was the opposite. The little that Garner knew told him that Hawk was a living contradiction. For starters, Garner had taken one look at him and thought he was going to be robbed, but Hawk had walked on past him without incident. Later, he had expected Hawk to be the dominant one in the bedroom, but he was actually quite passive. And by his appearance, Garner would have pinned Hawk as coming from a broken home, but he had very tolerant and accepting parents. Garner knew he was overthinking everything, so he turned off his brain and tried to simply enjoy the moment.

Garner looked at Hawk's nipple rings. He really enjoyed the sensation of having his nipples tantalized and especially remembered the sudden rush the teasing sent to his groin, so he could only imagine how intense it must be for Hawk. Not wanting to do anything that might be uncomfortable but still wanting to give Hawk pleasure, Garner started by putting the silver ring between his teeth and tugging on it gently. When Hawk stiffened and moaned, Garner tugged a little harder and twisted the ring back and forth. Hawk rewarded him with a little louder moan and grabbed the back of Garner's neck and pulled him closer against his chest. Garner opened his mouth wider, covered the nipple and ring, sucking on them both and jostling the ring around with his tongue. Hawk was now moaning continuously, bending slightly at the waist and holding Garner's head tightly against him.

While repeating the same act on the other nipple, Garner used his free hands to unbutton Hawk's jeans and push them down as far as he could reach. He released Hawk's nipple with a plop and knelt in front of him, forcing the man's jeans down to his feet. He lifted Hawk's feet one at a time and slipped his jeans completely off, taking his socks at the same time.

Garner was still on his knees, but his eyes slowly moved up Hawk's tall, slim frame. He gazed at Hawk's taut stomach as he tongued his belly button ring, and then his eyes continued up to Hawk's broad and muscular chest. When their eyes met, Hawk's normally blue eyes were now a dark steel gray, and his expression was one of pure lust.

With Hawk on display in front of him, Garner could now clearly make out the tattoos on the rest of Hawk's body. On his right arm, starting at the shoulder, was a three-eyed dog's head and what appeared to be a woman's hand. Below that was some sort of weird butterfly. His elbow had a diamond smaller than the one on his left arm. Running the length from his forearm down to his hand was another dagger, surrounded by an ocean. On his left leg was a rattlesnake that started with its head at Hawk's ankle and curled around and around until the rattle on its tail stopped at the top of Hawk's thigh. On his right shin was a female pirate holding a flagpole, waving a skull and crossbones flag that covered his right thigh. Garner stared in amazement at these works of art adorning Hawk's body and instantly saw how each and every one of Hawk's tattoos seemed to be a part of him, like a limb or one of his vital organs.

The sudden need to touch Hawk was overwhelming. He leaned forward and buried his head in Hawk's underwear-clad crotch and cupped his muscular ass cheeks. The aroma of laundry detergent mixed with Hawk's unique scent filled his nostrils. Garner inhaled deeply again and again, unable to get enough of the clean, pungent scent while he massaged and squeezed Hawk's tight ass.

Garner bit down on Hawk's length through his underwear and ran his teeth lightly up and down, coaxing a groan out of Hawk's lips and sending him up onto his tiptoes. Hawk ran the fingers of both hands the length of Garner's hair, pulling lightly through the shaggy parts, tightening his grip, and then running them through again. Garner moved his attention down to Hawk's balls and nibbled and bit at them through the cotton briefs until Hawk was rocking on his feet. In one quick move, Garner hooked his fingers in the waistband of Hawk's underwear and yanked them down to his ankles. Hawk needed no coercing and stepped out of them immediately, kicking them to the side and grabbing Garner under the armpits, pulling him up until they were again face-to-face.

Hawk plastered his lips to Garner's and tried to force his tongue into Garner's mouth. Garner didn't open to him and pushed back gently. "My way, remember?" he said to Hawk, earning himself a royally pissed-off look.

"I promise you won't be sorry," Garner said, taking Hawk's hand and leading him to his stateroom. When they reached the cabin, Garner urged Hawk to sit on the foot of the bed. He took a step back and slowly pulled his T-shirt over his head and tossed it aside. He seductively ran his hands over his chest and stomach, pinching his nipples a few times before moving down to his crotch. With one hand he rubbed his crotch repeatedly, while running his other hand through his hair.

Hawk watched him intently, pulling on his nipple ring and playing with himself the entire time.

When he was fully erect, Garner pulled down the waistband of his running shorts just far enough for Hawk to see the outline of his cock through his thin cotton briefs and slid his hand in and pumped himself. That action drew a moan from Hawk's lips, and Garner felt inspired to do more. He slipped his shorts all the way down to his ankles, stepping out of them and kicking them to the side while he continued to pump himself under his briefs.

Hawk stood and took a step toward Garner, but Garner stepped back, held his hand out, and pointed to the bed. Hawk backed up and sat down again, but didn't look very happy about it.

Figuring he couldn't keep this up too much longer without Hawk blowing a gasket, Garner sped up the process. He pushed his briefs down until his dick popped out, and hooked the elastic of his briefs under his balls. He pumped himself a few more times before pushing the briefs down and stepping out of them completely. Now totally naked, Garner continued to run a hand over his chest, up and behind his neck, through his hair, and back down to his abs, all the while pumping his dick slowly but deliberately.

Hawk stood again, but didn't make a move in his direction. Garner stepped up to him, went up onto his toes, and lightly brushed his lips across Hawk's. Hawk opened for him, but Garner withdrew. "Softly," he whispered. "Slowly." Again he brushed his lips over Hawk's. Hawk was now trembling, and Garner knew he was succeeding.

He leaned in once more and ran his tongue over Hawk's lips, licking softly, but this time Hawk didn't open. Instead, he closed his eyes, took a deep breath, and lifted his hand, gently stroking Garner's hair. Hawk leaned in and softly brushed his lips over Garner's, then kissed his way down to Garner's chin and then neck, tantalizing the sensitive skin with bites and kisses. While still nuzzling Garner's neck, Hawk slowly ran both hands down to Garner's thighs and just as slowly brought them back up again, lifting Garner's arms over his head. Hawk then buried his head in one of Garner's armpits and inhaled deeply, kissing and sucking one underarm and then the other.

Hawk kissed his way over Garner's chest, and Garner threw his head back when Hawk took one of his nipples into his mouth and sucked on it, bit softly, and then licked the sting away. Garner felt that rush he'd remembered and arched his back and hissed when Hawk did the same to the other.

Raising his hand and gripping the back of Hawk's neck, Garner forced Hawk's head into his chest. Hawk pulled back and stopped. "Softly," he said. "Slowly." Then he again brought his lips to Garner's nipple.

It took Garner a second to cut through the ecstasy and see that Hawk had just turned the tables on him. Garner chuckled and whispered, "You son of a bitch."

Hawk laughed seductively. "One good turn deserved another."

Garner pushed Hawk back until his legs hit the foot of the bed, and the two of them tumbled down with Garner sprawled out on top of Hawk.

This time when Garner's lips covered Hawk's, Hawk opened and Garner pushed his tongue in. When the kiss ended, Garner gave him another quick brush of his lips. "All I wanted was to take it slow," Garner said.

"All you had to do was ask," Hawk said, returning Garner's kiss. "Haven't done that in a while, but I can take it slow if that's what you want."

"Thank you," Garner said, sliding down the bed and stopping when his face was level with Hawk's erect cock. Hawk sighed and then moaned when Garner ran his tongue around the head of Hawk's dick, forcing an involuntary jump out of Hawk. He licked down to Hawk's balls and took them both in his mouth, lightly biting at the loose skin and pulling. Hawk's moans turned into gasps when Garner lifted his legs and ran his tongue around his opening, pushing in and out and then circling again.

Garner licked his way back up, lowering Hawk's legs and taking Hawk into his mouth. He moved slowly, swallowing Hawk up to the hilt, holding him there and then easing back up before repeating the process. By this time Hawk was thrashing in the bed, gripping at the sheets, and slowly turning his head from side to side.

Hawk pulled Garner up to him. "I'm gonna come if you don't stop," he hissed. "This is supposed to be slow, remember?"

"I remember," Garner said, pressing his lips against Hawk's again. Hawk flipped him over and straddled his chest, rubbing his ass against Garner's cock, gyrating and moving up and down. Hawk licked his fingers and pinched Garner's nipples between his thumb and forefingers and twisted gently. He slid down and rested his ass on Garner's shins and buried his nose in Garner's crotch. Garner closed his eyes when he felt Hawk's tongue licking his balls and then his warm wet mouth surrounding them, gently massaging with his tongue.

Hawk licked his way back up, teased at Garner's erection, and took him into his mouth. Garner was long and thick and felt certain Hawk couldn't take him all the way in, but he lost his train of thought when that was exactly what Hawk did. He gagged once, but found his rhythm quickly and continued the oral assault, swallowing Garner deeply.

Suddenly Garner felt himself being flipped over onto his stomach as if he weighed no more than ten pounds. His cock was pointing down toward the foot of the bed and his ass was slightly up in the air. He felt his cheeks being spread apart and saw stars when Hawk's warm tongue licked from the head of his dick, up to the top of his ass, and all the way back down again, over and over, brushing ever so lightly over his opening and tormenting his cock simultaneously.

Garner's moans grew, and he began to wiggle when Hawk focused solely on his opening, licking and probing, driving him mad with pleasure. Hawk then grabbed Garner's cock and started stroking his erection in time with his licking motions and suddenly it was Garner fisting the sheets and burying his head in his pillow to muffle the sounds of ecstasy escaping his lips.

"Holy fuck," Garner murmured when Hawk slid a finger inside of him and began moving it in and out slowly, twisting and turning in unison with the stroking of his cock. When Hawk brushed against that little bump deep inside Garner's ass, a gasp escaped his lips, and he rose up to his hands and knees, pushing against Hawk's pleasing invasion.

Garner vaguely heard Hawk's voice and looked over his shoulder, but he quickly lost all conscious thought when Hawk's eyes locked on to his. The intensity of Hawk's gaze had Garner's balls tightening and him struggling to hold back his impending orgasm. This image of Hawk, all tattooed and pierced, tormenting him with pleasure and donning the slightest bit of a contented smile would be forever etched into his brain. In this particular moment, up on all fours with Hawk working his ass and cock and the image of Hawk burned into his memory, Garner could have died and never regretted missing out on the rest of his life.

It took every bit of mental and physical strength Garner could muster, but he twisted around and faced Hawk at the foot of the bed, slipped both hands under his armpits, locked them behind his back, and pulled as hard as he could while simultaneously turning back to the head of the bed. As a result, Hawk ended up sprawled out crossways on the bed in front of him with a very surprised look on his face. Garner lifted a leg over Hawk's long, lean body and straddled him. He lowered his head and brought their lips together in a crushing kiss as he stretched out on top of Hawk, bringing their erections together and grinding slowly.

Garner broke the kiss just long enough to reach over to the bedside table and open the drawer to retrieve a condom packet and the lube he'd made a point to return to its rightful home after their last encounter. He held up the condom and gave Hawk a questioning look.

"Hell yeah" and a seductive smile was the response he got, causing his cock to involuntarily jump between them.

Garner locked eyes with Hawk as he slowly opened the foil packet with his teeth and rolled the condom onto his length, never breaking their gaze. He flipped the top of the lube bottle, poured the silky-smooth liquid into his hand, and generously coated the condom. He turned the bottle over and squeezed a stream of lube onto Hawk's cock, fisting him and moving his hand up and down, making a point to brush over the silver loop piercing Hawk's mushroom head, which caused his cock to jump and spasm with each pass.

Garner squeezed the bottle again and filled his hand before slowly moving it down between Hawk's legs. Hawk sighed and closed his eyes when Garner's finger circled his opening, teasing and massaging, adequately preparing Hawk for what was coming next. Hawk threw his head back and gasped when Garner slipped one finger inside of him and then a second, loosening him up. When Garner found his spot, Hawk arched his back and came up off the bed.

"Now!" Hawk begged. "I want you inside me."

Garner slowly lifted Hawk's legs and draped them over his shoulders. Resting his ass on his ankles, Garner pressed up against Hawk's opening and slowly pressed in and stopped. But this time Hawk didn't pull him; he simply relaxed and gave himself time to adjust. After about thirty seconds, Garner pushed himself up to his knees and eased in a little farther and then stopped again, continuing the process until he was all the way in.

Hawk's hands were resting on Garner's thighs, guiding him as Garner started to slowly move. "Feels so fucking good," Hawk murmured, transferring one hand to his cock and leaving the other resting on Garner's thigh. Garner lifted Hawk's legs off his shoulders and held them up by the ankles, giving him more access as he continued his unhurried, rhythmic thrusts.

"Fuck, this is so hot," Garner said, looking down at his cock as it disappeared inside of Hawk over and over again. Garner liked the fact that there was no roughness to their lovemaking this time. He had thoroughly enjoyed, even more than he cared to admit to himself, the rough-and-tumble sex they'd had earlier in the day, but somehow it pleased him that Hawk didn't seem to need anything hard and fast right now either. He stared down at his lover, and Hawk looked perfectly content, head thrown back and eyes closed, to ride the wave of the slow and steady treatment Garner was bestowing on him.

Garner dropped Hawk's legs down around his waist and leaned forward. Hawk rose up to meet him and their lips came together again in an intense kiss. Their tongues fought for dominance, and just like the first time they'd kissed, Garner thought the bar piercing Hawk's tongue felt foreign but not at all unpleasant. Garner continued his leisurely thrusts, keeping up this position until his back protested, and then he slowly rose back up onto his knees, bringing Hawk's left leg with him. Garner wrapped his left hand around Hawk's calf and held Hawk's foot with his right. He lightly bit and then licked at Hawk's ankle and foot while steadily pumping in and out of him.

"I'm so fucking close, dude," Hawk murmured, moving his hand up and down his length.

"Go for it," Garner said, picking up his pace. "I'm right there with you."

Garner pumped feverishly, trying to keep up with Hawk's hand. "Holy fuck," Hawk screamed, his dark gray eyes rolling into the back of his head. His shoulders and chest lifted completely off the bed and he fell back down again as he came in spurts, coating his stomach and chest with his thick white release.

The sight of Hawk's orgasm had Garner instantly on the brink. He felt a tsunami building from deep within, and when the first wave hit him, he screamed, "Jesus fucking Christ." Wave after wave consumed him as he filled the condom, still moving frantically in and out of Hawk. When the effects of the last surge were gone, Garner collapsed on top of Hawk, their sweaty bodies sticking together as their heavy breaths mixed into one loud sound.

"My God," Garner whispered into Hawk's neck as he slid to Hawk's side. "I don't think I've ever come so hard."

Hawk chuckled as he brought his fingers up to Garner's chest, which was now covered with a mixture of his come and their combined sweat, coating his fingers in the mixture and sticking them in Garner's mouth.

"Yum," Garner said as he held Hawk's hand steady while he licked his fingers clean, kissing each one before releasing it. Garner reached down between them, tugged at the condom still sheathing his semierect cock, and tossed it onto the bedside table, the weight of the loaded condom making a plopping sound as it came in contact with the granite top.

"Damn," Hawk said. "That's a shitload of come. No pun intended," he quickly added. "You know, shit—load—come all in the same sentence."

Garner laughed. "I got it. I *told* you I came really hard."

Garner gave Hawk a quick peck on the lips and then rolled out of bed. He collected the used condom, dropped it into the trashcan in the head, and returned with a warm, wet cloth. He cleaned Hawk's chest, cock, and ass, folded the cloth in half, and ran it over his chest. He tossed the cloth into the head and climbed back in bed.

Garner turned onto his side, fluffing his pillow and tucking his left arm underneath for support before he laid his head down. He draped his right arm over Hawk's chest and watched it go up and down. Hawk's breathing appeared to be back to normal, and his eyes were closed, but he brought his hands up and laid them on top of Garner's and rested them there.

Garner studied Hawk's face closely. "Did you know that after you have sex, the muscles in your face really relax and you lose that stressed look you normally carry around?"

Hawk raised his head up and opened one eye. "Dude, that's the weirdest fucking thing."

"Why?" Garner asked. "Sex relaxes a lot of people."

Hawk dropped his head down again. "Not that," he said.

"What then?"

"Justin just told me the exact same thing at happy hour today."

"Who's Justin?"

"My best friend. The guy you saw me leave with earlier tonight."

"Oh, right," Garner recalled. "You had sex with Justin at happy hour?" he asked.

Hawk lifted his head and opened his eyes. "What? No!" he replied. "He was referring to my *just laid look*, as he calls it, after our tryst this afternoon."

"Wow! That's a relief," Garner teased. "Well either way, he's right."

Hawk smiled and laid his head back down and once again closed his eyes. "I'll be sure to tell him you said that."

"You sleepy?" Garner asked, wanting to see if Hawk might be up for a little conversation. With Hawk in his current state, Garner thought this might be a good time get him to open up about himself a little.

"Not really. Why?"

"Oh, I don't know," Garner answered. "I thought we might talk a little."

Hawk raised his head and opened that one eye again, giving Garner a skeptical look.

"Never mind," Garner said, closing his eyes. "It was just a thought. We can just lie here and enjoy the afterglow."

"Oh Jesus," Hawk said, the corners of his mouth forming a light smile. "That sounds like a line someone might use on an infomercial selling dildos." He laid his head back down on the pillow and once again closed his eyes.

They lay there in silence for a minute or so, Garner content just to listen to the sounds of Hawk's breathing.

Hawk broke the silence. "Okay. What do you wanna talk about?"

"Nothing in particular," Garner replied. "I mean, I'm curious about a few things, but it's okay, really. They're probably none of my business anyway."

"Yes, I have my share of deep, dark secrets, if that's what you're thinking," Hawk volunteered. "I'm just not a big talker when it comes to personal stuff, but that doesn't mean I won't answer your questions."

"Well for starters, you got your boat because someone willed it to you. I was kinda curious about who that was."

"My father," Hawk answered without hesitation.

"Wow, a fishing minister," Garner commented and then smiled. "Sounds heavenly."

"Not exactly," Hawk replied. "I said my father, not my dad."

"Wait," Garner said hesitantly. "You were adopted?"

Hawk nodded without opening his eyes.

"Ooooh, now I get it," Garner replied. "But that means you must have found your biological parents at some point."

"Nope! Never cared about them and certainly never looked for them," Hawk said, his voice devoid of any emotion.

"Then how did your dad—no, your father—leave you the boat?"

"Apparently *he* knew *me*, or at the very least, *knew* I existed."

"And he never tried to meet you or develop any sort of relationship?" Garner asked inquisitively.

"Nope."

"How did you find out about the boat?"

"One day out of the blue, I received a registered letter from some legal aid attorney in Jacksonville informing me that my father had passed away and left me a fifty-five-foot fishing boat and enough money to get a captain's license and maintain the boat for at least five years. They needed to know where it should be delivered," Hawk explained. "Apparently, he'd been living in north Florida for the last thirteen years of his life doing fishing charters."

In his mind, Garner was trying to put all the pieces of Hawk's life together when he thought of another question. "How old were you when you were given away?"

"From what I've been told, my birth parents gave me up for adoption the day I was born, and I spent the first nine years of my life in foster care."

"That must have sucked," Garner said.

Hawk didn't respond right away, and Garner decided not to press the issue.

Then Hawk spoke. "Yeah, it bit the big one. I've heard there're a lot of loving families and good homes in the foster-care system, but I never got to see any of them. From as far back as I can remember, I mostly went from one bad situation to another. Just before my tenth birthday, I was adopted by the people I call my mom and dad, and that's when things started to get better for me."

"Were you ever abused physically or sexually?" Garner asked.

"It depends on what you identify as abuse," Hawk said. "Was I beaten? Sure. A hell of a lot, as a matter of fact. Was I talked down to and made to feel less than the family I was living with? Sometimes. Did one of my foster dads stick his dick up my ass? No." Hawk hesitated for a moment. "Dude, abuse comes in many forms."

"You know, Hawk," Garner said. "This is so weird because I had a feeling—" Garner stopped midsentence, deciding he probably shouldn't go there. "Oh never mind, it's not important."

"No. I want to know," Hawk said. "You can't just stop like that, dude, and leave me hanging."

"I'm sorry, but I don't want to offend you or sound like an uptight asshole, although I've been called that on more than one occasion."

Hawk laughed. "Imagine that," he said.

"What does that mean?" Garner asked incredulously.

"Oh, nothing. Never mind," Hawk said through a smile.

"Now look who's leaving who hanging."

"If you must know, the first time I saw you standing on the dock hosing off your boat, you looked about as uptight as a guy can get. And when I walked past you, you looked terrified, and you didn't even acknowledge me. As a matter of fact, I referred to you as the uptight guy until I heard your name at the cabaret."

"Oh really!" Garner said. "Cut me some slack. You scared the fuck out of me. I mean, you're not the typical boater. Honestly, how many boaters do you know who come to the marina at that hour of the morning half-naked?"

"Touché," Hawk said without further explanation.

Garner smirked. "And just for the record, my friend, you had a nickname as well."

Hawk raised an eyebrow. "Me? Oh this I've gotta hear."

"Mr. Clean."

"That bald dude from the cleaning-supply commercial?" Hawk asked.

"Bingo."

Hawk tilted his head to the side, apparently thinking about it. "I can totally see that. I like it."

Garner snickered and slapped his thigh. "Of course you would."

Hawk rolled his eyes. "So now that nicknames are covered, where were we?" Before Garner could answer, Hawk said, "Oh yeah. You were going to fill me in on this feeling about me."

"No," Garner corrected. "I was going to, but I decided against it."

"Dude, that's not fair," he said. "Now I'm intrigued. And besides, I'm sure it's nothing I haven't already heard. Relax, I don't offend easily."

Garner thought about how and what he was going to say and decided the best way was to just come out with it. So he did. "After I saw you on the dock yesterday morning, you really piqued my interest. And after connecting with you today and our very rough tryst this afternoon, I found you even more intriguing. I mean, on so many levels you are nothing like you appear to be. In fact, you are exactly the opposite of how I would have stereotyped you."

Hawk frowned but didn't respond, causing Garner to backpedal a little and justify his statement. "I know it sounds awful when I use the word 'stereotype' out loud, but the real truth is that most people meet someone for the first time and categorize or pigeonhole them from the get-go. And I'm sorry to say, mostly because of my profession, I'm one of those people."

Hawk cocked that one eye open again and waited. When Garner hesitated, Hawk said, "Go on," in a dubious tone.

"I guess I was so intrigued with you—and still am, by the way—that I started putting together everything I knew about you. Ya know, to try and figure out what makes you tick. Now this is where it's gonna get a little iffy, so if you want me to stop, tell me now and we'll talk about something else."

Hawk pushed himself up and rested on his elbow, cradling his head in his hand. He looked right into Garner's eyes. "Are you kidding, it's just getting good," he said. "I can't wait to hear this."

"Ooookay, but remember your words before you hit me," Garner teased.

Hawk smiled and rested his hand on Garner's hip, but he didn't promise one way or the other.

"So here's everything I knew about you when I came up with my analysis earlier today. You're a scary dude. You're covered in tattoos. You're pierced all the hell over, and you like really rough sex."

"So far your description of me is pretty accurate," Hawk said.

"Sooooo," Garner began. "Let's start with the sex. There are a shitload of possibilities that are pretty well documented. Studies have shown that some people who like really rough sex can have serious fears of intimacy and or a mental and physical disconnect between love and sex.

"Other studies suggest that adults who like rough sex can also be associated with childhood physical or sexual abuse. In a lot of cases, the victim doesn't believe he or she deserves to be loved in a gentle, loving, or nurturing way. And continuing with the abuse theory, domination and power can also play a role. In those cases the adult feels that he or she had no power to stop the abuse when it was happening, so they must exert that power now. But that one didn't apply to you, for obvious reasons," Garner explained, rubbing Hawk's ass. "You can be pretty submissive, at least so far."

At that comment, Hawk opened his mouth to speak, but Garner held a hand up to stop him. "Please let me get everything out before you start waling on me."

Hawk closed his mouth and shook his head.

"Now let's talk about your tats and piercings," Garner suggested. "If you hadn't told me that your parents were ministers who were rational, accepting parents, I would have guessed that your parents had been unwed teenagers with drug and or alcohol addictions that cared little or nothing about you or your upbringing.

"I also considered that you could have been a child of a single working mother who wasn't around a lot, and you had no real male influence in his life. Any of those options could have had a negative effect on you and your self-esteem, causing you to act out in appearance and behavior."

Garner squeezed Hawk's hand. "You okay so far?"

"Are you done?" Hawk asked.

"Almost," Garner said, rubbing his palm over Hawk's stomach. "After I learned you had loving and supportive parents, I was stumped and back at square one. But now that I know you were adopted and have heard some of your story, I now realize I wasn't that far from the truth. But I want to clarify. I'm not judging you. And I'll go out even farther out on the proverbial limb and say that I'm very attracted to you and am enjoying immensely getting to know you, and not as a psychological project. As a person.

"Here's the kicker. Everything I've said so far can be supported in many psychological studies, journals, and reports. Hell, a person can usually use the Internet to find a study or multiple studies that he or she can use to support any particular theory or belief. It's just out there, but none of it should be taken as gospel. In fact, a lot of it can just be written off as psychobabble that has nothing to do with a person's true motivation. In my opinion and experience, psychology is a study at best.

"With all that said, a person could have had the most loving parents in the world, the most normal childhood ever, and just simply love tattoos, piercings, and rough sex just for the sake of loving it. In which case, disregard everything I just said. It's all crap."

"Are you done now?" Hawk asked with no expression.

Garner nodded and waited to get his due.

"First of all, what are you, dude? A fucking psychiatrist?"

Here it comes! "As a matter of fact, I am—or was anyway," Garner explained. "Still licensed but no longer practicing."

Hawk rolled his eyes, but Garner didn't detect any outward signs of anger. "Sounds like you're still practicing to me."

Garner chuckled. "I guess it kinda does," he said wryly. "It's just... when you've done it for as long as I have, it's really hard to turn off. Especially when the human psyche still amazes me, even after sixteen years of education and practice. But... there's a light at the end of the tunnel. I'm hoping the longer I'm away from it, the less desire I'll have to analyze everyone."

Hawk suddenly got an inquisitive look on his face. "So how long *have* you been away from it?"

"Let's see," Garner said, doing the math. "One month preparing for the trip, two months on the water initially, almost two months in Savannah while my engine was replaced, and two weeks from Savannah to Key West, so not quite six months."

Hawk nodded. "So here's a question for *you*."

"Shoot," Garner said.

"What made you give up your practice for this?" Hawk asked, waving his free hand through the air and then laying it back down on top of Garner's.

"Burnout," Garner replied. "When your brain doesn't have an off switch, you never get any downtime. I just got burned out and decided I couldn't do it anymore."

"Got it," Hawk said. "But I'm pretty sure, based on your analysis of me, you still miss it."

"Guilty as charged," Garner replied. "But wait! Before we jump subjects, you never really commented on that."

"On what?"

"My analysis."

"Oh, that." Hawk looked up at the ceiling and appeared to be chewing on the inside of his cheek while he contemplated his answer. He looked back at Garner. "To be honest, a lot of what you said could be considered spot-on, and some of it I'll need to think more about. But some of it was just plain old crap. As it applies to me anyway."

Garner felt his eyes widen and his jaw drop.

"What?" Hawk asked in a suspicious tone.

"I guess I just didn't expect that response."

"What? You expected the scary dude to get all defensive, go apeshit, and call you crazy?"

"Yeah," Garner replied. "I kinda did."

Hawk shook his head. "There you go stereotyping again."

"Sorry, you're right," Garner said. "So can you tell me what was spot-on, what needs considering, and what you think was crap?"

"I could, but I'm not Dr. Smarty Dude," Hawk said wryly. "I want to see if you can figure that one out on your own."

"Fair enough," Garner said before leaning in and placing a gentle kiss on Hawk's lips.

When Garner withdrew, Hawk said, "Okay, it's your turn."

"Okay, what do you want to know?" Garner asked.

"Start at the beginning."

Garner gave Hawk the *Reader's Digest* version of his life to date, covering his family and upbringing, his education and career, his failed relationships, his burnout and retirement, buying his boat, his stay in Savannah, and eventually how he ended up in Key West.

"So you run too, huh," Hawk said, stifling a yawn.

"Wait! What?" Garner asked. "I don't run?"

Hawk raised an eyebrow. "Seriously?"

"I mean, yeah, I seriously suck at relationships, so I guess you can say I run from *them*," Garner admitted. "But I don't think I'm running from anything else."

"If you say so," Hawk replied, laying his head back down on the pillow and closing his eyes.

Am I running? "I never thought about myself as being a *runner*," Garner admitted, tossing the idea around in his head. "Maybe I am running."

"Doctors are always the worst patients," Hawk said without opening his eyes.

FOR THE longest time, Garner lay there in silence thinking about the topic of running away. *I guess I could say I ran away from my family and my previous life? I was building a good life in Savannah, and I left there as well. Did I leave because Hank and Thompson were getting so close?*

Garner's thoughts were suddenly interrupted by Hawk's light snoring as he turned away and backed his ass against Garner's crotch so they were now spooning, Garner's arm again resting on his stomach.

Garner tightened his grip, rested his head on Hawk's shoulder, and closed his eyes. He listened to Hawk's peaceful breathing, mixed with the occasional snort, until he eventually gave in to slumber.

Sometime later, Garner felt Hawk slip out of his embrace. Garner opened his eyes to see Hawk's peacock staring back him as Hawk sat on the edge of the bed, resting his elbows on his knees and cradling his head. A couple of minutes later Hawk stood and paused like he was trying to make a decision.

He must have to go to the bathroom. Maybe he's disoriented.

Before Garner could ask if he was okay, Hawk took a step. And then another, moving right past the head and going out into the salon.

Garner slipped out of the bed, still naked, and walked over to the doorway. He leaned on the doorjamb, folded his arms over his chest, and crossed his bare feet at the ankles. He observed Hawk picking up his scattered clothing and putting them on one by one. When Hawk was completely dressed, he put his socked foot on the bottom step.

Garner cleared his throat. "Leaving without saying goodbye?"

Hawk stopped but didn't turn around. "I didn't want to wake you."

"Oh come on, Hawk," Garner said. "We can be honest here. The first time I sort of understood, but this time? Is this your MO?"

"I'm sorry," Hawk said, taking another step. "I never stay."

"No need to apologize," Garner said. "I run from relationships too, remember? But hey, at least you helped Dr. Smarty Dude determine which part of his analysis was spot-on."

Hawk stopped again. This time he turned around and when their eyes met, the expression on Hawk's face was painfully obvious, even in the dimly lit cabin.

"Does the term 'fear of intimacy' ring a bell?" Garner asked, turning and disappearing into his cabin. He heard the sound of the companionway door sliding open and closing again as he crawled back in bed.

CHAPTER EIGHT

HAWK STEPPED onto the dock, bent down and picked up his Doc Martens, and slowly walked the three slips over to his boat. He felt like a heel sneaking out on Garner, but he was glad that Garner had caught him. In Garner's stateroom, he'd tried to convince himself to stay, but something deep inside of him just wouldn't allow it.

The words Garner had said to him, "Does the term 'fear of intimacy' ring a bell?" flooded his ears. The fact was that Garner's analysis had been right on the money. In so many ways, except for the sexual abuse, he'd hit the nail right on the head. But hell, he might as well have been raped, then he'd have one more thing to blame his lame behavior on. Hawk suddenly remembered Justin recounting his story about being raped and regretted his thought as soon as it occurred to him.

Hawken Bristol, you are majorly and severely fucked up, my friend.

He threw his shoes into the cockpit of his boat, climbed on board, and opened the door to the salon. The boat was in total darkness except for a dim light filtering its way into the salon from a lone lamp he'd left on in his V-berth. Hawk welcomed the darkness. It kept him from having to look at his face in the large wall mirror behind the couch. He glanced at the clock on his way to the galley. *Four thirty-five in the morning.* "Jesus," he said to himself. "Garner and I talked for almost four hours."

He took a beer out of the refrigerator, twisted off the cap, and threw it in the sink. He went back to the salon, plopped down on the couch, and took a pull off his beer. The cold liquid felt good against his parched throat. *Four hours?*

"That's probably the longest conversation I've had with anyone other than Justin in who knows how long," he said out loud.

The simple fact was that he liked the damn guy. He'd known him all of one day, but over the course of that day, they'd had sex twice, once hard, fast, and rough and once slow and easy, and he'd enjoyed both times immensely. In addition, in that one day, he'd shared more about himself and learned more about someone else than he had in all the years he'd been in Key West.

Sure Garner was a little uptight, but he'd also pretty much confirmed that he had issues of his own. That fact alone made Hawk feel like his pile of crap might not immediately stand up and sing "Crazy Train" by Ozzy Osbourne. And they'd both said at one point or another they weren't good at relationships, so there was really no real pressure there.

Hawk, you've already broken your golden rule and tapped the guy twice, so what have you got to lose? He runs from relationships, and you apparently have intimacy issues, among others, so it sounds like this is a purely sexual thing and probably is going to be over before it starts. Why not enjoy the ride while it lasts?

His mind made up, Hawk downed the rest of his beer, stepped out of the salon into the cockpit, hopped back onto the dock in his sock feet, and marched right over to *AquaTherapy*. He walked into Garner's stateroom and stripped, pulled the covers back, and slid into the bed. He moved his back against Garner chest and nuzzled his ass against Garner's groin.

"Keep that up," Garner said, "and we're never going to get any sleep."

Hawk stilled and reached behind his back, found Garner's arm, and wrapped it around his waist.

He felt Garner tighten his hold. "Welcome back."

"Fuck intimacy issues," Hawk said. "Good night."

Hawk felt the bed begin to shake from Garner's laughter. After a while it settled once more, and Garner kissed him on the shoulder and whispered, "Good night."

⛵

HAWK WOKE to the sound of a cell phone ringing. When Garner rolled over, Hawk turned with him and snuggled his chest up against Garner's warm back. He listened as Garner slapped the bedside table a few times in search of his phone.

"Hello," Garner said in a sleepy voice.

"Oh hey, Hank. Is everything all right?" he asked, rising up and leaning on his elbow.

"Good, glad to hear it. What the hell time is it anyway?"

Hawk felt Garner lay his head back down onto his pillow and stretch out again. "No shit? It can't be noon."

Noon? Hawk opened his eyes and rolled over onto his back and looked at the porthole over the bed. The sunshade was pulled, but light was beaming in around all the edges.

"No, Hank, I believe you." Hawk heard Garner say into the phone as he too rolled over onto his back.

Time for a little fun! Hawk lifted the covers, threw a leg on top of Garner, and straddled him, Garner's eyes widening with each passing second. Hawk pulled the covers over his head, and he slid down to align his face with Garner's crotch.

"This weekend?" Garner asked. "Sure, I'd love to see you guys. Who's gonna cover the marina?"

Silence.

"Oh, Bubba. Yeah, he'll do fine. I imagine that most of the snowbirds are already where they're going to be by now."

Hawk heard a gasp when he took Garner's cock into his mouth. He buried his face in Garner's groin, nuzzling his nose deep into Garner's pubic hairs and inhaling deeply before he started moving up and down.

"Oh, nothing. Just a frog in my throat," Garner said, apparently thinking quickly on his back and starting to move along with Hawk's efforts.

Hawk chuckled around a mouthful. *More like a frog in* my *throat.* He pulled all the way off and then went back down, taking Garner's now fully erect cock all the way up to the hilt.

Hawk's ears perked up when he heard Garner say, "Fishing charter? Yeah, sounds like fun, and I know just the guy. Yep, Saturday morning. I'll see if he's available."

Hawk nodded, giving the go-ahead while never missing a beat.

"As a matter of fact, I know he's available," he heard Garner say. "I'll take care of all the details.

"What time—" Garner started, stopping short when his voice cracked. Hawk smiled against Garner's groin and kept right on moving. *God, I'm loving this.*

Garner cleared his throat. "No really, I'm fine. What time do you think you guys will arrive?"

More silence.

"Yeah, with the traffic, six o'clock sounds about right. ... I'm looking forward to seeing you guys too. ... Drive safely, now, and give Thompson a hug for me. ... Okay, Hank. See you Friday afternoon."

Hawk heard the cell phone hit the bedside table. He had a pretty good idea of what was coming next.

"You little shit," Garner hissed and started to sit up, but Hawk picked up his speed and applied more pressure, and Garner fell onto his back again. "Jesus, Hawk, I'm so close."

Hawk continued his steady movements and prepared himself when Garner arched his back and tensed up just before he shot his load down Hawk's throat. Hawk continued to work Garner's cock until he'd milked every drop out of him, then released him and popped his head out from under the covers to see if Garner was still alive.

Garner was lying back, still breathing hard, with his forearm resting over his forehead and a huge smile plastered on his handsome face.

Hawk smiled in victory, slid over to Garner's side, and laid his head on Garner's chest. Hawk could hear and feel Garner's heart beating in double time and gave himself a secret "attaboy" for a job well done.

Garner wrapped his arm over Hawk's shoulder and squeezed. "You realize you're going to pay for that, right?"

"I hope so," Hawk said without raising his head. "So, a little birdie told me I have a charter on Saturday."

"A little birdie, huh?"

"Now who's Hank?" Hawk asked. "Are he and Thompson the guys from Savannah you helped work out their issues?"

"One and the same," Garner replied. "You'll really like them. They are such great guys. Because of the actions of others, they were cheated out of so many years together."

"That sucks," Hawk said. "But from what you've told me, it appears they are on track now?"

"Yeah, they're real good."

"So," Hawk said. "I gathered they're arriving on Friday afternoon?"

"And heading back on Monday morning," Garner added.

"That's such a long trip for just a couple days."

"About ten hours each way. But that's all the time they can spend away from the marina." Garner rolled Hawk over and climbed on top of him.

"Enough about my friends," he said. He leaned forward and took one of Hawk's nipple rings into his mouth and tugged on it fairly hard, causing a moan to escape Hawk's lips. He released it and circled his tongue around and around the sensitive area, kissing his way up to Hawk's neck. "I have some collecting to do," he whispered, scooting down and disappearing under the sheet.

"And I'm ready and willing to pay."

AFTER GARNER had collected on his debt, they'd both fallen asleep, wrapped in each other's arms.

Sometime later Garner woke and reached over and found the spot next to him was empty again. "Fuck," he said under his breath, frowning while rolling over onto his back and staring at the ceiling.

His frown quickly turned into a smile when he smelled something really good and heard noises coming out of the galley. He leaned up on one elbow and was about to get out of bed when Hawk walked in carrying two plates. "Hey, sleepyhead."

"Good morning again," Garner said, unable to contain his smile. He glanced over at the clock. "Or should I say good afternoon?"

Hawk shrugged. "I guess since it's almost four o'clock, good afternoon would be more appropriate. I hope you're hungry."

"Starved," Garner replied, sitting up and propping his pillow behind his back. "What are we having?"

"Broccoli and cheese omelets, country potatoes with olive oil and rosemary, crispy bacon, and dry toast, because you have no butter," Hawk recited, looking down at the two plates.

"Smells great," Garner shared. "I'm impressed."

"I could have done a hell of a lot better, but"—Hawk handed him the plate—"I was pretty constrained by the contents of your refrigerator."

Garner chuckled. "I guess I need to hit the grocery store soon."

"That would have been yesterday," Hawk said wryly, climbing into bed next to Garner. "Since it was so late, I skipped the coffee, but there's juice on your bedside table."

Garner looked over to see a little glass of orange juice resting on top of a paper napkin. "When did you put that there?"

"Just a few minutes before I brought the food in," Hawk said. "You were sleeping like a babe."

"Sorry," Garner said before taking a bite of his eggs and savoring the flavors. "Damn this is good," he said with a mouth full of eggs.

Hawk nodded.

Garner swallowed and took a sip of his orange juice. "Where did you learn to cook like this?"

"I was a private chef before I was a charter boat captain."

"Oh," Garner said and then took a bite of his potatoes. "Professionally trained?"

"Na, self-taught," Hawk admitted. "My degree is in architectural design, but I much prefer cooking and captaining."

"There you go again with the contradictions."

"There you go again with the stereotyping," Hawk responded.

"Damn, I hate it when you're right. But hey, promise me something," Garner asked. Hawk nodded. "As soon as I fuck whatever this is up royally and you can't stand the sight of me, please say you'll still cook for me."

"I'd promise that," Hawk said. "But remember… when things head south, you head south. Get it? That's a play on words."

Garner rolled his eyes. "I got it. But who knows, with your intimacy issues, you'll probably break it off first, and I won't have to run."

"Ha! Ha!" Hawk said. "This just might turn into a race to see who can fuck it up sooner."

"All kidding aside," Garner said. "What made you come back?"

Hawk chewed on his food and then swallowed. "I just figured we're both safe."

"How so?" Garner asked, holding a strip of bacon at his mouth.

"The way I see it," Hawk explained, "from the start, we've both made it perfectly clear that neither of us is looking for a relationship. As long as we both feel that way and don't expect anything more from the other person, I don't see any reason why we can't have a little fun. Besides, I'd already broken my golden rule."

"Which is?"

"I slept with you twice, and I never tap a guy more than once."

"Tap a guy," Garner repeated. "What a lovely term."

Hawk shrugged, taking another bite of his food. "That's the way I see it," he said when he'd swallowed. "You good with that?"

Garner nodded. "Yeah, I'm good with that. Especially since I get to stay in Key West. I mean… I'd hate to think I'd have to flee this place because you've gone and fallen head over heels in love with me."

"So now you can sleep peacefully at night knowing that will never, *ever* happen," Hawk replied. "And by the way, sarcasm does not look good on you."

"I'll remember that." Garner wiped his plate with his last piece of toast. "But if I were you," he added, waving the toast through the air, "I'd get used to it."

"I'll remember *that*," Hawk replied.

"Good."

Garner stood with his empty plate, took Hawk's, and headed to the galley.

When he returned and slipped into bed next to Hawk, the man was lying on his back, hands behind his head and feet crossed at the ankles, staring up at the ceiling. "Penny for your thoughts?"

"Oh hell no," Hawk said, rolling his eyes. "You're not getting me to talk about myself anymore. Especially now that I know you're analyzing every word I say."

"Come on," Garner begged. "What's left to say? I already know all your shortcomings."

Hawk looked over at him with a serious look on his face. "Are you kidding me? You've only just begun to scratch the surface."

Garner reached over and laid a hand on Hawk's chest. "All kidding aside, Hawk. Give yourself a break. Unlike me, you had no control over what happened to you before you were adopted."

"Wait. What do you mean *unlike you?*"

"Unlike you, the issues with my family were a direct result of decisions I made on some conscious or unconscious level. It all started when my father was diagnosed with Alzheimer's. He was my idol, and looking back now, I think I started to distance myself from him so I wouldn't have to watch him deteriorate to the point where I no longer knew him. I was a psychiatrist, remember?"

Hawk nodded.

"I knew exactly what to expect as his illness progressed. In other words, as you so plainly put it, I ran. And apparently I've been running ever since."

"I didn't mean—" Hawk said.

"No!" Garner said, stopping him midsentence. "You're smart, Hawk. You have common sense, and you hit the nail on the head when you pointed out doctors are the worst patients. There's a reason why doctors don't treat themselves. Because they can't. Throughout my career, after only one session, I could usually diagnose my patient's issues. But after thirty-seven years, I still can't see my own."

"But I really have no qualifications to analyze you," Hawk admitted.

"For someone with no qualifications, you got *me* pretty quick."

Hawk remained silent.

"The events in your life, on the other hand, were by no actions of your own. It kills me as a psychiatrist to see what the actions of some parents do to their children."

Garner stood up and started pacing. "When I was still practicing, I had a patient named Jasen who was five years old. He was blind from birth and diagnosed with a shitload of emotional problems, all as a direct result of his mother using crack cocaine while she was pregnant. That child will struggle with his blindness and suffer emotional issues throughout his life, all because of a conscious decision his mother made to use drugs."

Garner sat back down on the bed and ran his fingers through his hair. "All of this was out of Jasen's control, but yet he's the one paying for it in the end. How does a person live with themselves?"

Hawk rested his hand on Garner's leg. "I'm sorry."

"No, Hawk! I'm the one who's sorry," Garner said, laying his hand on top of Hawk's and looking him directly in the eye. "I own my shit. I caused it and I'll deal with it. But your shit was a direct result of a decision someone else made. But like Jasen, you're the one left to deal with the fallout."

"At least I see why you ran from your job," Hawk said. "I can't imagine dealing with that shit day in and day out. Especially the kids."

Garner took a deep breath. "How in the hell did we get from my asking you what you were thinking when I came back into the room to this? I haven't thought about this stuff since I left my job."

Hawk sat up and crossed his legs in front of him and took both of Garner's hands in his. "Maybe it's been in the back of your mind, and it was something that needed to be acknowledged before you could deal with it and put it away."

Garner shook his head. "How did you get so smart?"

"Don't get too excited," Hawk said through a smile. "After I was adopted, my parents sent me to therapy to make sure I was adjusting okay, and that was something I remember my therapist saying to me once."

"Thank you," Garner said while leaning in and stealing a kiss. "For listening, that is."

"Anytime."

Garner looked over at the clock. "Hey. I don't know if you have plans or not, but how about a shower and a sunset sail?"

Hawk shrugged. "Sure, why not."

"Wait!" Garner said. "You never told me what you were thinking about."

Hawk smiled. "I was thinking about how I haven't talked so much about myself in years."

Garner howled. "We're a pair, aren't we?"

"Sure looks like it."

Garner squeezed Hawk's hands. "You hit the shower, and I'll check the weather report."

As *AQUATHERAPY* motored around Sunset Key, Garner checked his anemometer. The wind was steady out of the south at about twelve knots. "Perfect," he said. "You wanna take the helm while I raise the sails?"

Hawk nodded and slipped behind the wheel.

"Just hold her off the wind until I tell you," Garner said as he cranked the winch and unfurled the bright white mainsail trimmed in a wide navy blue banding.

When the main was completely unfurled, Garner nodded at Hawk. He turned the wheel and headed directly into the wind, and Garner heard that familiar *woof* as the wind quickly filled the sail. *AquaTherapy* heeled over in the water about ten degrees and steadied as she picked up speed. Garner moved to the next winch and cranked, the jib slowly unfurling and luffing loudly until Garner tightened the sheet and she filled up with wind as well. *AquaTherapy* heeled over another few degrees as Garner trimmed the sails, until she was tuned perfectly to the wind and slicing through the crystal clear water.

"This is my favorite part," Garner said as he cut the engine. "Listen to that."

Hawk smiled as he listened to absolutely nothing but the occasional whistle of the wind though the riggings.

Hawk noticed that Garner seemed to be a different man on the water. Lighter somehow. The uptight vibe he gave off on land disappeared, along with the stress lines in his face. In fact, the expression on his face when he was unfurling the sails was almost giddy. He sat back and watched as Garner checked his surroundings, set the autopilot, and disappeared through the companionway door. He reappeared a few minutes later with two beers and a bag of potato chips. He handed a beer to Hawk and opened the chips, stuck his hand in the bag, and dropped it on the seat next to Hawk, keeping a hold of a handful of chips.

"Appetizers," Garner said through a smile. He looked up at the sky and took a deep breath, inhaling the rich salt air. "God, I love this." He sat next to Hawk and rested an arm over his shoulder. "This is exactly what the doctor ordered."

Hawk smiled and held up his beer bottle. Garner tapped the neck of his bottle against Hawk's, and they both took a pull.

Garner pointed across the cockpit. "Would you look at that?"

When Hawk turned, the sun had momentarily dropped behind a low-hanging cloud and the orange and red hues surrounded the entire cloud with rays of sun shooting out in every direction. For a split second Hawk thought that if he were a religious man, he might almost have to say a prayer or something. It was just that beautiful. But then just as quickly as it came, it disappeared as the sun started to peek out from the bottom of the cloud.

As they silently watched the scene unfold before them, Mother Nature didn't disappoint. The sky was filled with one spectacular moment after another until the fiery ball dropped below the horizon, leaving nothing but traces of orange, red, and fuchsia behind. With Garner's arm still hanging comfortably over his shoulder, Hawk felt his chest tighten and the slightest wave of panic when he realized he felt truly content. Before he could overanalyze the feeling, his thoughts were interrupted by Garner's voice. "Time to come about."

Pushing his feelings aside, he stood and saluted. "Awaiting my orders, Captain."

Garner laughed out loud. "You take the helm and I'll man the winches."

"Wenches?" Hawk teased. "I didn't know there were wenches on board."

"I said winches, you idiot. Now release the autopilot, turn her hard to port, and don't forget to duck."

"Aye, aye, Captain," Hawk shouted as he carried out his tasks.

When the boat came about, the boom swung from starboard to port, and both men ducked as it passed over their heads. Wind filled the mainsail, and Garner loosened the starboard jib sheet while cranking the winch on the port side. The wind caught the large sail and nosily blew it to port as well. *AquaTherapy* heeled over once again and sliced through the glistening water.

"Nice job," Garner said. "I'm gonna make a sailor out of you yet."

"Not sure about that," Hawk said. "I have a real need for speed, and I like my throttle too much."

Garner spun around and licked his lips. He grabbed a handful of Hawk's crotch and shook it. "I like your throttle too."

"Really? Is that the best you can do?" Hawk asked, shaking his head. "Oh, dude, that was pretty lame."

"You think so? I thought it was pretty damn clever," Garner replied. "You get it, right? Throttle." He squeezed Hawk's crotch again and then repeated the word while pointing to the throttle of his boat.

Hawk flashed a grin and rolled his eyes. "Yes, I get it, and I still think it was lame."

Garner released Hawk's crotch and hung his head, looking up at Hawk through his eyelashes.

"Stop with the puppy-dog eyes," Hawk said. "Do I look like the kind of guy that would react to that?"

Garner glanced up. "I have two words for you, Mr. Bristol: walking contradiction."

"Shit," Hawk said, looking away quickly, unable to mask the smile that consumed his face.

"What, no response?" Garner teased. "That's because you know I'm right. And for the record, I'll use my puppy-dog eyes any damn time I please."

Hawk figured he was catching Garner's giddiness because he started laughing and didn't stop until just before they entered the harbor.

Hawk took the helm and started the engine while Garner manned the winches, furling the sails and preparing the lines for docking. As soon as they were inside the breakwater, Hawk surrendered the helm and walked out onto the bow. When they passed *ReelCrazy* on their approach to Garner's slip, Hawk did a double take when he saw Justin sitting on the bow of his boat. Even from this distance, Hawk could see the all-knowing smile that was spread over Justin's face, and he could feel the sarcasm oozing out of his deliberate wave. "Shit," Hawk said under his breath. "I'm so busted."

Hawk watched Justin walk over to meet them at the dock, probably under the pretense of assisting them with the lines. "Hey, Butt-rah," he said, winking at his best friend as they pulled into the slip.

Justin smiled broadly as he caught the line Hawk threw him and secured it to the nearest cleat. Hawk jumped off the boat at midship and secured the spring lines and then the stern line until the boat was secure.

Justin walked down the finger of the dock and stood next to Hawk.

Garner shut down the engine and hopped off the boat. "Thanks for the help," he said, obviously recognizing Justin as Hawk's friend and extending his hand, "I'm Garner Holt."

Justin accepted the outreached hand. "Justin Morrison. Good to meet you."

"Hawk has mentioned you," Garner said.

"Has he now?" Justin asked, casting a sideward glance at Hawk and elbowing him in the ribs.

"Ouch," Hawk whined. "What in the hell was that for?"

"That was for not telling me you were going out sailing with a very handsome man," Justin said.

"In Hawk's defense," Garner offered, "we just decided at the last minute."

"We?" Justin questioned. "Did y'all spend the entire day together?"

"As a matter of fact we did," Garner said, looking over at Hawk.

Hawk offered Garner a weak smile and then turned to Justin. "Enough, Butt-rah," he said. "I'll fill you in later."

"Hawk, I do believe you've been keeping secrets from me."

"Enough," Hawk said again.

Hawk turned to Garner. "Do you need me to help you hose down the boat or anything?"

"Na, I can manage," Garner replied. "You two go along and catch up. Oh Justin, I have friends coming in for the weekend, and Hawk has agreed to let me charter his boat for a fishing trip on Saturday morning. You're very welcome to join us if you like."

Hawk started to feel a bit nauseous and wanted to crawl into a hole and bury himself.

"I might just do that," Justin said. "Thanks for the invite."

Hawk offered Garner another weak smile. "Thanks. I'll see you in a little while."

"I'll be here."

HAWK TOOK Justin back to his boat and waited until they got inside the cabin before he tore into him. "What in the hell do you think you're doing?"

"Nothing," Justin said. "Just being nice to your new boyfriend."

"He's not my boyfriend," Hawk insisted.

"Your new fuck buddy, then."

"For fuck's sake," Hawk said, running his hand over his shaved head as he quickly contemplated how much he should tell Justin. He finally threw himself down on the couch and 'fessed up. "If you must know, after I walked you home last night, we hooked up again, and yes, I spent the day with him."

Hawk watched Justin's eyes widen with disbelief.

"OMG, Hawk," Justin screeched. "In all the years I've known you, you've never, as you say, *tapped the same thing twice*, never mind spent the day with him afterwards."

Hawk had to laugh at that one. "Whoa! Now don't be getting ahead of yourself," he said. "This is nothing more than a fuck-buddy thing. He hates relationships, and you know my feelings on that subject."

Justin jumped on Hawk's lap and threw his arms around Hawk's neck. "Well, I'm just happy you're spending time with someone."

Hawk wrapped his arms around Justin. "Thanks, Butt-rah."

"I'm so happy I'm not even going to kick your ass for your poor taste in nicknames."

"In your dreams, pocket gay."

"That one either," Justin added. "Oh and just for that, tell Garner I'd love to join you guys on the fishing trip."

"Oh great," Hawk said rolling his eyes. "I'm looking forward to that trip."

"Do you realize you roll your eyes all the time?" Justin said, raising his leg and stomping on Hawk's bare foot.

"Fuck," Hawk hissed. "What was that for?"

"Not wanting me on your fishing trip."

Hawk threw Justin off his lap. "You get one of those in a lifetime, dude, and you just used your free pass," he said, lifting his foot up onto the couch and looking at his aching toes to make sure he wasn't bleeding. "The next time I kick your ass."

"Yeah, yeah, yeah," Justin said. "I'm shaking in my Nikes."

Justin looked at his watch. "Oh, gotta go. I have a cyberdate with Jeremy at eight, and I have to get lubed up."

"Christ, dude," Hawk said, still rubbing his toes. "I really don't want to know about that stuff."

"What time on Saturday?" Justin asked.

Hawk stood and limped over to the door. "I have to check the weather and the tides, but we'll probably pull out around first light."

"And what time would that be?" Justin asked sarcastically.

"I have no idea. You have a smartphone—look it up."

Justin frowned. "Just call me when you know," he said as he stepped through the glass door.

Hawk shook his head and waved as Justin hopped off the boat and ran down the dock.

Hawk limped over to the galley and rummaged through the refrigerator to see if he could scrounge up dinner for two. He pulled out a pork loin and a package of brussels sprouts. He found some quinoa in the cupboard and figured he had enough to work with.

He dug his cell phone out of his pocket to call Garner, but quickly realized they hadn't even exchanged numbers. He climbed off his boat, walked over to Garner's, and tapped on the hull.

A few minutes later, Garner popped his head out of the companionway door. "What's your cell?" Hawk asked.

Garner recited it, and Hawk plugged it in his phone.

"Here's mine."

"Wait," Garner said. "I don't have my phone with me."

He disappeared and returned a minute later, waving his cell phone in the air. "Shoot."

Hawk recited his number, and Garner plugged it in as well. "You hungry?" Hawk asked.

"You mean you didn't fill up on those apps I put out for the sunset sail?" Garner teased.

"Ah… no," Hawk replied. "My boat. One hour."

"I'll be there. What can I bring?"

"Bring wine if you have it."

"Wine it is."

Hawk walked back to his boat with a bounce in his step. Even with a tender foot, he was truly excited about cooking for someone, with no strings attached. *Well, maybe some strings. But only the good kind of strings.*

CHAPTER NINE

GARNER PRESSED the End button on his phone. "They're around the corner," he yelled, sticking his head in the shower. He and Hawk had spent the day together at the beach and timed it so they would get back to the boat in plenty of time to shower and get dressed before the boys arrived. But when they decided to shower together, one thing had led to another, and now they were running seriously behind.

Garner was standing in front of the mirror drying his hair when Hawk stepped out of the glass-enclosed shower. Garner kept one eye on Hawk's reflection in the partially steamed mirror. His piercings glistened from the moisture as Hawk reached for his towel and started drying off slowly, stopping every now and then to look up and lock eyes with Garner. *God he's hot!*

Hawk stepped up behind Garner and slipped his arms around Garner's waist. "That felt really good."

"Yeah," Garner agreed. "A hot shower always does the trick for me too."

"Dude, I wasn't talking about the shower."

"I know," Garner said with a wink. "It was so worth it. Even if we are running very late."

"I'll be ready in five," Hawk said, stepping out of the head into the stateroom, still drying off.

"I'm right behind you," Garner said, turning the blow-dryer off.

Hawk slapped Garner's ass hard. "I hope you'll be behind me later," he teased.

"Ow!" Garner said. "That stung." He stepped into his jeans and scowled at Hawk, trying to look fierce while fighting off laughter. "And after that move, you can count on it." They'd spent the last two days and nights together on one boat or the other, and so far, so good. Garner wasn't feeling any pressure, and it didn't appear that Hawk was either. Their conversations were getting easier, and each time they talked, Garner learned a little more about what made Hawk tick. Garner realized he'd thought it a million times, but Hawk really was a contradiction of himself. Take away the tats and piercings, and there was a smart, handsome, and witty man struggling to get through life with childhood wounds that never seemed to heal.

Garner wasn't the least bit nervous about introducing Hawk to Thompson and Hank because they would eventually see exactly what he saw, but he wished he'd given them a little warning. Hawk's appearance could be a little intimidating at first, as he well knew, but of course the circumstances surrounding their introduction were going to be very awkward.

Garner slipped into his flip-flops just as he heard Thompson's voice. "Anybody home?"

"Be right there," Garner yelled.

Hawk was buttoning his jeans, and he looked up, appearing to be a little nervous. "Is this shirt okay to wear?" he asked, holding up a red Henley.

"Absolutely. And don't be nervous; they're great guys."

Garner kissed Hawk on the lips. "I'll see you out there."

Garner stepped out of the cabin and picked up his pace when he saw Thompson standing in the companionway looking down into the salon, his sun-streaked blond hair falling over his shoulders and those emerald green eyes every bit as gorgeous as ever. "Permission to come aboard, Captain."

"Permission granted, you asshole," Garner replied. "Now get down here."

Thompson stepped down the stairs with Hank on his heels. *My God, these guys are as gorgeous as ever.* Hank's jet-black hair was shimmering, and his piercing blue eyes were sparkling like the Gulf of Mexico on a sunny day.

Garner hadn't realized how much he'd missed them until he saw them face to face. "My God. You two are a sight for sore eyes," he said, throwing an arm around each of their necks and pulling them in to hold them tightly against him.

After a solid hug, Garner released them and stepped back. "Let me get a look at you both. You look terrific. Love really agrees with you."

"Thanks to you," Hank said, punching Garner in the arm.

"Hey, I only put you on the right path. You made the road trip."

Hawk stepped into the salon and cleared his throat. Thompson and Hank both looked up.

"Hey, I want you to meet a friend of mine. Hawken Bristol, meet Thompson Gray and Hank Charming."

Hawk stepped up and shook their hands. "Nice to meet you. I've heard a lot about you. And please, call me Hawk."

Garner threw an arm over Hawk's shoulder. "Hawk has the fishing-charter boat we're going out on tomorrow."

"Great," Thompson said, looking Hawk over. "Man, those are some seriously cool piercings."

"Thanks," Hawk said.

"They really are," Hank said, stepping closer. "I almost got my ear pierced once. I'll never forget the place had a sign hanging in the window that said, and get this, 'Ears pierced while you wait.' I mean, really? What are you gonna do, drop your ears off and pick them up later, pierced and ready to go?" Hank shook his head, apparently still in disbelief. "Anyway, I chickened out at the last minute when I heard the woman ahead of me scream bloody murder."

"Can I?" Thompson asked, raising his hand to Hawk's ear.

"Sure," Hawk said, tilting his head to give him better access.

"Now that had to hurt," Thompson said, touching the half-dollar-size black disc filling Hawk's earlobe.

"Not really…," Hawk started. "Well, that's not exactly true. You start with a normal piercing, and then as the piercing heals, you increase the size of the discs until you get to the size you want. It smarts a little when you put the larger disc in for the first time, but your earlobe quickly adjusts and after a few hours, you don't feel a thing."

"You're more man than I'll ever be," Thompson said, shaking his head.

"Show them your tongue," Garner suggested.

Hawk stuck out his tongue and waved it around, showing off the silver bar piercing the tip of it.

Hank winced and looked away. "Oh man, now I could never do that. The anticipation of waiting for the poke alone would kill me."

Thompson piped up. "Damn, Prince, I thought you liked the anticipation of the poke?"

"Really?" Hank asked, glaring at Thompson. He turned to Garner and pointed an accusing finger. "I blame you for all of this. Thanks to you, this is what I've got to live with."

Garner covered his mouth with his hand, choking back laughter. He was absolutely amazed at how far Thompson had come in such a short time. He was like a new man, and Garner attributed it all to Hank's love and support.

"Prince?" Hawk asked.

"My last name is Charming," Hank said. "I got the nickname when I was a kid."

"Prince Charming?" Hawk said. "I get it."

"And I wouldn't have it any other way," Hank said, then kissed Thompson before swinging hard and smacking him on the ass.

"Oooouch," Thompson whined, rubbing his ass and looking back at Hank. "You said to be my witty and charismatic self."

"Yeah, but that was supposed to be at Garner's expense, not mine," Hank clarified.

Garner started to laugh and then realized what Hank had said. "Wait! What?"

At that point, all four of them lost it and roared with laughter.

When the laughter finally dissipated, Garner threw his hands up. "Let's get you guys settled so we can grab some beer and head topside and plan our weekend."

"We'll get our things out of the truck and be right back," Hank said, gesturing for Thompson to lead the way.

Thompson climbed the companionway stairs, mumbling to himself and still rubbing his ass. "I still think that was funny."

"It was, baby," Hank said, looking back over his shoulder and winking at Garner and Hawk.

"Well," Garner said, wrapping his arms around Hawk, burying his head in Hawk's neck, and kissing him. "Those are my boys."

Hawk raised his shoulder and bent his head against the ticklish assault. "They seem like really nice guys, and neither of them seemed the least bit afraid of me."

"It was early in the morning and you were half-naked," Garner said, stepping back and smiling. "Am I ever going to live that down?"

"Probably not."

Garner looked toward the door when he felt the boat tip from the weight of Hank and Thompson climbing back on board. Hank appeared in the companionway first and awkwardly stepped down the stairs, balancing two bottles of wine and a bottle of Scotch on top of a case of beer.

"Let me help you with that," Hawk offered, taking the wine and Scotch bottles and setting them on the counter.

"Thanks," Hank said. "Can you fit any of this beer in the fridge?"

"I have plenty, so we'll ice that down when we need it."

They all turned when they heard a thump as a duffle bag landed on the floor of the salon and then another and Thompson barreled down the stairs behind them.

"Gentlemen, you get the V-berth and the forward head," Garner said, pointing up the hallway. "Unpack, get comfortable, and meet us topside when you're through."

After a few minutes, Hank appeared in the cockpit barefoot, wearing a pair of khaki shorts and a royal blue T-shirt, which made his eyes bluer, if that was even possible.

He looked at the beer bottles in Hawk's and Garner's hands. "Excuse me? Why am I the only one up here without a beer?"

Garner reached into the cockpit fridge and pulled out a longneck, then twisted off the cap before he handed it to Hank.

"Whoa!" Garner said when he turned back and saw Thompson standing in the companionway in a bright pink, blue, and lime green, short-sleeve, button-up flamingo shirt and cutoff jeans.

"Nice, huh?" Thompson said, resting his hands on his hips and turning from side to side so that everyone could get a good look.

Hank rolled his eyes and took a pull off his beer and swallowed hard. "He spent hours in the basement looking for that shirt, digging through storage boxes that he still hasn't unpacked since he moved in."

"It's... colorful," Garner stammered. "Yeah that's it, very colorful."

"Nice shirt, dude," Hawk said, giving Thompson the once-over. "I like it."

It was Garner's turn to roll his eyes. "Honestly, Tommy boy, that's got to be one of the ugliest shirts I've ever seen."

"What are you talking about?" Thompson said, the shock and disappointment evident on his handsome face. "It's perfect. Come on, we're in Florida, and everyone knows flamingos go with Florida."

Garner looked over at Hank as he handed Thompson a beer. "God love him," Hank said. "There's always gonna be a part of him that's straight. I guess it could be worse."

"What's wrong with you people?" Hawk asked. "I think it's very cool."

"Thank you!" Thompson said, taking a seat next to Hawk and tapping the neck of his beer bottle against Hawk's. "At least someone here has taste."

After a few beers, they decided to take a cocktail stroll and check out all the other boats in the marina. In addition, Thompson and Hank were anxious to see if there were any good ideas they might be able to pick up and apply to their marina.

When they got back to *AquaTherapy*, satisfied they hadn't come across any obvious ideas or improvements they could steal, all four of them were starting to feel the effects of the beer. So because of Thompson and Hank's long drive and the fact that they had a very early morning ahead of them, they'd all agreed to stay in and order pizza. Besides, they figured they had two more nights to go into town and blow it out big time.

Since Hawk and Garner had already provisioned and fueled *ReelCrazy*, ordered an ice delivery for five thirty, and called Justin to give him a six o'clock departure time, they were all set there.

Garner ordered the pizza, and Thompson and Hank set the table while Hawk threw together a salad from ingredients he'd confiscated from both boats without touching tomorrow's provisions.

When they pushed away from the table, all of them were stuffed. They moved to the salon and sprawled out, Hank taking one end of the couch with Thompson on the floor leaning back and resting his head between Hank's legs, and Hawk and Garner on the other couch, Hawk stretched out with his head in Garner's lap.

"So?" Hank finally asked while gently running his fingers through Thompson's sun-streaked locks. "When are you two gonna tell us what's going on?"

"Going on?" Garner asked.

"Yes, Garner," Thompson said. "We're not stupid. Hank and I watched you guys all night, and neither of you can seem to keep your hands off the other."

Garner looked down at Hawk and then back up to Hank. "The short answer is absolutely nothing."

"Really?" Hank asked. "And the long answer?"

"Come on, both of you know my track record and how I feel about relationships. It just so happens that Hawk feels the same way. Right now we're simply enjoying each other's company and having a good time. When that's no longer the case, we'll go our separate ways."

"Hawk?' Thompson asked, apparently looking for confirmation.

"He's totally right," Hawk agreed. "Except for our first encounter, there was some spark between us almost immediately."

Hank tossed a questioning look over at the both of them. "Don't worry," Hawk said. "I'll fill you in on that later."

Garner threw his head back and rolled his eyes. "They can hardly wait, I'm sure."

Thompson looked up at Hank. "Sounds like there's a story there."

"Oh yeah," Hawk confirmed.

He continued by telling Thompson and Hank about Garner on stage at the drag show, which neither of them could believe, then seeing him later at the dance bar, where they had sort of played cat and mouse. And then eventually about the next day docking the boat and what ultimately followed.

"Anyway, we acted on our attraction big time, and it was good," Hawk said before pausing and looking up at Garner. "It was real good. And as I just told you, we did it again. But over the course of that one day and our two sexual encounters, we shared our experiences with dating, relationships, and fear of commitment and discovered that we had almost the exact same issues."

Hawk paused and then added, "For starters, I no longer felt like I was the only turd in the punchbowl. But more importantly, knowing someone else felt like I did and had similar issues took all the pressure or obligation away, and that was really liberating for me."

Garner smiled. "And for me as well," he said, playing with the loop in Hawk's eyebrow.

"Guys," Hawk said. "I haven't even had as much as a date in over ten years. I mean, don't get me wrong. I have sex—a lot of it—but up until Garner, never with the same guy twice. It feels really good to spend time with someone and not feel guilty when I'm done."

"Same here," Garner said, then dipped his head and kissed the top of Hawk's head. "So, gentlemen, what we have here works for us right now. Maybe not tomorrow or the next day, but for right now I'm very content."

"Me too," Hawk agreed.

Thompson shrugged. "Hey, man, with my past, I'm the last one to judge. If you're both happy, I'm happy for you."

"Me too," Hank said. "Besides, Gar, I really like knowing you're not alone all the time."

Thompson nodded and looked up at Hank, who was attempting to stifle a yawn. "That's my cue, gentlemen," he said. "It was a long drive, and we have a big day tomorrow. I think we're gonna turn in."

Hawk looked up at Garner. "I think we're right behind you," he said, hopping to his feet. "It was great to meet you both, and I look forward to a fun day tomorrow. Weather looks good, and hopefully, we'll catch some fish."

Thompson stood and offered his hands to Hank to pull him to his feet. "Come on, baby, time to put you to bed."

The men exchanged hugs, and just before they went their separate ways, Garner said, "It's really good to have you here. I miss you boys a lot."

Thompson smiled, nodded, and took a step toward their stateroom.

"Ditto," Hank said, joining him.

"Oh, and Thompson?" Garner said.

Thompson stopped and turned.

"Please don't wear that god-awful shirt tomorrow. You'll squash any chance we have of catching a fish."

Thompson looked at Hawk, who was standing behind Garner and shaking his head mouthing, "Not true."

"Fuck you, Garner," Thompson said. "I'm wearing it now just to piss you off."

And with that Thompson turned and disappeared into his stateroom.

THE NEXT morning Garner was awakened by the smell of freshly brewed coffee. He rolled over, stretched, and glanced at the clock. *Fuck! It's five forty-five. I set the alarm on my phone for four forty-five.*

Garner sat up, swung his feet over the side of the bed, and reached for his phone. It wasn't where he'd left it last night when they went to bed.

"Looking for this?" Hawk asked, waving a cell phone in the air and carrying what Garner hoped was a cup of hot coffee.

"As a matter of fact, I was," Garner replied in a sleepy voice. "The phone for sure, but right now, I want the coffee way more."

Garner reached for the coffee, but Hawk pulled it away just before he could wrap his fingers around the cup. He puckered his lips and leaned in.

"Bribery, huh?" Garner said. "I can assure you it is not needed." He gave Hawk a good morning kiss and gladly accepted the steaming cup of java. He took his first sip and looked up at Hawk. "I don't understand."

"Simple," Hawk said. "I woke up at four o'clock and couldn't go back to sleep, so I got up, took your phone with me so the alarm wouldn't wake you, and headed to my boat to get everything ready. After the ice delivery, I came back and started the coffee. And here we are."

Garner shook his head. "What a nice way to wake up."

"Good morning, ladies!" Hank said, banging on the wall right outside Garner's cabin. "Please tell me you're dressed and not doing the nasty. I don't think my eyes could handle that this early in the morning. Or any other time of the day, for that matter."

Garner smiled at Hawk. "Watch this," he whispered before raising his voice to answer. "One of us is dressed and one of us is naked, but feel free to come in and watch."

"Kinky," Hank said. "But no thanks. If I wanted to play that game, I have a naked man in my own bed. I think I'll just stand right here and listen instead."

"You're one fucked-up dude," Hawk yelled.

"Thank you," Hank replied.

Garner laughed. "No seriously, we're dressed, sort of. You can come in."

Hank peeked around the door. "I'm a little concerned about the *sort of* part of that statement, but I guess I'm man enough to take my chances."

Hank joined Garner and plopped down cross-legged on the bed, leaned against the headboard, and sipped his coffee.

"Is Tommy boy awake?" Garner asked.

"I brought him his coffee," Hank shared. "But that man is getting harder and harder to get up in the morning. I guess he's playing catch up for all those years he was up before sunrise."

Garner smiled weakly. "Good for him. How's he doing?"

Hank looked down into his coffee cup. "Really well, I think. I mean… he has his moments. But hell, we all do." Hank looked up and met Garner's eyes. "But I think after all these years, he's finally at peace and seems truly happy."

Garner nodded. "And you?"

"The happiest I've ever been," Hank admitted. "Seriously, Gar, I don't think I can ever say thank you enough. From the minute you walked into our lives, everything changed."

Garner waved his hand in the air. "Seeing you boys happy is more than thanks enough. And really, all I did was show you the way. You did the work."

"Yeah, but it still amazes me how it all worked out. Who would have dreamed when I towed you back to the marina, it would have had such a lasting effect on our lives?"

Garner rested his hand on Hank's leg and squeezed. "I'm a firm believer that things always work out the way they are supposed to."

"What in the hell is going on in here?"

It was Thompson's voice, and the others looked up to see him leaning on the doorjamb. "A bunch of old hens cackling and having a coffee klatch?" he continued.

"Says the mean old rooster?" Garner teased.

Hank uncrossed his legs and patted the bed in front of him. "Get over here, Foghorn Leghorn."

Thompson walked over to the bed. "I say, I say, boy… I think I just might take you up on that offer," he mocked and then kissed Hank on the forehead and settled between his legs, leaning back and resting his head against Hank's chest.

"You know," Garner said, "sooner or later everyone is going to have to get out of my bed if we're actually going to try and go fishing."

Hawk was still standing at the side of the bed up until this point. He suddenly kicked off his flip-flops and threw himself across the foot of the bed. "Well, until then, you ladies make some room for me."

They all looked toward the door again when they heard someone call, "Anybody home?"

"We're back here, Butt-rah," Hawk called out.

Justin appeared in the doorway looking like the Gorton's Fisherman with a scowl on his face and his arms crossed over his chest. "Already with the names, Hawken?" Justin looked back and forth at all the bodies sprawled out on the bed without giving Hawk time to respond. "Good morning, all," he said. "Ah, sorry to break up your little love fest, but no one was on *ReelCrazy*, so I came over here. The companionway door was open and I heard voices, so I came down."

"Not at all," Garner said. "The coffee's in the galley, and if you can find a spot on the bed, you're welcome to join in."

Garner pointed at Thompson and Hank. "Justin, meet Thompson Gray and Hank Charming. Guys, this is Justin Morrison, Hawk's best friend."

Thompson waved and Hank said, "Good to meet you, Justin," as he tried to push Thompson, who wasn't budging, off him so he could stand.

"Oh no. Please don't get up," Justin said. "It's nice to meet you guys as well."

Hank settled back against the headboard, smacked Thompson on the back of the head, and took another sip of his coffee.

"Ouch," Thompson said, rubbing his head and looking over his shoulder, apparently knowing why he got smacked.

"Thanks for the offer, but I've had enough coffee and Dramamine to send my system into a tailspin," Justin admitted. "So I think I'll pass. And as far as the bed, I don't know what you people are into, but whatever it is, leave me out of it."

"Yeah," Hawk said. "He's saving himself for his cyber boyfriend."

Justin narrowed his eyes. "Very funny, Hawk. At least I can count the number of men I've been with on one hand. If we tried to add up your conquests, we'd have to enlist the fingers and toes of the entire US Navy."

"Ouch," Garner said.

Hawk looked at Justin. "Cut a guy some slack, would ya? I've only been at it for fifteen or so years. I promise my numbers will increase."

Everyone laughed but Garner. He didn't know why, but Hawk's sex life with other guys didn't strike him as funny. He knew the guy wasn't a saint by any means and had slept around a lot; hell, Hawk had told him as much. But suddenly the thought of Hawk with another guy left a sour taste in Garner's mouth and was not something he wanted to think about.

Everyone was laughing and focusing on the back and forth banter between Hawk and Justin, so luckily Garner's change in mood went unnoticed. He quietly got up, went to the head, and dressed. One by one, the other guys followed Garner's lead, and eventually they all made their way to *ReelCrazy*.

DESPITE NOT being able to shake off the odd sensation settling in his chest, Garner made sure everyone had a great time, and the fishing trip was a huge success. Hawk had proven to be an excellent charter captain and all-around great fisherman. He'd taken them to his favorite fishing spots, and none of the spots had disappointed. Throughout the trip they'd caught Amberjack and Blue marlin in a variety of sizes, with Justin landing the last and largest catch of the day: a ninety-pound Yellowfin tuna, or Ahi as it was referred to by some.

When they arrived back at the marina, Garner watched Hawk skillfully clean the large fish, which provided more than enough steaks for dinner with plenty left over for everyone to have some to take home. They all pitched in and washed down the boat, then showered and changed and relaxed with a cocktail while Hawk prepared a gourmet meal featuring fresh seared tuna.

Later that night they hit the town, Hawk and Justin taking them to all of their favorite hangouts, ending up at La Te Da's for the late show. When they arrived, they had a drink in the lounge, and Garner discreetly slipped Austin a fifty-dollar bill to make sure Jack picked either Thompson or Hank to sing her duet with during the show.

As luck would have it, Jack was dressed as Dolly Parton and she picked Thompson, who, to his credit, hammed it up big-time while he sang "Islands in the Stream" with the blonde-haired drag queen.

After the show, Thompson and Hank got into one pedicab and Hawk, Garner, and Justin piled into another and whooped and hollered as they raced back to Justin's apartment, each promising their driver an extra twenty bucks for whoever got there first.

After saying goodnight to Justin, Garner, who had stopped drinking when they reached La Te Da, realizing one of them should be reasonably sober, watched over the guys as they stumbled the three and a half blocks to the marina in the tepid Key West air. When they arrived back at the boat, Thompson, Hank, and Hawk were well past tipsy, and Garner struggled to get them aboard *AquaTherapy* without anyone ending up in the drink. Hank came the closest, saved only by the fact that Thompson's hand was already down the back of his pants and Garner was holding on to Thompson.

Garner sighed when, by some miracle, they all made it back on board safely. Once down below, Thompson and Hank headed directly to their stateroom, offering slurred good nights without even bothering to stop for a hug. Garner helped Hawk back to his stateroom, and they barely made it to the bed before Hawk collapsed, fully clothed, and fell fast asleep, snoring lightly.

Garner peeled Hawk's clothes off and emptied his pockets, laying his phone and wallet on the bedside table. He quietly folded Hawk's jeans and Henley and laid them on the floor on top of his shoes and socks and then turned to gaze down at the handsome man lying in front of him. Sleeping as soundly as a newborn baby, Hawk was mesmerizing, his beautifully tattooed and pierced body practically still except for the rise and fall of his breathing.

In the quiet of the cabin, with his walls down and defenses almost nonexistent from the effects of the liquor, it took Garner only moments to realize why he'd begun to experience such odd feelings this morning. Tears stung the backs of his eyes and quickly ran down his cheeks as he admitted to himself for the first time that he was starting to develop feelings for this wounded walking contradiction of a man.

How could this have happened in less than a week? he asked himself. *Because you let your guard down knowing Hawk wanted no part of a relationship. You have no one to blame except yourself.*

Garner's tears flowed freely while he stripped, folded his clothes neatly, and then crawled into bed. He choked back a whimper when Hawk instinctively scooted his back against Garner's chest. Garner fought the urge to wrap his arm tightly around Hawk's waist and draw him close, but in the end he lost the battle and held on to Hawk as if his life depended on it.

Garner's heart nearly broke in two, and he couldn't hold back the whimper any longer as he admitted to himself what was coming next.

Do what you always do, Garner. Run!

CHAPTER
TEN

HAWK WOKE to the sound of his cell phone ringing. He turned over and winced from the headache pounding at his temples. He glanced at the clock and groaned. Seven fifteen.

He picked up his phone and looked at the caller ID. *Justin.*

He slid his finger across the bottom of the screen and lifted the phone to his ear as he rolled over onto his back. "This better be important, Butt-rah, or you're a dead man," he whispered, trying not to wake Garner.

"Hawk?" a gruff voice said.

Confused, Hawk looked at the caller ID again. It still said *Justin.*

"Uh yeah, this is Hawken," he replied. "Who is this?"

"My name is Sergeant White with the KWPD."

A cold chill ran down Hawk's spine and the haze of his hangover cleared as he put two and two together. *A police officer calling from Justin's phone. This can't be good.*

He sat bolt upright in bed. "What happened to Justin?"

"I'm sorry to have to call you so early on a Sunday morning," Sergeant White said. "But your name was the first one in his favorites list on his phone."

"I don't care how early it is," Hawk retorted. "What happened to Justin?"

"He's been in an accident," the officer said.

"What kind of accident?"

"He was struck by a vehicle on Duval while crossing the street in front of a coffee shop."

"What? Hit by car?" Hawk said, no longer able to keep his voice down. "How bad is it? Please tell me he's not...."

"Oh no," Sargent White interrupted. "He's alive, but he suffered a pretty serious head trauma. He's about to be transported to the Lower Keys Medical Center."

"Please tell me he's okay?" Hawk asked.

"He was unresponsive for a while, but he's conscious now, and that's about all I can tell you, son," Sergeant White said. "I suggest you get over to the hospital as soon as you can."

"I'm on my way," Hawk said before ending the call.

Hawk jumped out of bed and scanned the room for his clothes. When he turned, he saw Garner already up and putting his pants on.

"Over there." He pointed to Hawk's neatly folded clothes. "How bad is it?"

"I don't know," Hawk said, his voice cracking. He was shaking so hard he couldn't button his pants. "They won't tell me anything other than he has a serious head trauma and he's on his way to the Lower Keys Medical Center."

"Look at me," Garner said, grabbing Hawk by the shoulders. "Let's not jump to any conclusions. He's still alive, and we have to believe that he'll be okay."

Hawk took a deep breath and nodded. Garner ran a cloth over his face and brushed his teeth, then called a cab while Hawk did the same.

On the way out, Garner left a note for Thompson and Hank, explaining where they were and that he would call as soon as they knew something.

The hospital was on Stock Island, just one island over from Key West across the bridge on U.S. Route 1, but as far as Hawk was concerned, it could have been in Miami for how long he thought it was taking to get there. When the cab stopped at the emergency entrance in front of the hospital, Hawk knew he should be doing something. *We're here! Move, you idiot!* He looked down at his left hand and realized his fingers were gripping the door handle so hard his knuckles were white. They wouldn't budge. No matter how hard he tried, his fingers stayed wrapped around the handle. He looked at his right hand. It was locked into Garner's left, holding on tightly. When had that happened?

"We're here, Hawk," Garner said softly, handing the driver a twenty-dollar bill.

Garner tugged on his hand gently, but Hawk still couldn't move. "Hawk. Listen to me. It's going to be okay, but you have to let go of the door handle so I can help you out of the cab."

Somehow Garner's soothing voice gave Hawk the courage to break free. He released his grip, slid across the seat to Garner's side of the cab, and allowed Garner to help him out. Together they entered the hospital, still hand in hand, and Hawk wrinkled his nose at the strong antiseptic smell he always associated with hospitals.

They walked up to the information desk and Hawk attempted to speak, but his voice cracked and he stopped, realizing he was about to lose it. He sighed with relief when Garner spoke up. "I'm Doctor Garner Holt, and we're here regarding Justin Morrison. I think he was brought in a little while ago."

The attendant checked the computer records. "Yes, I see Mr. Morrison was brought in about fifteen minutes ago. I'm sorry. What was your name again?"

"Holt. Doctor Garner Holt."

"I'm sorry, Doctor Holt. I don't see your name listed on the hospital authorization paperwork signed by Mr. Morrison when he was brought in. And being a doctor, I'm sure you are very familiar with current HIPAA laws and my inability to give information to anyone not listed as next of kin."

Hawk heard the words "next of kin." "Me," he choked out, raising his hand. "I think that would be me," Hawk added, vaguely remembering Justin telling him that he'd listed him that way on his health insurance.

"And you are?" the attendant asked.

"I'm… I'm Hawk, Hawken Bristol."

The attendant checked the records again. "Ah, yes, Mr. Bristol, you are listed as next of kin."

The attendant read farther down the record. "It appears that Mr. Morrison is having a CT scan done as we speak. Please have a seat in the waiting area, and as soon as he's back from the scan, someone will come out and talk with you."

"But…," Hawk said.

"No, no, Hawk. It's okay," Garner said, squeezing his hand and tugging. "Let's take a seat, and they'll find us when he's back."

Hawk followed Garner's lead, and they found chairs side by side in the corner of the waiting room. Hawk looked straight ahead, staring at the blank wall across the room, but he felt Garner's grip tighten when he began to tremble.

"It's going to be okay, Hawk. Whatever it is, we'll deal with it."

After a moment, Hawk realized his head was moving up and down, but it felt like he was no longer in control of it.

Hawk fought the waves of panic as his body trembled, settled, and then started trembling again. His brain was on overload, and suddenly the blank wall in front of him appeared to be a video screen, flashing all sorts of pictures through his mind. He saw Justin flying through the air and rolling off the hood of a strange car. Then he saw him lying in the middle of the street alone and bleeding as the car sped up and rounded the corner on screeching tires. An image of Justin lying on a stretcher and being put in an ambulance came next, followed by an image of Justin's lifeless body lying in a coffin.

"No! No! No!" Hawk whispered as he released Garner's hand, stood, and began pacing.

Garner quickly stood, put both hands on Hawk's shoulders, and stilled him. "Stop it!" Garner said compassionately, as if he'd somehow seen the same images as those flying through Hawk's head. "Don't jump to any conclusions, Hawk. We just don't know."

Hawk blinked back the tears threatening to escape his watery eyes. "He's my only real friend, Garner. My best friend."

"That's not true," Garner said. Hawk felt strong arms wrapping around him and pulling him close. "I—" Garner paused. "I'm your friend, and I'm gonna be with you as long as you need me."

Hawk's subconscious picked up on some odd tone or hesitancy in Garner's voice, but he quickly pushed it to the back of his mind for later. In that moment, for the first time in his life, he realized he actually needed someone. He needed Garner. Hawk didn't know how long it would last, but for right now he damn sure needed the man.

"Hawken Bristol?" a voice yelled from across the sterile waiting room.

Hawk looked up to see a man in gray pants and a knee-length white coat standing at the attendant's desk.

"I'm Hawk Bristol!" Hawk said, rushing across the sparsely filled room and meeting the man halfway. When Hawk stopped, he was relieved to feel Garner right behind him.

"I'm Doctor Bridges," the man said with his arm extended. "I'm Mr. Morrison's neurologist."

"Hawk Bristol," Hawk repeated, shaking the doctor's hand, adding, "This is my friend Garner Holt. How's Justin?"

The doctor shook Garner's hand and addressed them both. "I just conferred with the radiologist who reviewed Mr. Morrison's CT scan, and Mr. Morrison has suffered a pretty severe head trauma."

"Exactly what does that mean?" Hawk asked, feeling certain he had that deer-in-headlights expression on his face.

"Well, the human brain is surrounded with cerebrospinal fluid that acts like a cushion or a buffer for the cortex," Dr. Bridges explained. "For lack of a better word, the brain *floats* in the fluid, which provides a layer of basic protection inside the skull. When the skull or head experiences some type of trauma, the brain is bounced around, but the fluid protects it and keeps the cortex from coming in contact with the inside of the skull. In the case of a severe head trauma, the fluid is not thick enough or sufficient to completely protect the brain, so in many instances, the brain slams against the inside of the skull case like a pinball and, as a result, can become badly bruised or severely damaged."

"How severe was Justin's trauma?" Hawk asked.

"I can't really answer that question right now," the doctor said. "There is a significant amount of blood mixed in with the cerebrospinal fluid, and his ventricles are dilated, indicating some swelling of the brain. The blood is a direct result of the trauma and will dissipate if the bleeding has stopped, but the swelling could become a problem."

"Jesus!" Hawk whispered, rubbing his head.

"No, wait!" Garner said, looking back and forth between Dr. Bridges and Hawk. "Before you jump to any conclusions, this is not an uncommon occurrence for this type of trauma."

The doctor looked at Garner with a questioning expression.

"*Dr.* Garner Holt, MD, PhD, and PsyD," Garner said.

Bridges nodded. "He's right, Mr. Bristol. The issue becomes more serious if the brain continues to swell and eventually fills the skull casing, causing further damage, which can result in paralysis, loss of speech and motor functions, or even death."

"Please tell me you can stop the swelling?" Hawk begged.

"We've already started Mr. Morrison on anti-inflammatory drugs, and we're watching him very carefully. We've scheduled him for an MRI in a couple of hours, and if his brain is still showing signs of swelling, we can take further action."

The blood drained from Hawk's face and he involuntarily reached for Garner. When their hands touched, Hawk grabbed hold and squeezed, needing the human contact, and braced himself for what was coming next. "Which means what exactly?" Hawk asked.

The doctor continued. "After the MRI, if we determine there is limited to moderate swelling, we can drill a hole through the skull and insert an intraventricular catheter through the lateral ventricle, which is the area of the brain that contains the cerebrospinal fluid, and monitor the fluid levels, releasing fluid through the catheter as needed, giving the brain a little more room to expand. Or if the swelling is moderate to severe, we can do a trephination, or burr hole procedure, which means we'll temporarily remove a portion of Mr. Morrison's skull to give the brain the room it needs to further expand until the swelling stops."

Hawk wasn't sure how to respond. Both options required holes in Justin's skull, and neither sounded pleasant.

"Were there any other injuries or trauma?" Garner asked.

"Besides the head trauma, Mr. Morrison has various lacerations, a broken wrist, and he's pretty badly bruised, but other than that, he's in remarkably good condition considering what he's been through."

"When can we see him?" Hawk asked.

"He's on his way up to the Neurointensive Care unit now, but by the time we get there, he should be settled in."

"Is he conscious?"

"Yes and no," Dr. Bridges said. "I was told by the EMT he was unresponsive immediately after the accident, then slowly regained consciousness during transport to the hospital. When he arrived, he was alert, knew his name, and was able to answer a series of questions used to determine basic levels of head trauma. He signed the paperwork giving us authorization to treat him and gave us your name as next of kin.

"But he was starting to show signs of distress, a second indication that the brain was indeed swelling, so we've since sedated him until we can determine the severity of his injury."

"Distress?" Hawk asked, looking at Garner. "What kind of distress?"

"It's okay, Hawk," Garner said, squeezing his hand. "In many cases a brain injury can cause a patient to act irrationally. I've seen patients wake up disoriented and try to pull their IVs out or attempt to get out of bed. I've even seen patients get extremely violent, and they can do all sorts of further damage to themselves and others. So this is good for him. It will also give his brain time to rest."

"If you say so," Hawk said, feeling a little relieved. He turned back to Dr. Bridges. "So, can we see him now?"

"Sure. I'll take you both up," Dr. Bridges replied. "Right this way."

Hawk held on tightly to Garner's hand as they walked down the hall and waited for the elevator. When the doors opened on the fourth floor, the doctor went up to the nurses' station and spoke quietly to the attending nurse, then waved Garner and Hawk over.

The doctor led them through a series of halls before they got to a set of secured double doors. The doctor swiped his badge over the reader and admitted them to a very large open area with a nurses' station in the center and glass-enclosed cubicles lining the exterior walls. They walked past three of these, each with patients inside hooked up to a daunting array of machines, before getting to Justin's room.

Hawk gasped and fought back tears when he saw his best friend. He released Garner's hand, walked gingerly up to Justin's bed, and stood staring down at him. "How long can we stay?"

"Just a few minutes," the doctor said. "The NICU allows family members to see patients every four hours for thirty minutes at a time. But it's okay for now. Take your time. In fact, I'll give you two a little privacy while I check his status reports."

Justin had a white bandage wrapped around his head, and his face was covered with scrapes and cuts, his skin ghostly white where it wasn't black and purple from the bruising. His left wrist was in a cast almost up to the elbow, and he had various other bandages covering his chest and arms. Hawk was sure there were more bandages on his legs but they weren't visible under the blanket covering his lower body.

Hawk panicked when he heard a beeping noise and looked at Garner.

"It's okay," Garner reassured him. "The IV is to keep him hydrated and to administer his medications. The other machines are monitoring his heart rate, breathing, blood pressure, and pulse rate, as well as his central venous pressure, or CVP, which reflects the amount of blood returning to the heart and the ability of the heart to pump the blood into the arterial system. And lastly"—Garner pointed to a bag hanging at the foot of the bed—"they will monitor his intake and output levels to make sure he stays hydrated and that fluids are passing through his system adequately."

Grateful for the explanation, Hawk backed away from the bed and stared at the still figure lying in the bed.

"Talk to him," Garner urged. "I, as well as many other doctors, believe the patient can sometimes hear you, even while in a drug-induced comatose state. Let him know you're here and he's all right."

Hawk stepped up to the bed and took a deep breath. He had to be strong for Justin.

"Butt-Rah," he said softly, taking Justin's right hand. "I don't know if you can hear me, but Garner and I are here. But don't worry about anything. You're going to be fine."

Hawk's voice started to crack and he looked away, not wanting Garner to see him losing it.

When he could speak again, Hawk continued. "You're in the Neurointensive Care Unit and we can't stay with you all the time, but I'll be here as often as they allow me to. If you wake up and I'm not here, don't worry. You're not alone. I'll be right outside in the waiting room." Hawk paused to clear the lump that was forming in his throat. "They are going to take you down for an MRI shortly, and as soon as we get the results from the doctor, I'll call your parents. I'm sure they'll want to fly in and be here for you too."

"Where are they?" Garner asked quietly.

"In California," Hawk whispered. "Justin told me he was a late baby and that his parents were pretty up there in age now, although in good health."

Dr. Bridges reentered the room just as Hawk heard a plastic bag on the bedside table ringing.

"That's Mr. Morrison's things," Dr. Bridges said, gesturing toward the ringing bag. "You may want to take his cell phone and wallet with you for now."

Hawk picked up the bag and held it in his hand. "I'll just take it all until he needs it."

The doctor nodded. "I'm sorry, gentlemen, but I'm afraid we'll need to take some vitals before they take him down for the MRI."

Taking Justin's hand, Hawk said, "We have to go for right now, but I'll be back as soon as they let me. Remember, you're not alone." He stopped when his voice started cracking again.

"Thanks, Doctor," Garner said. "We appreciate everything."

"I'll come and get you as soon as I get the results of the MRI."

Garner nodded as he took Hawk by the hand and led him out of the NICU.

When they reached the waiting room, Hank and Thompson were waiting for them.

All four men exchanged embraces, and Garner brought them up to speed on Justin's condition while Hawk sat silently clutching the plastic bag tightly in his fingers.

"How about coffee?" Thompson asked.

"That would be great," Garner said. "Hawk?"

"Yeah. Sure," Hawk said without looking up.

"He takes it black," Garner added.

Thompson and Hank disappeared down the hall in search of a coffee machine or the cafeteria, whichever they found first.

"You okay?" Garner asked, looking down at Hawk.

Hawk nodded but didn't respond.

"I really need to pee," Garner said. "Will you be okay until I get back?"

Hawk nodded again.

"I'll be right back. If the doctor comes out for any reason, do not go anywhere without me. Okay?"

"'Kay," Hawk mumbled. He jumped to his feet and wrapped his arms around Garner's neck, plastic bag still clenched between his fingers. "Thank you," he said. "I don't think I could have done this without you."

"You won't have to," Garner said. "Like I said, I'm here as long as you need me."

With that, Hawk released him, and Garner gave him a wink and took off in search of the bathroom.

Hawk rubbed his head. There was that tone again in Garner's voice.

Hawk sat back down, and the plastic bag sounded again. From the annoying sound of ducks quacking, Hawk knew it was definitely Justin's e-mail notification. He searched through the bag and found Justin's cell phone. He pressed the e-mail icon, and Justin's inbox popped up. He scanned the messages for anything important and saw that the last three were from Justin's cyber boyfriend, Jeremy.

Hawk felt like a voyeur reading Justin's private e-mail, but this was a unique situation, and suddenly feeling very protective of his best friend, he opened the first one and starting reading.

Dearest Ben, I'm looking so forward to finally meeting you tomorrow. It's taken us far too long. I know that was my fault, but I couldn't leave the ship. But just know I can't wait!

Hawk shook his head. "Butt-rah, or should I say Ben, you little shit," he said under his breath. "You finally decided to meet the guy in person and you didn't even tell me."

Hawk looked at the date. It had been sent last night while they were out. *Holy shit! He's coming today.*

Hawk closed that message and opened the next.

Hey Ben, Haven't heard from you since early last night. Is everything okay? XXOO, Jeremy.

"No, everything is not okay," Hawk mumbled. *Do I let the poor bastard know what's going on or leave him hanging?*

Not making a decision either way, Hawk closed that e-mail and opened the last one, which had come in thirty minutes ago while he and Garner were with Justin.

Getting really worried, Ben. Not like you to not respond. Not getting cold feet, are you? I'm at the Coast Guard station now, but leaving just before lunch. I won't have time to change so I'll be in my blue working uniform. You have no idea how much I'm looking forward to meeting you in person. After twenty-two months you're all I can think about. See you at Aqua, five o'clock sharp.

Hawk leaned back in the chair, stretched out, and closed his eyes. He thought about his options and kept coming back to the same conclusion. He needed to make sure this guy was on the up and up. Not knowing what Justin told Jeremy about what he did for a living, he decided to go with something very general. He hit reply on the last e-mail and started typing.

Sorry it took so long to respond. Went out with friends last night and got in very late. Been in meetings all morning, but looking so forward to our date. I have meetings all afternoon so I probably won't get time to e-mail again but will see you at five. Looking so forward to it.

Hawk reread his e-mail and then hit Send. He opened the photo gallery on Justin's phone and flipped through the photos until he found a picture of a handsome guy in a U.S. Coast Guard uniform. "Bingo," he said out loud.

"Bingo what?" Garner asked, sitting next to him.

Before Hawk could say anything, Hank and Thompson walked up with coffee and pastries and took a seat across from Garner and Hawk.

While they sipped their coffee and waited for the doctor to come back out, Hawk filled them in on Justin's history, the rape, and the details surrounding his two-year cyber relationship and the e-mails about their rendezvous at Aqua this evening.

All three looked at him quizzically. "Look," Hawk explained, "Justin said he thought he was in love with the guy, and if Jeremy is really in love with Justin, he has a right to know what's going on. But before I bring him into Justin's life, I want to make sure the guy is who he says he is."

"So let me guess. You're going to Aqua this evening," Garner said.

Hawk nodded. "Do you think I'm crazy or out of line?"

"Not really," Garner said.

Thompson and Hank nodded their heads in agreement.

"He's your best friend and these are extenuating circumstances," Garner continued. "In a normal situation, I would tell you to mind your own business. But for someone who's been through what Justin has, and the fact that he's finally going out on a limb and taking a chance, this could be a crucial point in his mental recovery. I say go for it."

"It's settled, then," Hawk said. "I'll be at Aqua at five o'clock sharp."

GARNER SAT watching Hawk pace like a caged tiger while he waited for the doctor to come out with MRI results. Thompson and Hank dozed off and on, changing position every so often in the uncomfortable hospital chairs.

Last night Garner had lain awake most of the night planning his escape. Right after Thompson and Hank left on Monday morning, he was pulling out of Dodge, weather permitting.

He wasn't yet sure how he was going to tell Hawk. They had in essence signed a pact. Had an arrangement, an understanding of sorts: nothing emotional between them, just sex and companionship. *But lo and behold, I had to go and fuck that up royally.*

Watching Hawk now, so vulnerable and completely unsure of himself, pacing back and forth, concern for his friend written all over his face, made Garner's heart ache for him. Up until this morning, Garner hadn't thought Hawk would have cared one way or the other if he stayed or left. But seeing the way Hawk had clung to him when he got the news about Justin, almost as if Garner were his only lifeline, had shaken his resolve. Hawk was relying heavily on him emotionally, and Garner knew he couldn't let him down.

But ultimately, he couldn't let his emotions get in the way of his decision. As soon as Justin was out of the woods and Hawk could stand on his own two feet, Garner was out of there.

Hawk stopped pacing and looked up every time he heard the double doors open and close, but this time when they did, Dr. Bridges stepped through and scanned the waiting room.

"There he is," Hawk said. Garner rose to his feet, as did Thompson and Hank. When Dr. Bridges spotted Hawk, he started toward him, and they all met him halfway.

"I have some news for you," the doctor said.

Garner felt Hawk reaching for his hand, and he grabbed it and held on tight.

"It appears that, for now, the swelling is fairly minimal, and the blood in the cerebrospinal fluid seems to be dissipating. I don't feel that either procedure I told you about earlier will be needed at this time."

Garner felt Hawk squeezing his hand, and he squeezed in return.

"We will do another CT scan in about four hours, and then one more late this afternoon and continue to watch him closely," the doctor went on. "If the next scan shows no increased swelling, I think we'll be in pretty good shape. And if he continues to improve, I'll start reducing his medication, and he'll slowly start to regain consciousness.

"However, let me caution you. If the next scan shows additional or increased swelling, depending on how severe, we will have to reevaluate our entire plan at that time."

"Got it," Hawk said. "I understand completely."

"Good day, gentlemen," Dr. Bridges said. "I'll keep you posted if his condition changes."

Hawk grabbed the doctor's hand and shook it so hard Garner thought he was going to break the man's hand off. "Thank you so much, Doctor. Can we see him again?"

Dr. Bridges looked at his watch. "Sure," he said. "Visiting hours start in about five minutes. Remember, you guys can go in only two at a time."

Hawk nodded. "Thanks again, Doc," Hawk said as the doctor turned and disappeared down the hall.

"That's all good news, right?" Hawk asked, looking at Garner.

"It is good news," Garner agreed. "If he continues like this, he'll be home in no time." *And I'll be gone.*

Since Hawk and Garner had already been to Justin's room, Thompson went with Hawk, and Garner and Hank would go in when they returned.

As soon as the other two men were gone, Hank sat down next to Garner and looked him in the eye. "What's going on with you?"

"What do you mean?"

"Don't give me that crap, Gar. I know you," Hank said. "I saw the way you were looking at Hawk when he was pacing, so tell me what the fuck is going on?"

Garner sighed. "I fucked up is what is going on."

"How?" Hank asked. "What do you mean you fucked up?"

"Hawk and I. You know, we had this thing," Garner said, hanging his head.

Hank nodded. "Yeah, you told us Friday night."

"Well it was supposed to be no strings, no emotional attachment, just good times and sex. And when it was over, it was over."

"And...?" Hank asked.

"I fucked up and got attached," Garner said, looking up at Hank through his eyelashes.

"I knew it," Hank said, slapping his knee. "I could see it in your eyes, the way you looked at him, the way you laughed. It was as plain as the nose on your face. That's great, Gar. I knew it would happen eventually."

"No, not great, Hank."

Hank tilted his head to the side. "Why not?"

"Hawk doesn't want this, and neither do I. We each made that very clear to the other before anything ever got started."

"Have you asked Hawk how *he* feels?" Hank asked.

"Of course not."

"Why not?"

"Because we both agreed, and I'm not going back on my word!" Garner snapped.

"Fuck that, Garner. Haven't you noticed how the man's sticking to you like glue, like you're the only thing keeping him together?"

"He's scared and alone, Hank," Garner said. "Nothing more and nothing less."

"Bullshit!" Hank replied. "I'd bet my life there's more to it than that."

Garner just shook his head. "It doesn't matter. I suck at relationships, and Hawk has the worst fear of intimacy issues I've seen in my career. It would never work, and frankly, I don't have the ability to bounce back anymore. It's easier to not even go there. The minute I tell him I have feelings for him, he's gonna panic and bolt."

"So let me guess, you're gonna bolt first?" Hank asked with a disgusted expression on his face.

"I'm afraid so," Garner replied.

Before Hank could say another word, Hawk and Thompson came out of the NICU.

"He looks better," Hawk said, sitting on the other side of Garner and taking his hand. "His color is getting back to normal. I mean, he still has the bruises, but his skin is not so pale. But you guys go in and tell me if you think I'm right."

Garner stood, but Hawk didn't release his hand and stood with him. Hawk threw his arms around Garner's shoulders and pulled him close. "I can't thank you enough. I don't think I could have gotten through this morning if you hadn't been here."

Over Hawk's shoulders, Garner watched Hank eyeing up the two of them and shaking his head. Garner blinked away tears, and his voice cracked when he spoke. "I'm so glad I was able to be here for you."

"It's okay, dude," Hawk said when he realized Garner was crying. He ran his fingers through Garner's hair and rubbed circles over his back. "He's doing so much better now. I think everything's going to be okay."

Garner broke their embrace, stood up on his tiptoes, and kissed Hawk on the forehead. "Everything is going to work out just fine. You'll see." He turned and headed for the double doors, and Hank fell in line behind him.

When the doors closed behind them, Hank laid a hand on Garner's shoulder.

"Not now, Hank," Garner said, shaking free of his hand.

Hank spent a few minutes at Justin's bedside and then looked Garner in the eye. "You can't keep running, Garner. Eventually, everything you're running from is going to catch up with you."

Garner raised a hand to silence Hank and looked back down at Justin.

"I'm out of here," Hank said, making a beeline for the door.

Garner took a seat and rested his elbows on Justin's bed and took Justin's hand in his. "I'm so glad you're going to be okay, Li'l Man. You gave us quite a scare. Didn't anyone ever teach you to use a crosswalk?"

Garner swallowed the lump that was forming in his throat and continued. "Hey listen, I'm gonna have to be leaving soon. Yeah. I knew I wouldn't stay forever. I mean, I never do, and I kind of fucked up and started to develop feelings for Hawk, and we both know how that would end. I know you're probably thinking I should stay and make it work, but it wouldn't, and besides, Hawk hasn't asked me to. Anyway, I just wanted to make sure that once you're all healed up you'll continue to take care of Hawk for me. You and me are probably the only ones who know he's not the tough guy he pretends to be. He really needs someone he can count on. Someone who will keep him in line, ya know?"

Garner was losing the battle to keep his emotions in check. Tears flowed freely down his cheeks. "I wish I could stay," he went on, wiping at his cheeks with the back of his hand, "but I just can't. He and I would never work out. We have too much baggage between us, and we would be over before we got started. And probably kill each other emotionally and physically in the process. We both agreed that we wanted nothing more from the other than a good time, and somewhere along the line, for the life of me I can't figure out where, I messed up and started to care."

"When were you gonna tell me?"

Startled, Garner looked up. Hawk was standing in the doorway, skin almost as white as Justin's and tears running down his cheeks.

Garner looked back down at Justin, incapable of speech at that moment. Hawk took a few steps inside the room and closed the door. "What if I told you I fucked up too?"

A sliver of hope that maybe, just *maybe*, awoke in Garner. But then he realized what he was considering and quickly recognized that it would never work. Hawk didn't want a relationship, and neither did he? Right?

"It wouldn't change anything," Garner said, glancing at Hawk apprehensively. "We're both the same damaged goods we've always been, and I don't see that changing anytime soon. In either of us."

Hawk hung his head. "I guess you're right," he said. "But what if I told you I was a better damaged guy when I'm with you?"

"I'd say I was too," Garner agreed. "But how does that change things?"

"It doesn't really," Hawk said. "I guess the fact that I haven't slept with a guy more than once in over ten years and you come sailing into Key West and suddenly we're inseparable was all due to the 'no expectations' thing. You're right. With emotions comes expectations, and once all that started to happen, I'm sure everything would go downhill from there."

Garner nodded. "It's been less than a week," he said. "We're not naive little schoolboys. We're fucking adult men who know people don't fall in love in a week."

"Yeah, I guess you're right," Hawk said. "It's not love yet, but I am feeling something."

"I'm feeling something too, but you know how this will play out," Garner explained. "I run physically and you run emotionally. Eventually, we'd both be left out in the cold, and I don't think either one of us wants that. Personally, I can't handle it again."

Hawk looked down at the floor as if all the answers were written in the shiny gray and white tile under his feet. "Then I won't ask you to," he said.

Garner closed his eyes. *I knew it!* "Thank you," he said, feeling a pang of disappointment. "I think that's best. We understand each other too well. That's probably why we got off to such a great start."

"When will you pull out?" Hawk asked.

"As soon as I know Justin is okay and I get a long enough weather window to cross the gulfstream."

"I see."

A nurse knocked on the glass door and pointed to her watch.

Garner nodded and stood. He walked over to Hawk, put his arms around him, and nestled his head against his chest. "We've got a little more time. Let's enjoy what we have and not let it get away from us. Your memory has got to sustain me for a long time."

Hawk wrapped his arms around Garner, kissed the top of his head, and nodded.

They said goodbye to Justin with a promise to be back at the next visitation.

When they got back to the waiting room, Thompson and Hank were still sitting in those damned uncomfortable chairs, not looking too happy. Hank had obviously filled Thompson in on what was going on with Garner and Hawk. They both stood and smiled when they saw Hawk's arm draped across Garner's shoulder.

"Don't get excited, guys, I'm still leaving," Garner said. "But we're gonna make the best of the time we have left."

"Hey, listen," Thompson said. "Now that we know Justin is going to be all right, unless you guys need us, we're gonna head home."

"Really?" Garner asked. "I wish you wouldn't. I don't know when I'll see you again."

"Well, the way you keep running, my guess would be never," Thompson said abruptly. He rested his arm over Hank's shoulder. "You know, Gar, I know what running is like. Hell, I did it for most of my life. But you showed me how not to be afraid and how to face my fears head on. Hank, and especially I, will always be grateful for that. If I weren't so angry with you right now, I'd compare you to an angel who sails into people's lives, changes everything, and then sails away as fast as you came. But one day, man, you're gonna run out of wind, and what happens then?"

Garner could think of nothing to say. He was certainly no angel, but Thompson was right about one thing. One day he would run out of wind. Life, circumstance, and probably his own choices had screwed him up royally, and there was no way out for him.

Snapping out of his thoughts, he asked, "Can you give me a lift back to the boat? I'm gonna get some clothes for Hawk and me in case we have to stay the night."

"Sure thing," Thompson said. "We need to get our stuff anyway, and we'll bring you back to the hospital on our way out of town."

"I'd appreciate that."

Garner kissed Hawk on the cheek and stepped away so Thompson and Hank could say their goodbyes.

The men embraced and exchanged a few words Garner couldn't hear, then slapped each other on the back and separated. Hank stepped away with tears in his eyes.

"You boys come down and I'll take you fishing anytime you like," Hawk said, shoving his hands in his pockets. "I'm serious, please don't be strangers."

"I promise we won't," Hank said, looking around. "I guess that's it, then; we'd better get a move on."

"Oh!" Hank pulled his wallet out, dug for a business card, and handed it to Hawk. "Please call us if Justin's condition changes," he said. "Or if Garner is gone and you need anything, anything at all, we can be back as fast as our truck will carry us."

Hawk's tears were flowing freely now as he stepped up and wrapped his arms around Hank and held on tight. "Thanks, man, I'll do that."

The thought of Hank and Thompson coming down to see Hawk and the three of them just hanging out without him stung more than Garner thought it would, but the thought that Hawk might need them because he wasn't there was like a dagger through his heart. He hung his head and silently cursed himself.

Thompson and Hank headed toward the elevator. Garner kissed Hawk one last time and followed his friends.

The mood was somber, and no one said a word during the ride back to the boat. When they got to the marina, Garner went over to *ReelCrazy* and grabbed a change of clothes for Hawk and then joined Thompson and Hank on *AquaTherapy* to pack a change of clothes for himself. He walked into the head, and Hawk's toothbrush was lying on the counter next to his. He picked them both up, along with his hairbrush and a stick of deodorant, and shoved them into his backpack.

When he finished, Thompson and Hank were packed and standing with their bags at the bottom of the companionway stairs. Garner nodded. "I'm ready."

"We are too," Hank said. "I guess this is it, then. Goodbye, Garner."

"How about if we just say *so long*?" Garner asked. "It doesn't sound so final."

"If that makes you feel better, sure," Thompson said. "So long, Garner. I'll be forever grateful for everything you did for us. And if you ever find yourself in our neck of the woods, you always have a place to stay."

"I appreciate that," Garner said.

The three men did a group hug and made their way up the stairs and to the truck.

After a quick stop at a Wendy's drive-thru to get Hawk something to eat, they reached the hospital. Garner leaned up and rested one hand on Thompson's shoulder and the other on Hank's. "You guys—" He stopped, too choked up to speak. "I love you both," he barely managed to say before he lost it completely. He climbed out of the truck and sat on a bench in front of the hospital and cried like a baby as he watched his friends drive off, probably for the last time.

CHAPTER ELEVEN

HAWK WAS sitting in the corner of the hospital waiting room. His head was flooded with so many mixed emotions he was having trouble sorting them out and assigning them to the specific saga going on in his life.

He was thrilled that Justin was improving with each visit to the NICU and that his prognosis was getting better and better. But Hawk was also processing Garner's departure, which, surprisingly, made him feel like he had a bit of a hole in his heart. His emotions were raw, and he couldn't figure out if Garner's decision to leave was so damn difficult to take because of what he'd been through with Justin or something else. *Could I have really gotten this attached to someone in less than a week?* Hawk wasn't completely sure, but he decided it wasn't likely. He never got attached to anyone.

He battled internally for a while and finally convinced himself it was just the scare with Justin that had his emotions running rampant. And besides, it didn't matter either way; Garner had already made the decision to leave. And although he was going to miss the man, he figured it was probably for the best, especially considering all their personal baggage.

But a little voice way in the back of his subconscious kept rearing its ugly head. *You told him you couldn't ask him to stay. But... why couldn't you?*

"Oh hell no!" Hawk mumbled.

He shook his head in an attempt to clear the obviously insane voice and tried to focus on his best friend.

Hawk was watching the clock and anticipating his next visit with Justin when Sergeant White from the KWPD stopped by to check in on the patient and fill them in on what had happened. According to statements from the eyewitnesses and the driver of the car, Justin had been crossing the street in front of the coffee shop when an elderly driver turned the corner and struck him. Based on her statement, by the time she saw him, it was too late to stop, but she panicked and hit the gas pedal instead of the brake and ran him down at about thirty miles per hour. Also according to witnesses, Justin was thrown about ten feet in the air, landed on the roof, and rolled down onto the trunk and into the street, where his head struck the pavement. Sergeant White wished Justin well and excused himself, leaving behind a copy of the police report and saying it was completely up to Justin if he wanted to press charges or consider a civil lawsuit.

Hawk looked at the clock again. Twenty more minutes. He stretched out again, folded his arms over his chest and closed his eyes. Shortly after Garner had left with Hank and Thompson, he'd made the difficult call to Justin's parents, and the conversation had gone as well as could be expected. Naturally, they were very alarmed and wanted to get on a plane immediately, but Hawk had convinced them that Justin's condition was stable and improving by the hour. If all went well, he would probably be able to go home soon, and he would need them more when he got home than he would while he was in NICU. He promised to update them with each visit, and they seemed satisfied and content to wait at least until tomorrow before making a final decision.

The double doors opened, signaling the next round of visiting hours. Hawk was heading in that direction when he saw Garner stepping off the elevator with a backpack slung over his shoulder and what looked like a Wendy's hamburger bag.

He waved him over.

"How's the patient?" Garner asked.

"I think he's doing better," Hawk replied. "I could have sworn he squeezed my hand during my last visit, but it could have just been my imagination. I'm just about to go in to see him now."

"Do you mind if I join you?" Garner asked.

"Of course not," Hawk said. "Let's go."

Garner put the backpack and food down next to Hawk's chair, and they started walking. "There's food back there when we get done."

"Thanks," Hawk said. "Oh, I forgot to tell you, the nurse confirmed during my last visit they have him scheduled for another MRI in—" Hawk looked down at his watch. "—about an hour from now. I feel like this one will be the deciding factor in his condition."

"How so?" Garner asked.

"If the previous swelling has gone down," Hawk explained, "I think we're home free, but if the swelling is worse, they'll probably have to do one of the procedures the doctor mentioned, and things could get more complicated."

"I've got my fingers crossed," Garner said.

The two men walked the rest of the way in silence. Hawk felt that familiar ache in his heart and still didn't know if it was Justin or Garner causing it. That little voice popped into his head again. *You can always ask him to stay.*

"No, I can't!" he said.

"Can't what?" Garner asked.

Embarrassed by his outburst, Hawk simply said, "Oh, nothing. I was just thinking out loud."

The two men spent the next thirty minutes with Justin, one on each side of his bed. Hawk could have sworn Justin looked even better than he had the last visit and was convinced things were looking up. Both of them spoke to him, reassured him he was going to be fine and that he wasn't alone. Hawk told him quietly that he'd spoken to his parents, and they were concerned but fine and would be here as soon as he needed them. While they were still there, the transport came to get Justin for his next MRI.

Hawk panicked for a second. "It's not time," he told the nurse. "Is something wrong?"

"No, honey," the nurse replied, taking his hand. "They're just ready for him a little earlier than expected. It's all okay."

Relieved, Hawk turned to Justin and took his hand. "You're going for your next MRI now," Hawk told him. "We won't be far and we'll see you at the next scheduled visiting time."

Hawk watched them roll Justin's bed out into the hall and stepped out of the room and watched until he couldn't see him anymore.

He felt Garner's breath on the back of his neck and wondered how much longer he'd get to enjoy that familiar feeling.

You can still ask him to stay!

AN HOUR later Dr. Bridges came out and found them in the waiting room. "I have good news, gentlemen. I just conferred with the radiologist regarding the latest MRI, and the anti-inflammatory medication seems to be doing its job. The brain is no longer swelling, and the existing swelling is diminishing."

Hawk involuntarily found Garner's hand again and squeezed. He took a deep breath and looked up to the ceiling. "Thank you, Doctor."

"My pleasure," Dr. Bridges said. "This is the kind of news I love to share."

"So what next?" Hawk asked.

"I'm going to slowly start reducing the medication that's keeping him in the induced coma and see how he responds. If all goes well, he should be totally conscious by tomorrow morning. We'll do some tests to see if there is any further brain damage, but right now all indications look good."

"Yes!" Hawk said, sporting a huge smile. He shook the doctor's hand, pumping it a few extra times before he let the man get back to work, then threw his arms around Garner's neck. "It looks like he's going to be okay."

He released his hold on Garner when the realization of what he was saying sank in. *Justin is going to be okay, which means Garner will be leaving.* He felt a stabbing pain in his heart and finally knew the feeling had nothing to do with Justin. "I guess now that Justin's going to be okay, you'll be leaving soon, huh?"

"Probably," Garner replied. "I checked the forecast on my phone a little while ago, and it looks like tomorrow is the best opportunity for the three-day weather window I'll need to make the trip, so I'll probably head out at first light."

Hawk smiled weakly. *You can still ask him to stay*, the little annoying voice kept saying. But Hawk did his best to ignore it. "What's it, about two hundred fifty miles to Andros?" he asked.

"Two hundred and eighty or so," Garner replied.

"How long will that take you?"

"Depends on the wind and currents," Garner said. "If I have to motor the entire way, it could take as long as forty-eight hours. If I can sail and have the currents in my favor, I can make it in as little as thirty hours."

"I guess you'll need to provision the boat before you leave. Right?"

"Yeah, I'll do that tonight."

Hawk nodded. *You can still ask him to stay*, the little voice reminded him once more.

GARNER AND Hawk were sitting silently in the same spot they'd occupied most of the day. It was right at four o'clock when Garner looked at his watch. "What time are you heading over to Aqua to meet Jeremy?"

"I have a cab picking me up in thirty minutes," Hawk said. "Why?"

"No reason. I was just curious."

"It's a fifteen-minute ride over, so that should give me plenty of time," Hawk explained.

"Have you decided what you're gonna say?"

Hawk shook his head. "Not really. Who knows if he'll show up, or even look like his picture, for that matter. But if he does show up, before I say anything, I need to make sure he's legit."

Garner looked at Hawk. "How are you going to do that?"

"By watching him closely, for starters," Hawk said. "I plan on sitting in the corner and observing the guy, just to see how he acts."

"And then what?" Garner asked.

"If it was me in his situation, I would sit fairly close to the door and keep an eye on it. When five o'clock comes and goes with no Justin—or Ben, as he calls him—I would start to get a little nervous. When five thirty comes with no sign of my date, I think I would start drinking heavily, but hang around just in case. After a couple of hours, I think I would give up and get out of there."

"I see you've given this some thought," Garner said.

"There's little else to do while I sit here and wait for my next opportunity to see Justin," Hawk said. "I think my biggest challenge is going to be to catch Jeremy between the time he realizes that Ben isn't coming and before he starts drinking heavily. That will be key."

"Because if he's too wasted, he won't be able to comprehend what Justin has done and why," Garner surmised.

"Bingo."

Hawk look at his watch and down at the backpack. "I'm gonna change my clothes, wash my face, and brush my teeth before I go."

"Oh yeah, right," Garner said, picking up the backpack and handing it to Hawk. "Everything's in there."

"Thanks."

Hawk disappeared into the men's room, and Garner was left alone to ponder his situation. His rational brain was having an internal battle with his emotional brain about leaving Hawk, but luckily his rational brain was winning.

Besides, even if you wanted to, Hawk hasn't asked you to stay. He made it perfectly clear from the start that he wanted no attachments. It's better this way.

A few minutes later, Hawk came out of the men's room carrying the backpack. "Thanks again, I feel much better," he said, offering it to Garner.

"No problem," Garner said, taking the backpack and dropping it at his feet.

"Look. I've been thinking," Hawk said. "I haven't asked you to do this, but promise me you won't leave."

Garner couldn't believe his ears. He sat up a little straighter in his chair and looked up at Hawk.

"At least until I get back," Hawk said. "I'd hate for anything to happen and neither one of us be here. I'll stop by the desk and give the hospital permission to talk to you if anything happens."

"Oh, yeah, that's a good idea," Garner said, easing back down in his chair. "Don't worry about Justin. I won't leave him alone."

"Thanks," Hawk said through a weak smile. "I better head downstairs before someone nabs my cab."

Garner stood. "Good luck," he said.

The two men simply stared at one another, neither wanting to make the next move. "I hate this awkwardness between us," Garner said.

"Me too," Hawk agreed. "It's amazing how things can change so quickly."

Fuck it! Garner opened his arms and Hawk immediately stepped into them.

They embraced and Garner heard what he thought was a small whimper. He heard Hawk clear his throat. "I'll be back as soon as I can," he said, stepping back and turning without looking back.

Garner stood frozen in place and watched Hawk walk away. He had so many things he wanted to say, but he couldn't find the right words.

He said nothing.

HAWK PAID the driver and slid out of the cab. He looked down at his watch. Four fifty-five. With road construction and rush hour traffic in full swing, the trip had taken him longer than he'd estimated. He stood in front of Aqua, his heart pounding, hoping he was doing the right thing. He had to know, for Justin's sake, if this guy was okay. For all he knew, the guy could be some kind of gay basher, stringing Justin, and who knows how many other guys, along while at the same time waiting for a chance to strike. He took a deep breath and walked in.

Hawk saw heads turn and felt eyes on him when he stepped through the door. And although he tried to focus, his eyes were still adjusting to the dimly lit room, and he couldn't see a damned thing. He walked to the far end of the bar, ordered a beer, paid the bartender, and moved to a back corner, where he could have a full view of the club, and took a seat. Within minutes his vision was back, and he spotted the handsome guy in a blue uniform whose picture he'd seen on Justin's phone sitting at the bar, very close to the door, just as he would have done.

He smiled. So far, so good. He leaned back and sipped his beer while he waited to see what was coming next.

As Hawk had expected, each time a patron would walk through the front door, Jeremy's head would spin around. When he didn't recognize the patron, he would turn back around and stare at his drink. As time passed and each patron wasn't Justin, Jeremy seemed to get more and more disappointed.

While Hawk observed Jeremy, his mind wandered back to the cat and mouse game he'd played with Garner in this very bar, and he smiled. But Hawk's smile turned to overwhelming sadness when the playful memory was replaced with the reality that Garner was leaving tomorrow.

He shook the thoughts from his mind. *Not now, Hawk. You've got a job to do.*

It was nearing six o'clock, and Jeremy was now slouched over his third drink, looking grim and defeated.

Now's the time to make your move!

Hawk stood, walked over to the bar, and took the empty seat next to Jeremy. He ordered another beer, took a sip, and put it down on the cocktail napkin in front of him. He looked at Jeremy, who was staring down at his drink and continually stirring it with a cocktail straw. Round and round.

Jeremy must have sensed Hawk's gaze because he turned and gave him an odd look. Hawk nodded, but Jeremy didn't respond. He just turned back and started stirring his drink again.

"I'm Hawken," Hawk said, still staring at Jeremy.

"I'm waiting for someone," Jeremy said without looking up.

"I know," Hawk said. "You're waiting for Ben, right?"

Jeremy sat straight up on his stool. "How did you know that?"

"Ben is a friend of mine," Hawk said.

"Where is he?" Jeremy asked with concern in his voice. "Is he okay?"

"He's gonna be," Hawk said.

"Oh good—wait, what?" Jeremy stammered. "What do you mean he's *gonna* be?"

"He was in an accident this morning, and he's in the hospital," Hawk explained.

"What hospital?" Jeremy asked. "I've got to go to him."

"I'll take you to him in a little while," Hawk promised. "But you and I have to have a talk first."

"No!" Jeremy said. "I want to go now. If you don't take me to him, I'll just go to every hospital in Key West until I find him."

"You can try, but you won't find him," Hawk assured him.

"Why not?"

"Because his name's not Ben."

GARNER WAS sitting at Justin's bedside, resting his forehead on their joined hands as the tears streamed down his face. He found the oddest comfort in talking to someone who he thought was listening, but who couldn't respond, and he babbled incoherently about everything going through his mind.

Garner stopped talking when he heard something that he could have sworn sounded like, "Don't go," in a weak, almost inaudible voice. He looked up. Justin's eyes were still closed, but his head was moving back and forth like he was in some sort of distress, and his eyeballs were moving under his eyelids.

"It's okay, Justin," Garner said in a soft voice. "It's Garner, and I'm right here. You're going to be all right."

Garner knew from experience that Justin was slowly coming out of the induced coma and would be disoriented for a while. He continued to talk to him in a soft, steady voice, and within a few minutes, Justin's head slowly stopped moving and he seemed to be settling down again.

"That's it," Garner said, still holding Justin's hand. "Come out of it slow and easy. Take your time. No rush at all. We have all the time in the world."

Garner felt Justin squeeze his hand ever so slightly.

"I'm right here, Justin," Garner said softly. "It's Garner."

"Water," Justin said.

Garner raised the head of the bed just a little and poured a cup of water from the pitcher on the bedside table. He peeled the paper wrapper off a straw lying next to it and put the straw and cup up to Justin's lips. "Just one sip and very slowly, Li'l Man," Garner instructed.

Justin took one draw off the straw as instructed, and Garner pulled it away. "That's it," Garner said. "Good job."

"Hawk?" Justin murmured.

"No, Justin, it's Garner," Garner explained slowly. "Hawk had to leave, but he'll be back shortly."

"No," Justin said. "Hawk. He. Needs. You," he choked out. "Don't go."

What the fuck? Garner was amazed at how quickly Justin was coming down off the medication. *The little shit was listening the entire time.*

"Okay, Li'l Man," Garner said. "I hear ya. Now you just rest and let us take care of everything."

Justin settled down again and drifted off into slumber.

"I'll be damned," Garner said out loud.

When his time was up, he went back to the waiting room and decided to freshen up. He took a sink bath in the public restroom, changed clothes, and brushed his teeth. He sat back down in his and Hawk's corner and waited for Hawk to return—or his next opportunity to see Justin, whichever came first.

HAWK WAS in the front seat of a silver Honda Accord, speeding back to the Lower Keys Medical Center. He looked down at his watch. Eight twenty.

He and Jeremy had talked for about two hours before he was convinced Jeremy was not an ax murderer and truly had sincere feelings for Justin. Hawk had taken his time explaining everything to Jeremy in great detail, trying to make him understand where Justin's head was and why he did some of the things he did.

During their conversation, Jeremy's emotions seemed to have run the gambit. One minute he was surprised and very angry with Justin for lying to him. The next he was sad for Justin but foaming at the mouth to get revenge for what Andrew Kincaid had done to him. But in the end, although he wasn't happy about it, he seemed to understand Justin's actions and why he was so cautious with his heart.

It was eight forty-five when Jeremy parked the car and the two men raced up to the fourth floor, trying to make the eight-thirty visitation, which lasted until nine o'clock. Hawk figured they would at least get to see Justin for ten minutes or so before they got thrown out, but when they reached the waiting room, Garner was still sitting in their spot and the double doors were closed.

Garner stood and walked in their direction. "Eight-thirty visitation was cancelled due to a code blue."

Hawk's heart dropped to his feet. "Not—"

"Oh no, sorry," Garner clarified. "Not Justin. In fact, Justin is starting to come out of the medication. He squeezed my hand, had a sip of water, and even mumbled a few words."

"That's great news," Hawk said as a broad smile spread across his face.

Garner looked at Jeremy and back to Hawk.

"Oh, sorry!" Hawk said. "Garner Holt, meet Jeremy Stanton."

The two men shook hands. "Good to meet you," Garner said.

"So there are no more visitations tonight?" Jeremy asked.

"Unfortunately not," Garner said. "Not until six o'clock tomorrow morning."

"Damn," Jeremy said, looking around. "I can't believe we missed it. Can one of you guys tell me where I can find a bathroom?"

Both Hawk and Garner pointed simultaneously, and Jeremy nodded. "Thanks."

As soon as Jeremy was out of earshot, Garner turned to Hawk. "He's here, so I guess he passed the test."

"And then some," Hawk said. "I think he's a good guy."

"So what did Justin say when you saw him last?" Hawk asked.

"He said your name and some other mumble jumble," Garner said, stretching the truth a little bit. "He's still pretty heavily sedated."

"But that's a good sign, right?" Hawk asked with concern in his voice.

"Absolutely," Garner said. His hands were in his pockets, and he was looking everywhere but at Hawk.

Hawk sensed Garner was about to make his break, and he wanted to make it as easy on him as he could. "Hey, why don't you go ahead and get out of here. I know you didn't get much sleep last night and you still have to provision the boat before you leave in the morning."

Wow! I guess he's pretty anxious to get rid of me, Garner thought. "Okay. You're probably right. I have a lot to do."

"Look," Hawk said. "The Publix is open twenty-four hours, and it's on the way back to the marina."

"Appreciate that," Garner said. "Do you have the cab company's number you used earlier?"

"Oh, yeah. I'll call one for you right now." Hawk searched his phone, hit recall, and walked away as he put the phone to his ear. "As soon as possible" was all Garner heard before Hawk ended the call.

"They should be downstairs in minutes," Hawk said. "The guy said they had a cab in the area."

"Great, thanks." Garner walked over, took Hawk's dirty clothes out of his backpack, folded them neatly and put them on a chair, and slung the backpack over his shoulder.

"I guess this is it."

Before Hawk could reply, Jeremy returned from the bathroom.

"I'll walk you down," Hawk said.

"That's okay," Garner replied, turning to Jeremy. "It was good to meet you, Jeremy. Listen I don't know what's going to happen with you and Justin, but if you hurt the Li'l Man you're gonna have me to deal with. You got it?"

Jeremy shook his hand and said, "Yes, sir."

"I insist on walking you down," Hawk said.

Garner nodded.

Once in the elevator, Hawk opened his arms and Garner stepped into them, resting his head on Hawk's chest. "You be careful out there," he said, his voice cracking.

"I will," Garner said. "And I'll never forget you, Hawken Bristol."

Hawk felt the tears sliding down his cheeks and knew if he didn't break this up, the sobs were coming next. He thanked the heavens when the elevator doors opened and Garner backed out of his arms.

"Likewise, Holt. Thank you for everything. Keeping me together and what you did for Justin. You are a true friend, and I'll always remember that."

"Please say goodbye to Justin," Garner said. "I mean, I did when I was with him, but who knows if he heard me or not."

"I promise."

Garner looked toward the glass doors and when Hawk followed his gaze, he saw the cab just pulling into the porte-cochere. "Your chariot has arrived," Hawk said with tears still running down his cheeks.

Garner took Hawk's face in his hands and brushed the tears away with his thumbs. "You're a good man, Hawk, and you deserve all the happiness in the world. Don't you ever forget that." Garner kissed him gently on the lips, turned, and walked away.

When the cab drove away, Hawk unknowingly sat on the same bench Garner had sat on earlier and cried like a baby.

CHAPTER
TWELVE

GARNER HAD the cab pull into Publix, and he stocked up on provisions for his journey. When he got back to the marina, he paid the cab driver, loaded one of the carts with his groceries, and pushed it down the dock. He reached his boat and looked the three slips over to see *ReelCrazy* swaying back and forth in the gentle current. He smiled fondly. He realized that he truly would never forget the scary, funny, handsome, and unpredictable Hawken Bristol. What an impression that man had made on his life in just under a week. *Crazy!*

Garner put his groceries away and secured the cabins. He went up to the helm and checked his fuel, programmed the waypoints to Andros into his GPS unit, pulled out the appropriate charts and charted the same course as a backup, and finally checked all of his safety gear.

Exhausted, Garner kicked off his shoes, poured himself a glass of wine, turned on the weather radio, and sat on the couch listening to the pre-recorded loop one more time to make sure everything was still a go for first light.

When the loop finished and he was satisfied that the weather was holding, he turned the radio off, downed the last of his wine, and decided there was nothing more he could do until the morning.

He walked into his stateroom and stopped short when he saw Hawk's ball cap, a T-shirt, a pair of his gym shorts, and his flip-flops on the floor in a neat pile next to the bed. He lifted the small pile of clothing and held them to his nose. He could smell Hawk's scent all over them, and the aroma sent a jolt to his groin like no other. Unwilling to give in to his desires, he put the cap, shorts, and flip-flops in a plastic bag. Garner kept Hawk's T-shirt, folded it, and laid it on his pillow.

Closing the plastic bag, he took it over to *ReelCrazy* and put it just inside Hawk's door, then returned to his cabin.

He undressed, sat on the edge of his bed, and unfolded Hawk's shirt. He pulled the T-shirt close to his chest and finally climbed into bed. The last thing he remembered was inhaling Hawk's wonderful scent over and over again until he fell asleep.

Sometime later, Garner was awakened by a familiar dip on the opposite side of the bed. He opened his eyes and saw Hawk's beautiful, steel-gray eyes looking back at him.

Garner opened his arms without saying a word, and Hawk fell into them, crushing their lips together in a warm, desperate kiss.

"Need you" was all Garner could say through their kiss as he laid back and allowed Hawk to straddle him, never breaking contact. Garner whimpered when Hawk slowly moved over and buried his head in the crook of Garner's neck and nibbled at the sensitive areas Hawk seemed to remember each time they made love.

"I need you now," Hawk said as he slid down even farther, brushing his lips over Garner's nipples and then taking Garner into his warm mouth. Garner was instantly hard, throwing his head back and arching his back from the sensation. Hawk moved up and down on him slowly and deliberately, causing goose bumps to appear all over his body. Hawk stopped long enough to retrieve a condom, opened it with his teeth, and started to slide it onto Garner's length.

"No," Garner said, stopping him. "You. I need to feel you inside me. Please."

Hawk rose up on his knees, his erection staring Garner in the face, and slowly rolled the condom on. He reached for the lube, coated his finger, and slid it slowly inside Garner. Garner again arched his back and hissed. "More," he said. "I need more."

Hawk eased another finger inside, and Garner brought his knees up and lifted his ass off the bed using his feet, giving Hawk more access. "Move!" Garner said. "Please move."

Hawk started slowly working his fingers in and out of Garner's opening, searching for that magical spot Hawk himself knew so well.

Garner let out a loud moan, letting Hawk know he'd hit his mark. Behind the lids of his closed eyes, Garner saw the biggest fireworks show of his life. One with a finale that repeated every time Hawk rubbed his target.

"You now!" Garner heard himself beg breathlessly. "Please, Hawk, I want to feel you inside me. I have to."

Lifting Garner's legs and resting them over his own shoulders, Hawk positioned himself at Garner's opening and slowly pushed in. Garner pushed against him and Hawk stopped. "No, please don't stop," Garner pleaded.

Hawk pushed again, working himself in a little at a time until he was in all the way. He slowly withdrew and pushed in again.

"Yes!" Garner said. "Hawk, please."

Hawk picked up his speed and force as Garner thrashed his head from side to side and pumped his own length vigorously. "Harder!" Garner said. "Please, Hawk! I need to feel… need to remember. Want to always remember you! Remember this!" He knew he was begging but didn't care. Didn't care either that tears were streaming down his face.

Garner opened his eyes and saw sweat mixed with tears staining Hawk's cheeks, once again solidifying their connection in every way. Hawk was beautiful as he breathlessly drove in and out, giving Garner exactly what he needed.

Garner felt his orgasm building and pumped himself harder, screaming when the first spasm landed on his neck, the second and third spasms hitting his chest and stomach, continuing until he was utterly spent.

Hawk pulled out of him, peeled the condom off, and stroked himself feverishly until he too screamed and came in streams on Garner's stomach, mixing their release.

Hawk hung his head and Garner knew not whether it was from exhaustion or shame, but he lifted his head up by the chin and smiled. "Thank you."

Hawk fell to his side, breathing heavily as Garner reached over and used Hawk's T-shirt to clean their combined seed. He rolled onto his side with Hawk pushed back against him, and they both gave way to the exhaustion.

WHEN GARNER opened his eyes, his first thought was of Hawk. He felt the other side of the bed and raised his head to look around, but he soon realized he was once again alone. Out of desperation, he sniffed the air to see if he picked up any scent of breakfast being prepared or even fresh coffee being brewed, but he smelled nothing of the sort. *Was it all a dream?*

He rolled to the edge of the bed and winced when he felt the stinging and burning at his opening. *I guess that answers my question.*

Garner pulled himself out of bed, made coffee, and showered, all in the early morning darkness. Each time he moved a certain way and felt the sting, he was thankful to be reminded of the events of the previous night. He dressed and stepped through the companionway door just in time to see the sun peeking above the horizon. He started his engine, disconnected his shore power and water, released his lines, and pulled out of the marina. He stared closely at *ReelCrazy* as he passed by, but there were no signs of Hawk. He waved anyway, just in case Hawk was onboard, and smiled weakly, remembering it all. Garner made the turn out of the breakwater into the open ocean and looked back one last time, not sure what he was looking for, but happy to cast one last glance over Key West and the home of Hawken Bristol.

CHAPTER THIRTEEN

HAWK AND Jeremy were standing in front of the double doors at five minutes before six waiting for the first visitation. "Thanks for covering for me last night while I went to say good-bye to Garner," Hawk said. "I would have never left Justin alone if you hadn't been here."

"I know," Jeremy said. "It's the least I could do. You guys have been here around the clock."

The double doors suddenly opened, and Hawk and Jeremy made their way down the corridor to the NICU. "I think it might be a good idea if you stay outside for a few minutes until I can tell him that you're here," Hawk suggested.

"You're probably right," Jeremy agreed. "But please hurry."

Hawk chuckled. "I will."

Hawk rounded the corner and stepped inside Justin's door. To his surprise, Justin was awake, sitting up, and the nurse was helping him with a cup of water.

"Good morning, sunshine," Hawk said. "Look who's awake?"

"If you must know, I've been up since three o'clock this morning, trying to figure out what in the hell is going on here," Justin said in a raspy voice. "I'm still a little groggy from the meds, but I understand I was in an accident."

"So Nurse Ratchet here filled you in, then?" Hawk asked, smiling at the nurse.

Justin smirked, but also smiled at the nurse. "What little she knew," he said. "Which wasn't very much."

"Sorry," the nurse said.

Justin waved her off with his good hand. "Not your fault."

Justin looked around Hawk and out into the hall. "Where's Garner?" Hawk felt his smile fade, and he lowered his eyes. "Hawken Bristol, please tell me you didn't let him leave?"

"It's complicated," Hawk said.

"Oh, Hawk," Justin said. "You finally found a man who liked you for who you are and one you liked just as much, whether you'd admit it or not, and you let him get away."

"Like I said, Justin, it's complicated."

"Complicated my ass," Justin said, leaning forward.

"Now, Mr. Morrison, you can't get too excited," the nurse said, pushing Justin back down on the bed.

"Hawk, somewhere around five o'clock this morning I panicked because I remembered bits and pieces of conversations you and Garner both had with me when I was knocked out. It took a while to piece it all together, but the gist of what I remember is you wanted him to say he wanted to stay, and he wanted you to ask him to stay. How could two adult men fuck this up?"

"What are you talking about, Justin?" Hawk said. "You must have been hallucinating."

"Hawk!" Justin said very slowly, looking over at the nurse. "Did you and Garner not have a conversation in this very room about fucking up and developing feelings for one another?"

"Yeah, but—"

"But nothing, Hawk," Justin said. "You both agreed to no attachments and you both got attached. How is that bad?"

"Because we both suck at relationships."

"Most people do, Hawk, but that's doesn't keep them from trying, especially when you find someone you click with so well."

"He's right," Nurse Ratchet said.

"So now you're gonna gang up on me?" Hawk asked. He turned back to Justin. "He never said he wanted to stay."

"And you never asked him to."

Hawk threw his hands up in the air and started pacing and rubbing his head. "I told him I fucked up too, and that I was feeling something, and he shot me down."

"He's scared, Hawk, but instead of trying to reassure him, what do you go and do?" Justin asked. "You agree with him and his stupid reasoning, and you both leave it at that."

"Well, what the fuck? What do I do now?"

"You go after him."

Hawk continued to pace. "God, I wish you'd stick to your own relationships." *Oh shit! Jeremy.*

"After last night, I probably don't have a relationship anymore."

"What's that supposed to mean?" Hawk asked.

"After talking to you, I finally agreed to meet Jeremy in person. He was meeting me at Aqua last night at five o'clock. And guess who didn't show up?"

"Wait one second," Hawk said before walking out into the hall.

When he rounded the corner with Jeremy, Hawk thought Justin was going to jump out of the bed. "Jeremy?"

"Justin?"

Justin eyes widened. "You know my real name?"

"He knows everything," Hawk said. "He and I had a long talk at Aqua last night."

Justin looked back and forth between Hawk and Jeremy. Jeremy smiled and nodded.

"And you forgive me?" Justin asked.

"I do. But...," Jeremy said, "if you ever lie to me again, you're a dead man."

"I promise," Justin said, holding his hand out.

Jeremy walked up to the bed, took Justin's hand, and bent down to kiss him.

"No," Justin objected. "I haven't brushed my teeth in over twenty-four hours."

"I don't care," Jeremy said as his lips covered Justin's.

When the kiss ended, Justin looked over at Hawk. "What are you still doing here? Please go and get Garner."

"Take my car," Jeremy said. "I won't need it for a while."

"Thanks," Hawk said through a huge smile.

Hawk took off running at breakneck speed. Instead of the elevator, he took the stairs two at a time until he reached the ground floor. Hawk drove carefully but quickly as he thought about what he needed to do to catch up to Garner.

When he got to *ReelCrazy*, he started the engines, looked at the GPS to determine Garner's presumed course, disconnected power and water, and released his lines. He looked at his watch. Seven fifteen. *He's only got about an hour and a half on me. I'm sure I can catch him.*

When Hawk rounded the breakwater, he gunned the engines, and *ReelCrazy* climbed on top of the water and hit thirty knots in under thirty seconds. She was spraying white water on either side of the hull as far as fifteen feet out and throwing a six-foot wake, but he didn't care. At least people saw him coming. Hawk adjusted his course and paid special attention to the Automatic Identification System, AIS, feature on his GPS unit, which told him all the registered boats within a certain vicinity. In addition, he took out his binoculars and started scanning the horizon.

AQUATHERAPY WAS cruising along in one- to two-foot seas at 8.2 knots with her sails tuned perfectly as she took the fifteen-knot wind off her starboard bow. It was a beautifully clear, warm, and sunny morning, but Garner's wounded heart by far overshadowed the beauty of the day. The boat was on autopilot, and he was sipping his third cup of coffee, wondering how in the hell he had let himself get in this position.

Garner missed Hawk already. He probably would have stayed had Hawk given him any indication that he wanted him to, but the die was already cast. They had set the ground rules at the beginning, and although it was clear they'd each developed feelings for the other, Garner hadn't wanted to be the one to put himself out there and admit they *might* have a chance. Evidently, Hawk felt the same way, so they'd gone their separate ways. Regret warred with inertia, leaving Garner paralyzed. The ocean that usually soothed him now seemed vastly lonely.

Garner jumped when his VHF radio sounded through the quiet of the morning.

"*AquaTherapy*, this is *ReelCrazy*. Over."

Hawk? Garner froze, not trusting his own ears.

The VHF radio sounded again. "*AquaTherapy*, this is *ReelCrazy*. Over. I know you're out there, Garner."

Garner picked up his radio handset with a trembling hand. "This is *AquaTherapy*. Over."

"*AquaTherapy*, switch to channel seven two. Seven two."

"*AquaTherapy* switching to seven two."

Garner reached down and tuned his radio to channel seventy-two. "This is *AquaTherapy*."

"Turn around and come home," Hawk said. "We're gonna make this work. Over."

Garner smiled. "Where in the hell are you? Over."

"Look behind you. Over."

Garner stood and looked aft, and he could see *ReelCrazy* way off on the horizon, barreling toward him throwing off a bright white spray that could probably be seen for miles.

"You crazy bastard," Garner said. "Over."

"Call me whatever you like, just come home. Over."

"Aye, aye, Captain," Garner said as he dropped the radio handset and got to work coming about. He spun the wheel hard to starboard, ducked when the boom passed overhead, and loosened the port jib sheet and started vigorously cranking the winch on the starboard side. The jib switched sides with a *woof* as it again filled with wind. *AquaTherapy* came about with ease and started heading in the opposite direction.

Five minutes later, Garner was looking through his binoculars and could actually see Hawk on the flybridge, yelling his fool head off, his smile glowing.

In another ten minutes Garner started his engine and dropped his sails, anticipating their rendezvous.

Garner idled in the royal blue water and Hawk circled and motored up to his port side. He tossed Garner the bowline and then the stern and he cleated the spring line on his own. When the boats were secure, Hawk stood on his gunwale, giving a mock salute. "Permission to come aboard, Captain."

"Permission granted. Now get your ass over here."

Hawk jumped onto *AquaTherapy* and tackled Garner, both men falling against the vinyl seating and landing on their asses.

"What in the hell are you doing?" Garner asked.

"For once in my life, I'm taking a chance," Hawk said. "Will you take one with me?"

Garner covered Hawk's lips with his own. When the kiss ended, Hawk opened his eyes. "Am I to take that as a yes?"

Garner rolled his eyes. "Of course that's a yes."

Hawk beamed, and his eyes turned as bright as the ocean. "Good. Now let's go home."

SCOTTY CADE left Corporate America and twenty-five years of marketing and public relations behind to buy an inn & restaurant on the island of Martha's Vineyard with his partner of fourteen years.

He started writing stories as soon as he could read, but only recently for publication. When not at the inn, you can find him on the bow of his boat writing m/m romance novels with his Shetland sheepdog Mavis at his side. Being from the South and a lover of commitment and fidelity, most of his characters find their way to long, healthy relationships, however long it takes them to get there. He believes that, in the end, the boy should always get the boy.

Scotty and his partner are avid boaters and live aboard their boat, spending the summers on Martha's Vineyard and winters in Charleston, SC, and Savannah, GA.

Visit Scotty at http://www.scottycade.com and Scotty Cade on Facebook and Twitter. You can contact him at scotty@scottycade.com.

Also from SCOTTY CADE

Sunrise Over Savannah

Thompson and Caroline Gray were living their dream until Caroline's untimely death just two years after they'd bought the Thundercloud Marina. When Caroline died, she left Thompson alone and emotionally disconnected—until Thompson's longtime friend and towboat owner Hank Charming tows Garner Holt, a recently retired psychiatrist, and his boat into the marina for repair. Thompson and Hank are both drawn to the sailboat captain, but for very different reasons.

Since high school, Hank has secretly carried a torch for Thompson, even though Thompson remained committed to Caroline, even after her death. Hank is totally caught off guard when his initial attraction to Garner makes him realize this stranger might be the one to help him move on with his life. Thompson establishes a platonic friendship with Garner and starts to see the psychiatrist as his only lifeline to sanity. Life improves until Thompson sees Hank and Garner together, and old feelings Thompson thought were long buried begin to resurface. Garner quickly identifies the unresolved feelings between Hank and Thompson and decides to tap his professional skills and work behind the scenes to help Thompson and Hank see what has been right in front of them all along.

http://www.dreamspinnerpress.com

FINAL
ENCORE
Scotty Cade

The Love Series from SCOTTY CADE

http://www.dreamspinnerpress.com

Also from SCOTTY CADE

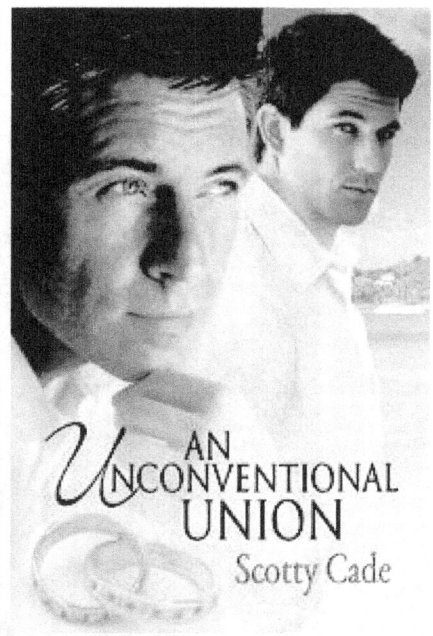

Made in the USA
Coppell, TX
10 November 2021